How could I refuse her? In the past I would have pulled back . . . There was no going back now. I could not deny my lover as I had done too many times before, nor could I ignore the fire burning through my whole being. I knelt in front of my queen and began to feast on her bounty.

Visit

Bella Books

at

BellaBooks.com

or call our toll-free number

1-800-729-4992

52 Pickup

BONNIE MORRIS
E.B. CASEY

Bella
BOOKS

2005

Bella Books, Inc.
P.O. Box 10543
Tallahassee, FL 32302

Printed in the United States of America on acid-free paper
First Edition

Editor: Anna Chinappi
Cover designer: Sandy Knowles

ISBN 1-59493-026-0

For all the lesbian couples out there:
Live well, laugh well, love well, with joy and gratitude.

About the Authors

Making her writing debut in *52 Pickup*, newcomer E.B. Casey is a native New Yorker with authentic New York *tawk* and wit. By day, she's a seasoned educator and athlete. By night, she's usually pretty tired.

A popular women's history professor at two major research universities, Bonnie Morris is the author of five other books, including the 2001 Bella Books mystery *The Question of Sabotage*. Her short stories, both academic and erotic, have appeared in more than forty anthologies. When not lecturing in the classroom or working at women's music festivals, Dr. Bon can be found sharing laughter and love with her favorite softball pitcher, E.B. Casey.

Contents

Odd-numbered chapters are by the professor, Bonnie Morris.
Even-numbered chapters are by the pitcher, E.B. Casey.

From the Authors

This is a collection of playful erotica, meant to be read in bed. We chose the concept, 52 Pickup, with the idea of creating fifty-two different stories—one for every Saturday night in a year. Each story is short enough to be read aloud as a "teaser" or to complement a romantic moment with humor, arousal, or intrigue.

I had already published five books and had written five more when I met E., and it was a titillating pleasure to find on the shelf of her city apartment an anthology of erotica which included one of my own short stories. She had read my erotica before we ever met! Wordplay became a central part of our courtship: the competitive gift of gab between a Jewish girl and her Irish lover. When E. shyly mentioned that she, too, wrote erotica and showed me a manuscript I found moving and well done, I began nudging her to consider writing for publication. The next thing we knew, we were writing together—our first effort was an essay about our lives as a long-distance couple—and we spent countless giddy hours making up playful titles for stories we thought we might put together someday.

For a writer, nothing could be more intimate than coauthoring. Even risking our professional reputations with public erotica says much about our level of trust and our inability to resist joining the great lesbian party out there. The stories poured out like foreplay, the result of more than two years of laughing in bed at the story scenarios we invented in our minds. We're both pretty vanilla, and have kept the level of graphic sexual detail fairly mild, hoping rather to engage the reader's sense of situation—comical or wild. We hope you enjoy the results.

—*Dr. Bon, the professor*

The professor has well described the origin of this writing, so I will not cloud its description with my own perception and interpretation. I will only say, "Yeah, that's what happened!" I was always one to throw out one-liners and to use my New York wit, bur I never imagined myself sitting down and actually creating so many characters and scenarios flavored with puns, innuendos, and romantic excursions. It has been fun and tiring at the same time.

For the reader, I hope we have brought you a bit of literary stimulation as well as the other kind. But for that you may need more than just a story. Soft candlelight, soft music, dark chocolate, and a fine partner would do the trick. I am sure you will find enjoyment with this winning combination. The professor and I from time to time have found ourselves using one of the lines from a story and chuckling out loud. Perhaps you may find yourself recalling a story or a scene and having a "moment." Whatever is your pleasure, my wish is that the stories have contributed to it in some way.

This is my virgin voyage in this writing genre, but I hope in the future to share with you many more trips down romance lane. Until then, enjoy!

—*E.B. Casey, the pitcher*

Chapter One
The Pitcher's Mound

They play on asphalt, these tough city girls, and "softball" it ain't. I've seen the fervor, heard the angry yells, watched at least one player take a ball to the face and go reeling off the fence, but against all that toughness, the pitcher's eyes were soft. She strode up to the mound that was a chalk mark in a burrow and no more. I huddled, frozen, whining, on a bench, a visitor, outsider, not a jock. I huddled in my Polarfleece and watched.

The pitcher's legs began beneath her collarbone—they walked her out and held her up to God. I'd never looked at legs much, mostly faces, but this girl had *thigh*. When she bent her knees, slightly, the planet went: shift. Long lean legs and just a bit of ankle in the chill, just a creamy ankle at the sock. When I felt my brain begin to form the word *creamy*, I knew I was in trouble on that bench. When the pitcher warmed up, I warmed up. And in my mind, I touched the pitcher's mound.

1

How come they move me, these athletic dykes? Me, I was a bookworm. I played *jacks*. I played *hopscotch*. I stood sulking in the outfield wanting to write in my journal, I stood fish-faced below the basket trying to hurl the ball upward through the hoop. I could twirl a yo-yo, I could ride a bike, I could ride a wave, and that was it. And yet. These girls, these women, home-run hitters, filling out their uniforms, chomping past in cleats.

Geraldine had brought me to this game, my old college roommate, now a busy lawyer, and she had clients to meet with while I was visiting her and so took me to the park nearby her office. "Check them out," she said. She knew me well. So here I was, chillin' in both senses, but not in my five senses, if you dig. I was grateful for my oversized cat's-eye sunglasses, hiding my expression. OH! Struck out! "My" pitcher grinning, beaming, nodding to her team: "Took care of *that*." She walked off the mound and dumped her glove, accidentally knocking my cell phone off the bench. It crashed into two pieces.

"Geez, I'm sorry."

"I'm not."

She squinted down at me in nonrecognition. "Huh?"

"I mean so what if you busted it. Fine. This way my friend can't call me and interrupt the game. I want to see you win."

The pitcher's eyes were blue. "Ya rootin' for me?"

"You win, I'll buy the beer."

"I'll take a soda, but you're on."

"Or make it dinner," I amended, but she was up at bat.

The pitcher had long fingers, to go with long eyes, long thighs, and I was all long sighs by now, wishing I had a butterscotch drop or something to suck on because my mouth was watering. Here came the ball, low and inside. *Smack.* The ball was somewhere in Cambodia. My pitcher, now my hitter, loped around the bases like a wolf, her teammates screaming "MAURA!" So, that was her name.

"You're good, Maura," I praised as she heaved onto the bench, rubbing her instep.

"Aw, I was better when I was nineteen."

"Yeah? I can't say the same for myself. I'm better now, at what I do well," I dared.

She considered this, and I wondered if I'd gone too far. Damn it! How I push when I'm attracted! Then Maura spoke: "Didn't you say you were waiting for some friend to call and come get you?"

"Just an old college friend. She's busy. I'm . . . at liberty."

Maura slurped water from an old cracked bottle with a peeling Wonder Woman sticker on its plastic front. She looked out affectionately at the asphalt field where her teammates were wrapping up a victory. "On a day like this, it sure feels good to be up on my mound."

I wanted to be up on her mound myself. To bury my face in it, share the grass stains, shout out "opening day." I'd wait to be invited. How come I liked her so? Those long legs, those blue eyes. And how long had it been, for me? And was I hot enough to score? I thought I might be.

An inning's never longer than when you're cold, with no coffee, and hoping for a date, I watched them win. Watched Maura. Come on, baby. Pitch it to me. Find my sweet spot. Her hand fell on my shoulder: "Where's my soda?"

I jumped up, stupid. "That was great! Uh—can I help you carry anything? Your hat? Your glove? Your water?"

"Nobody touches my glove but me; I won't even take it out of state." So I shouldered her bat and the water.

Maura had a car parked two blocks over, and I assumed it would be dingy inside with sweaty workout gear and sneakers. To my surprise, the entire car interior was lined with Barbie dolls. Maura noted my ironic expression and explained, "I'm a bit of a collector. If you laugh, you're dead."

"I won't laugh," I promised, shoving aside a prom-night Barbie and settling into the front passenger seat.

Inside of two seconds I was practically lying down as Maura expertly pressed the seat adjuster and sent me flying backward into

3

horizontal comfort. Barbies in provocative golf shirts tumbled into my lap—or was that Maura's hand? Her eyes were twinkling. "Let's play ball."

"Batter up." I hadn't expected THIS.

A warm scent of Ben-Gay mixed with Nivea lotion rose from Maura's forty-something knees as she straddled me there in the Barbie-mobile. I wondered if anyone might come looking in the windows, then realized dusk had fallen. "I thought you wanted a soda," I gasped out.

"I got something better to sip now," she said huskily, and slipped her tongue into my mouth.

Chapter Two

Midnight in the Garden of Good and Plenty

The mail arrived containing the long-awaited invitation to Janet's annual New Year's Eve party. Her parties were famous for their outlandish themes and elaborate settings as well as the gourmet menu overflowing caviar and champagne. I would wait with anticipation for the personalized perfumed stationery, chuckling inside at Janet's choice of theme and specialized party favors. This time the invitation ignited warmth in the pit of my stomach that had been dormant for a whole year. I had not allowed myself to feel the intensity of my desire since that night in the garden. I had searched for a whole year, attending other parties hoping she would show up. For a brief moment she turned my existence from complacency to ecstasy and then she was gone. I have not loved another since.

We met at Janet's last party—a sixties hippie theme. I caught her eye from across the room and we smiled at each other as if we were old friends. She was the most beautiful woman in the room, standing softly in her long peasant dress. Coming to rest gently upon her breasts were her love beads hanging delicately from her neck. The strobe light was flickering still images of her radiant smile and dark eyes. I was instantly drawn to her, bewitched by her presence. I slowly made my way across the room, grabbing two glasses of champagne from a passing waiter, never taking my eyes off of her.

"You look thirsty," I said as my eyes danced along the soft outline of her body.

"Yes, this is exactly what I need," she responded in a deep sultry voice. My heart began to ache as I felt my limbs become heavy with each word that dripped off her tongue. She had lured me in like a spider's prey into her web.

"Your costume fits you well," she commented, as her eyes rested upon my chest. I had decided to go with a simple pair of tie-dyed jeans and T-shirt with a brown suede vest. Her long fingers reached out to touch the fringes on the vest, brushing the back of her hand against my breast. I felt my stomach tighten as her knuckle grazed my nipple that had begun to protrude from the moment my eyes fell upon her. People were dancing, music was blaring, and Janis Joplin saturated the room with her blues rhapsody. None of it penetrated my senses. I could only see her face, hear her voice, feel her touch. I was lost in her eyes as she kept her hand on my vest and my leg rested against her thigh.

"I would like to get some air. Would you join me?"

A cagey little smile appeared across her lips. She slowly lowered her hand into mine and began to lead me to the veranda. We inched our way through the crowd. From behind I could breathe in the jasmine scent of her hair as she gently squeezed my hand

Does she know what a bewitching effect she has on me? Was this a game she played? Or did she feel the same energy that was pulsating through my body? I shook these thoughts from my head.

I didn't care what she thought. No analysis. No speculation. Just be. I had never let myself be swept away like this. She was enchanting, and I wanted to lose myself in her mystery.

We reached the veranda still holding hands. Couples were moving in and out of the party. Some were roaming the grounds while others sat in the shadows exchanging caresses and long kisses. She continued to lead me down the concrete staircase into the garden as the party noise faded into the distance. We twisted and turned our way through overgrown ferns and tall green hedges. She moved at a pace as if she had a specific destination— she had been this way before. Our journey ended with our arrival to a small clearing. The moon illuminated our surroundings, allowing me to see only a small statue of some Greek goddess and several stone benches positioned in a circular formation. She let go of my hand and raised her sights to the moon above. I moved toward her, placing my hands around her waist, leaning in so my lips brushed gently against her cheek.

"What is your name?" I whispered into her ear.

"Reddy."

"I sure am," I stammered.

She chuckled. "No, silly, that's my name."

Our eyes met once again as the party crowd in the distance began the final countdown—the last few seconds left in a year and the opening chapter of a new one.

"You are the most beautiful woman I have ever met," I exclaimed.

She smiled and let go of a throaty giggle. "I am here for you and only you," she murmured.

Nine, eight, seven . . .

"This moment is for us to take. It can be the beginning or the end," I said as she glanced away acknowledging the chorus of voices counting. *Six, five, four . . .*

"Can it just be a moment, yes?" and she led me toward one of the benches. *Three, two, one . . .*

I kissed her with all of my being. I wanted the kiss to be endless like the darkness that surrounded us. She lowered herself down, inviting me into her arms. *Happy New Year!*

I felt the fire rise within me as I kissed her lips, burning into my memory their taste and texture. She felt magnificent under me. Her dress ascended over her head, revealing skin as soft as the moonbeam shining upon us. She stretched her arms above her head as my mouth began its slow descent along her throat, the edge of her shoulder and resting upon her breast. I was lost in her beauty, her delicacy. She was an angel surrounded by light and love, yet she was real to the touch of my fingers within her, moaning and lifting her body from the bench with each new sensation.

Our moment reached finality as the passion she ignited relinquished within me. Not a word was spoken between us. She covered herself with her dress as she walked back toward the party. I followed her out of the clearing, trying to find my way through the darkness, searching for her shadowy figure with every turn along the path. I could not keep up as the distance between us grew. I began to weave my way through the darkness at a quicker pace. The music was louder as I emerged from behind a large bush and the veranda appeared in front of me. She was gone. Where did she go? I hadn't noticed Janet standing on the veranda peering down at me.

"Hey, where ya been? Ya missed New Year's," she announced.

I stared up at her, trying to catch my breath.

"I went for a walk in the garden," I stated.

"Seems more like a sprint. Y'all right?" she asked.

"Yeah, I'm fine. You didn't see a pretty blonde in a peasant dress come through this way, did ya?" I asked subtly.

"Oh, so that's what gotcha outta breath, huh?" She had a devious smile on her face.

A smile came to my face as I dropped the invitation and my car keys onto the hallway table. With remembering that incredible moment at midnight came all of the questions left unanswered since. Would she be there again this year? Where did she disappear to that night? Who was she, really?

My apartment door flew open and Crystal came barreling in. A longtime friend and confidante, she had tried to counsel me and encourage me to let go of my mystery woman.

"Oh, I see you got Janet's invitation. Are you going?"

"I guess so," I said, lost in my thoughts.

"You're still thinking of that woman, aren't you? Get her out of your mind, babe. She has haunted you for too long."

"Yeah, you're right." But it was a half-hearted response.

"You know, you never told me her name."

"Reddy. She told me her name was Reddy."

Crystal's eyes were bulging from their sockets as her jaw dropped to her chin.

"What?" I said excitedly. "You know this woman? All this time you knew her and you didn't say anything!" I was ready to pounce on her.

"You never told me her name before," she said defensively.

"Who is she, Crystal? Do you know where she lives?" I was ready to explode inside.

Crystal could barely speak. She sat frozen in the cushioned chair looking up at me as if I had spoken some heresy.

"Babe, Reddy is, I mean was, Janet's first and longtime partner. She died almost ten years ago during one of Janet's parties. She overdosed while partying with some lowlife out in the garden behind Janet's house. That's why Janet has these extravagant parties each year. They are given in her memory."

Chapter Three
Syrup on the Glass

My girlfriend was still asleep and snoring gently with the sweet rasp of a skateboard scraping against the curb when I crept out of bed to admire my neck in the mirror. There, just above the collarbone, the soft spot had turned reddish blue and oval where her teeth had nudged my skin last night. "Harder," I had whispered to the darkness. "Come on, pretty baby. Leave your mark." "Never want to hurt you," she had murmured back, hovering above me like a hot benevolent glider in midair, but I insisted. "Yes, a wee one." Just that spot to show the world where her mouth met me. Just a gaudy splash to wear home on the plane.

Now in the untested morning light I leaned across the sink and thought, "Our bodies blend together just like syrup on the glass." I knew what I meant. Dreamily splashing cold water on my face, preening at the mirror and tugging my pajama top, I let my thoughts reel back to 1981—the year I lived in Israel, at twenty.

There was a café all the students loved, affectionately called "The Cage" for its barred wallfront, just across the road from the gates of Tel Aviv University. I was alone the first time I ventured inside, an exchange student from America, with my bad clothes and my bad Hebrew and my long unraveling braid. I wanted a milkshake, which was listed on the menu in three languages, but when I placed my order the counterman confused me with his questions. "A chocolate shake?" he bellowed. "Yes, OK. *Beseder*," I replied.

But then he asked me, "What flavor ice cream?" Well—hmm, now, wouldn't it be chocolate? But perhaps this was a cultural test, a trick. I boldly chose banana, and then waited, acting cool.

Here's the way they shook milk at the Cage. A chocolate shake meant chocolate-flavored *syrup* squirted in gorgeous looping latticework on the inside of a clean soda glass. Then, as this pattern hardened just slightly, just tenderly tumescent, the whirr of a blender, there's your ice cream flavor, in my case, banana, whipped up and poured into the chocolate shell. I held up the heavy glass, now as fancy to my eye as any crystal goblet. Through the clear globe I watched the crisscrossed syrup lean against the ice cream, streak, then melt. It hung suspended, frozen by the ice cream, changing as I drank and let in air, fading, dripping, chocolate mingling into the banana, art as well as flavor, a palette for my palate. Then my hunger was fed.

I made it last a long time, sucking down that sweetness, but in the end I put down the glass, and on its rim a dainty drop of syrup, reminding me that this was a masterpiece.

Well. I've learned that lovemaking is messy-sweet like that. My girlfriend leaves her flavor in my mouth. Sometimes vanilla, sometimes teaberry. She blends me like a milkshake, stirring, swirling, my mouth is watering. I need to eat. I feel the chill steal over me. The tasting. Her syrup makes a pattern on my glass.

Chapter Four
Jump Start

"How could I be so stupid?" Taylor shouted over the Joan Jett tape blasting from the car's stereo. *"I should a seen it comin', I knew she was cheatin' on me!"*

She had just left Morgan's house, her girlfriend for the past three years, who was getting more than her nails done by the beautiful Danielle, her manicurist. Both Taylor's mind and car were racing down I-95 after she just walked in on the two of them in the shower. It was a cold winter's night. Taylor drove with no destination in mind. She had a need for speed and some loud tunes. That was her fix for when she got hot under the collar. She would just drive her car until her engine cooled down.

"Oh man, what now!" Taylor saw a car's hazard lights flashing in the distance, along with a person standing in the middle of the road waving their arms. Taylor hit the brakes before she ran over

the lunatic. Standing in her headlights was a woman. It wasn't just any woman. To Taylor it was a vision of beauty. She stood in front of Taylor's car, her silky brown hair flowing in the icy wind. Her long black coat covered most of her, but when the wind blew, she could see the leather miniskirt she wore and a pair of legs that were as long as I-95.

"*My God! What is that? Who is that?*" Taylor whispered aloud. Her eyes were wide open as if she herself was a deer caught in headlights. The vision walked as quickly as her black leather boots would allow her over to Taylor's window.

"Please, my car's battery died. Could you give me a jump?"

Taylor tried to release the words stuck in the back of her throat, but all that came out was "Sh . . . sh . . . sure."

"I would be so grateful if you could." Her voice, though seasoned with a hint of desperation, was a melody to Taylor's ears.

Taylor stepped out of her car and could not feel the ground beneath her feet. She was immune to the cold as she slowly made her way to her trunk. She fumbled for the cables, moving as if she was in a dream, and there was nothing she could do to speed things up. She bumped into the fender on her way toward the vision's car.

"I have been waiting so long for someone to come along. You are an angel."

"N . . . n . . . no problem," Taylor stammered. She leaned under the hood to locate the positive and negative cells on the battery while she tried to keep her heart from jumping out of her ski jacket.

"Maybe I can pay you for your kindness?" the woman inquired.

"No, that's OK." Taylor felt beads of sweat forming on her forehead, though the latest weather report declared below freezing temperatures for the night.

"Well, perhaps I can reward you in some other way." And before Taylor could respond she felt a slight pressure against the back of her leg, climbing its way from the back of her knee up her thigh. She quickly deduced, "*It's her fingers!*"

Taylor remained motionless while her head went into overdrive. *"Come on, girl! Make a decision, yes or no. Right now."*

Thoughts and images sped across her mind. She saw her and Morgan's first chance meeting at the bookstore. She saw their first date, and their first kiss in front of Morgan's house. She replayed their first time making love. She remembered how Morgan acted so shy when Taylor unbuttoned her blouse and revealed her soft, tanned breasts. How Morgan buried her face into her neck when Taylor moved her fingers over her body, making her moan as she stroked her so tenderly. Holding Morgan after making love was like holding a precious gift, delicate yet strong. She held those moments, lying beside each other in the darkness and solitude of her bedroom, as sacred. She then saw Morgan in the shower with Miss Hand Specialist. Her eyes winced with the emotional pain from the memory of this image. She slowly turned to face the mysterious woman. Her eyes met the dark brown pair looking back at her with a seductive smile in them. They held each other's gaze. It seemed like an eternity.

"Would you like me to jump-start it now, or would you like the pleasure?" Taylor said, returning the same devilish smile. The woman moved closer, placing her leg strategically between Taylor's, and taking hold of the zipper on her ski jacket, whispered into Taylor's ear, "Baby, the pleasure is all mine."

Chapter Five
The Bush Pilot

I'd been stationed in Tanzania for almost a year when I realized I was running out of supplies. Up until the morning I used my last slip of toilet paper, I'd barely noticed—or cared about—my isolation from the "real" world. I worked out of a simple straw-and-mud hut in a remote corner of the game reserve; all of my attention was focused on wildlife preservation, specifically the habits of giraffes. I was up well before dawn to make notes in my journal. I stalked giraffes, elephants and baboons all day long with my camera and binoculars. About once a week I caught a ride or walked miles through Masai country to the nearest lodge with Internet service and filed my reports back to the zoological society I worked for in New York. I'd joke with the lodge staff in my bad Swahili, drink a cup of excellent coffee or chai bora, then go back to my hut. Occasionally, watching baboons mate or catching sight of a female reedbuck lifting her tail for receptive sex, I'd realize I was having no "wild life" of my own. I missed it—but in Tanzania, homosexuality is illegal, Masai girls are ritually circumcised, and I kept my lusty nature to myself. I didn't want to cause an international incident, or, perhaps, an international affair.

Looking through my trashed hut for toilet paper that day, I knew I'd either have to go back to stocking banana leaf in the outhouse again or tear up the back pages of a magazine, when suddenly I thought I heard an elephant trumpeting in the distance. Funny, it didn't sound like a *tembo* warning call. Soon I discerned the ongoing whine of an airplane engine, not an animal noise after all—boy, I'd been out here a long time. I knew there was a landing strip at the north end of the game park, but no one had warned me about a party coming in.Usually those flights were private tour groups of rich Westerners (or, more recently, Japanese) landing in the bush for a prepaid photo safari.

I squinted at the sky. It was a small white two-engine plane without any corporate logo I could see. The pilot seemed to circle above me intentionally. I thought I observed a wave from a gloved hand. Thick babao trees, their trunks ravaged by elephants, obscured the landing of the plane, but soon the engine's roar died down and I assumed there'd been no trouble with our runway—really it was just a strip of red African earth, hard-packed and dung-flecked. Sensing I might have company later on, I hastily did my business with the banana leaf and resumed my planned morning with my animal pals.

"*Jambo! Haribu?*"
"*Jambo. Mzere. Npenda coffee? Chai?*"
"*Asante sana, rafiki.* But you speak English, I assume?"
The pilot wore leather pants, leather jacket, and a ripped black T-shirt printed with HAKUNA MATATA—Swahili for "no wor-

ries." I noticed a sparkle of eye makeup just below her thick and handsome brows, and quickly took stock of my own appearance: these months in the remotest parklands hadn't included much daily hygiene, let alone regular primps in a mirror. Did I still own a mirror? I'd given up shaving away any kind of body hair I might be growing, and most of my shirts and brightly patterned kanga cloths were stiff with repeated bug repellent applications or the occasional stumble into a pile of animal dung. I did remember to put on chapstick with SPF 30 every day, so I figured my lips still looked somewhat approachable, and I was wearing my favorite sun hat that day, with the New York Liberty WNBA logo, not quite faded.

The pilot grinned. "Are you Dr. Annabel?"

Cover blown. "The one and only. They call me Bela here. Do I look professorial enough?"

"You look like you've been doing what they hired you to do back in New York. They sent me out here to bring you some supplies and to get your notes—there's a mail strike on, did you know?—and I've got some papers from the office that you need to sign now to extend your grant. I think I also have some good old American snack food for you, toilet paper, Tampax, film, batteries, your tax forms, and a sweater from your mother that you totally won't need in *this* heat."

What a bounty! It was Hanukkah in July! Tampax! Toilet paper! Granola bars and even a jar of pickles! Batteries for my vibrator! I pressed the bulky packages to my braless breasts. "Would you like sugar in your coffee, Miss . . ."

"Actually, it's Captain. But you can call me Chex."

Chex. I stirred raw sugar into the Kilimanjaro brew, mentally warming to the situation. In truth, I was warm all over. That's partly life on the African plain, but I had to admit the inner fire wasn't exactly extinguished by the arrival of a pilot in leather for breakfast.

Chex helped me through my bashful awkwardness by unloading the delivery bags while I threw the hut into a sort of order.

How long had it been since I entertained a female who wasn't a baboon or an elephant? At least Chex was unlikely to pee down my shirt. Or had trends gone so wild in dyke U.S.A. during my time abroad that . . . *naw*.

"Mind if I sit on your . . . bedding?" Chex laughed aloud at my sofa-sleeper, really a pile of tapestried pillows gone to seed with a few bright kangas tossed on top. She spread her legs as she lowered herself, thighs creaking amicably. "Mmm." She sipped at the coffee as if we were in the most chic New York café instead of a zoologist's Tanzanian hideout. "Good stuff."

We sat like that, companionably, the Tanzanian heat causing beads of sweat to well up between our breasts, for maybe an hour, talking about life back home, about the moral and social complications of being white Western women in African service. Taking each other's moral, political, ethical temperatures while, I suspected, we were also checking each other out on an entirely different internal heat monitor. You can't study the mating habits of animals, the body language, for most of your adult professional life and not recognize when a female of any species is relaxing into what we call the *receptive* position. There was Chex with her legs apart and her pupils dilated, and no one around for miles. So what if the Kili coffee barely masked the aroma of giraffe dung beyond my doorway? Aren't we all just animals, ourselves?

Had I forgotten how to *do it*, in my isolation, my loneliness? Did I need help to get me started? Someone who knew her way around a woman's needs?

A bush pilot, in other words?

I made a show of opening my mail, my mother's packages, the contracts from my very distant office. Outside, I heard every nameable species getting it on. And the Lord God named them all. And they were being fruitful and multiplying. My zoologist brain recognized every squeak and groan, howl and shriek, hoot and trumpet of animal love. I ticked off the species in my mind. Dik-dik. Grant's gazelle. White-bellied bustard.

Chex in the receptive position, waiting for my move.

18

Did I have the nerve? To pilot into the bush of the bush pilot? I might, I thought, turning to look at the beautiful creature who had literally fallen out of the sky. I just might.

Formalities, in Swahili. "*Uko peke yako*?" I asked her. Are you . . . here on your own?

On her own, free and easy. No partner, I gathered. No worries. *Hakuna matata*.

I fumbled for my next line. And like a good pilot, she seized the controls. "Would you like to come over here?" She patted my bed.

Without thinking, I responded in Swahili: "*Vizuri, nitapenda kuja*." I'd love to come. And we burst out laughing.

Outside, the elephant shifted her enormous ears. The giraffe and zebra paused. I had for so long taken notes on them, now they tuned into me and to the human animal noises they had never heard before. The zoologist was laughing. The zoologist was moaning. They knew better than to come close. The sweet scent of our bodily fluids warned them back. I had learned from my wildlife pals to respect the forceful realm of what came naturally, and, following my better animal instincts, I mated and marked my territory, at last.

Chapter Six
Late Night Omelet

Something told me I was in for a surprise tonight. Call it a gut feeling, call it female intuition, call it three bourbons with beer chasers, but something was talking to me at two in the morning when I walked into that diner and sat down in the booth by the window.

It was saying loud and clear, *"Baby, fasten your seat belt, you are in for the ride of your life!"* Could it be true or was it the liquor talking? I was betting on the booze until she stood at my table to take my order.

"What'll you have?" she said, holding her pen to her pad, never looking up from the paper. I peered over the menu with my bloodshot eyes. She was a tall drink of water, all right. A strawberry blonde with fingers so long they could make pencils jealous. I started to speak but my tongue was stuck to the roof of my mouth.

I gulped the water in front of me, hoping it would come unglued. She looked up from her pad to see what was taking so long. Our eyes met. Those green eyes melted into me like butter on a hot griddle. I was finally able to remember a few words and I put together a sentence.

"You got some eggs?" I asked her.

She took a long time answering, like she had to think about her stock. Finally with a short smile creeping through the sides of her mouth she said, "Yeah, we got eggs. How ya like dem eggs?"

I caught on to her little game fast. I was a player, and she knew it. So it was my turn to raise the ante.

"Can you make me a three-egg omelet?" I was testing the waters to see if she was a swimmer or was she just the type that likes to dip their big toe in once and a while.

"Yeah, I can do that. How's about some home fries and toast to go with it?" She was slick, but I knew how to handle the fast ones.

"OK," I said, "I can get into some of that."

"Can I getcha some coffee while you're waitin'?" She was working it real hard, but I wasn't backing down either.

"Yeah, some coffee."

"How ya take it?"

This was my big move. I was throwing in all of my chips. I doubled down and was going for broke.

"I take it light and sweet," I said in my best sultry drunken stupor voice. And then I added, "Just like my women."

"I'll be comin'"—she hesitated while tapping her pen softly on her pad—"right up with that coffee."

I leaned back against my seat feeling as proud as a prize-winning pig at the county fair.

We exchanged glances as she and the last customers at the counter exchanged money. She slammed shut the register, bid the lovely couple good night and headed into the kitchen without taking those emerald eyes off of me. Just thinking about those long fingers serving my meal was bringing on that nice warm feeling inside. The one that starts between your legs and makes its way up

21

through you and settles somewhere around your throat. I sat playing with my utensils, waiting for her to come through those swinging doors and serve me a plate of pleasure along with my omelet.

It got quiet. Too quiet, I suppose. No sounds of clanging pots or sizzling grease could I hear going on in the kitchen.

"Hey, darlin', where's my omelet?" I shouted toward the swinging doors. But still, I couldn't detect any movement taking place back there. This started to stir up part anger and part curiosity in me. Like a bit of heaven and hell rattling around inside having a tug of war. Did she stand me up? Leave me hanging here? Or maybe . . .

I took leave of my booth and made my way toward the door. I peered first through the frosted windows only to see a shadowy figure on the other side. She was in there, all right. But I needed to investigate further. Like a "recon" team, I needed to penetrate behind enemy lines and advance my position. So I decided to invade her territory. I flung open the doors.

"Honey, where's my . . . *Oh my Lord! What have we here?*"

Well, there she stood like a pinup calendar girl—a Miss July, and the fireworks were about to go off in every part of my body. Her strawberry blond hair was falling about her naked breast and there was only a white apron separating me from having the main course. She was leaning back against the butcher block counter, kinda spread-eagle like. She was waiting for me to come through the doors, and I had obliged. The sight of her definitely wet my appetite. She threw those pair of jade jewels with their seductive look my way.

"The cook's gone for the night, how's about some home cookin' instead?"

I slowly moved toward my luscious entrée, disposing of my dinner jacket along the way.

She moaned in my ear as my lips nibbled on her neck, lighting her pilot light under her burner. I was going to make this spicy dish simmer for a few minutes, letting my fingers work her dough under her blond locks. I gently kneaded her, molding her form to my hand, feeling them rise with each tender squeeze as her mouth-watering tongue slowly stirred mine. I was turning up the heat and bringing her to a boil. I moved my way down this blond buffet, finding her beautiful tenderloin under her apron with sweet drippings enticing to the palate. I feasted upon her, wanting seconds and thirds. The voice in my head egged me on until her piece de resistance came to its finale. I held her in front of me, letting her plate cool while inhaling the intoxicating aroma of her bountiful body. A smile made its way to my face as I looked into her glossy green eyes.

"Now," I said slyly, "how's about that omelet."

Chapter Seven

I Was a Drag King Sandwich

She went down to the bar and knew nobody. She'd been away too long. Funkily dressed out in a Hang Ten belt from 1971 and striped jeans, an alligator tooth necklace around her neck, she tripped down the magic stairs into sweaty dyke culture, public eroticism, young perfect bodies and middle-aging bodies like her own. How had she come to feel so at home in this public eroticism, drag kings onstage rubbing packed crotches, femmes in the audience screaming for candy?

She surveyed the room for familiar characters: it couldn't have changed that much in the four months she'd been gone. What happened to that cool character everyone knew as "Autumn Leather"? Had she quit the scene, as she so often threatened to, and gone back to the Southwest to fight brush fires? What about Amber, whom everyone envied because she landed that job waxing women's bikini areas at the Smoother You salon? Had everyone graduated and left town?

24

There. Over there. Greta, the biker anthropologist, taking notes in the same old wax-spattered journal, pausing now and then to bite her girlfriend's neck. Greta would know.

She tossed her worn leather jacket atop an equally worn leather bar stool and ordered a shot of Stoli on ice. "What's the word, Greta the Great?"

The anthropologist had gone drag king that long winter. "It's Greaser now, but good to see you, mate." Long sideburns, long chaps, but no chapstick. She barely recognized her. But Greta/Greaser's girlfriend was the same. Moody, sulky, petulant, pierced and snarling. "Oh, it's *you*," the girlfriend offered in welcome, then stalked off to the bathroom, probably to apply more sparkle-dust to her already quivering cleavage.

She was left alone with Greaser. "Still writing about king life? But now you are one. Lean back against me and talk about it."

Greaser's flannel back pressed to her own cotton shirtfront. The biker/writer/king mused eagerly in a voice made raw from the effort of shouting above retro lounge classics. "I got it all figured out, Stace. I got it going here. See, one minute I was writing a paper about it, the next I was onstage and loving it. They hollered for more. I'm going on the road with the kings!"

The girlfriend returned, glaring, and having overheard this last bit, hissed, "There ain't nothing on the road that she can't get at home, nothing out there I can't give her or better."

Greaser shifted. "I know, honey. But you regret more the things you didn't do. I gotta be a king. Just let me try."

They were warming up to fight, and she didn't want to hang around for the flying ice cubes, the shattered Cosmo glass. She pulled back and released Greaser's warm, tight body. She thought, I had you once. I took you. I had my fingers in the folds of your old Levi's. What's your little femme got that's so tasty?

It was hot in the bar. Some straight boys had pushed onto the dance floor, shirtless, catcalling at the drag kings and their women. It happened every once in a while when the kings were staging a show, mean testosterone from the street. "Get them out of here!" the manager shouted, setting loose a bouncer as built and shaggy as a Newfoundland dog. Gay men slammed down their Cosmo glasses and rushed to defend dyke tomboys. The straight boys fled. The kings cheered. Greaser took notes.

She really had been away too long. There was no one here to touch the way she once touched, knees beneath the bar stool, a breath mint passed from mouth to mouth that time. No one who remembered that night when she was out on the dance floor with one king in front of her and one pressed up behind, making a drag king sandwich. It didn't have to be so bittersweet, nostalgia. The bar was younger now.

"Excuse me," said a voice.

She turned to look right into Sammy's dreads. "Sam!"

The queenly king was smiling. "Heard you were back, baby. But I never thought you'd come back looking *this* good." Warm arms, scent of China musk, cigar in a work shirt pocket. A Jamaican vision.

She opened her mouth to shout for sheer gladness and had about a mile of Sammy's tongue, just like that, that quick.

Spinning strobe lights, ashtrays full of gum wrappers and matchbooks, girls with big legs in cheap cargo pants and girls laced up in corsets. It wasn't much, just home. Just home again, and Sammy. Just hands down in her pockets, Sammy's hands. Sammy pulling her onto the floor and whispering louder than any hip-hop sound track, "Baby's back."

They danced. Moshing together, wide open pores. Greaser slipped up and ground on her from behind, making a sandwich of the three of them. She could feel the room throbbing like a crotch on a pony ride and the sweat was shining on her own collarbone, the smoky air just one alert level below choking, but the dress-up cologne of kings and femmes overlaid in pearly sheen, seductive. And she was neither king nor femme but loved them both and all. Could it ever be this good again?

Sammy had a delicate long finger in the small of her back, heading southward in no hurry.

It might even get better.

Chapter Eight

Long Train Coming

Mary Beth was a looker. She was your typical college coed. She had shoulder-length blond hair, blue eyes that made the sky jealous, a pair of 36B's up front and a 27-inch waist right below. She would walk across the campus and heads would turn. Her smile made anyone stumble over the cobblestones. She was all that and more. Mary Beth was a well-bred blue blood—attending Exeter and now Vassar, raised in Connecticut, and spending summers abroad.

Yet inside lived a wild woman. She was a woman who never said no to any experience, big or small, good or dangerous. She lived life on the edge but always pulled back just in time.

It was a balmy night in late September, and all the sororities were hustling the freshmen to sign up to pledge. My good friend Samantha, Sam to me, dragged me out to a pledge party at one of those Greek-named houses. Sororities just ain't my scene. I'm more of the blues-playing-candlelit-cheap-wine-smelling-bars kinda girl. I like an atmosphere that lets a woman get up close and personal with that special someone they met just fifteen minutes earlier. For me, it's at the bar, on the dance floor, or in the bathroom stall. It's the moment that counts, if you know what I mean. But Sam is my friend, so I bit the bullet. I threw on my neatest pair of jeans, a black T-shirt, and my leather jacket and headed out to throw back some punch and eat sugar cookies.

The house was filled with girls that looked liked they just stepped out of the latest issue of *Cosmo*. My "gay-dar" was up and running, but something told me I was going to be the lonesome dyke swimming in this pond of females with not a blip on the screen. After wading through a sea of cashmere sweaters and pearl necklaces, I finally made my way to the makeshift bar set up in the common room. There she was. She was propped up on a bar stool wearing her tight black jeans and an even tighter white tank top underneath the silk blue blouse that opened enough to reveal an ever-so-slight line of cleavage. She was surrounded by two or three little princesses, all in their Ann Taylor best. But she was their queen, and she held court with her outrageous stories that I couldn't help but overhear.

"Hey, it's time to sing our sisters' pledge song!" someone shouted from the next room.

All the princesses scampered away onto the veranda, deserting their queen. From the corner of my eye, I could see her staring at me, wondering who was this odd girl out.

"Hi, I'm Mary Beth," she said. As I turned to acknowledge, her eyes caught mine and pierced through my leather jacket and my "tough girl" act that I was throwing her way.

"I'm CJ."

"Nice to meet you. Are you thinking of pledging?" she asked.

"I don't think I'm their type," I said with a superior smirk on my face.

"You're probably right, but you certainly are my type," she

declared emphatically. I suddenly found moisture running down my shirt due to the punch I sprayed halfway across the fake bar.

"Look what you did to yourself. Here, let me help you." She picked a few napkins up off the bar and began to soak up the punch, pressing her napkin-filled hand across my chest. I soaked up the sweet-smelling perfume emanating from her hair. It was intoxicating.

"This isn't going to dry, and it will leave a major stain on you. Come with me and I'll fix you up."

She was already leaving a stain on me.

She took me by the hand. She had the softest hands, but her firm grip revealed a strong, no-nonsense woman. A woman who knew what she wanted and most likely got it nine times out of ten. So was this going to be the ninth or the tenth time? I found myself having very little choice. I was being pulled up the staircase to her room as well as being pulled toward her by the power of her being. In a blink of an eye she became my queen, and I would do her bidding.

She threw open her bedroom door and pulled me in. Before I could speak, she filled my mouth with her luscious tongue, pinning me against the door with her arms. We had left the party downstairs and began our very own one flight up. We tore madly at each other's clothes, saying little to each other, letting our fingers and lips speak of our desire. She lay back upon the bed, letting my eyes take in every inch of her beautiful frame, burning her naked image in my memory forever. She softly moaned *"yes"* as I pressed my fingers within her and she . . .

The organ began to play, jolting me back to reality. The congregation stood, but I was slow ascending due to the wetness between my legs from my trip down memory lane. Two years have gone by since that night when our passion for each other was ignited. It was intense.

Then she did the "proper" thing. She met Tom, the soon to be six-figure-earning stockbroker.

I was now standing with a hundred of her closest friends witnessing their marriage.

She began her long walk down the aisle. Our eyes met, and she threw me a wink and a smile. It was that same smile that pierced my heart two years ago. I looked once more into those deep blue eyes that placed me in a trance whenever she glanced my way. Now, she was the queen once again in her long flowing wedding gown, a veil upon her head encircled with diamond-like stones. She proceeded down the aisle, standing tall, so sure of herself. Like the cat that ate the mouse, she smiled as if she had a secret. She did. We did.

Did anyone else know? I didn't care. I will always be hers. So I returned her wink and her smile, knowing that our pact that we made two years ago was still in place. She would always be my queen, and I would still do her bidding!

Chapter Nine
The Brass Ring

I had her in the Haunted House. The roller coaster would have been too messy—we tried something like that on Space Mountain in Disney World once, and her dark glasses went flying off into Neverland, and I got a kink in my back. But the Santa Cruz Beach Boardwalk? That's a slower-paced, infinitely hip scene, more surfer boys and chicks in flannel than at any theme park. You can be as quirky as you like there, lost amid the characters and corn dogs, dripping wetsuit bodies in the fog. You can try to have some loving there.

Why the Haunted House? Because that's where it all happened when I was seventeen.

In August 1978 I was seventeen and baby-dyke jailbait. I was walking around in a pre-lesbian funk, or, to use folk troubador Alix Dobkin's excellent phrase, I was suffering from "pre-lesbian tension," not ready to claim what I was but nonetheless walking around with a copy of Ruth Falk's *Women Loving* in my schoolbag, and I'd

31

checked *Rubyfruit Jungle* out of the library a couple of times. I was on vacation with my parents and had just told my mother, *I think I like women*, and I had a really bad haircut and wanted everyone to just leave me *alone*, you don't *understand*, the way it is when you're seventeen and brainy and dig girls. So they dropped me at the boardwalk while the rest of the family went shopping for a picnic, and that's when I noticed two actual lesbians holding hands in front of the Haunted House that afternoon in August 1978.

These women were *dykes*. Both were in their early thirties, which to my seventeen-year-old eye meant forty or fifty or a hundred. They wore matching weather-beaten denim jackets and had matching weather-beaten faces, free of makeup, which crinkled into smiles as I looked at them curiously. One said something to her friend, who turned back toward me and nodded. Then both of them stood quite still, gazing back at me, with something like a friendly and calm acknowledgment.

They were real lesbians—I knew this. Not only because they looked very much like the photo of lesbian activist Jill Johnston that I had recently cut out of *Ms.* magazine and hidden away, but also because they were so unlike all the other women on that carnival midway: they were open, brave, *together*. Probably *partners*, my brain rolled out the word like a spitball. I knew I was staring. But they were staring back. They were evaluating me just as boldly and smiling at me with what I recognized as recognition.

They recognized *me*.

Yeah, I'd recognized them. But this was something new. Caught looking, I was nodded to: a sister. They knew I'd soon be batting for their team. This would be me in twenty years or so. I stood alone in the great dyke stare-down, wondering who'd blink first. I wanted, twenty years hence, to have their open, smiling stance, my face still makeup-free, my clothes still boots and denim, my hair uncut, unstyled, and at my side a woman, not a man.

But did I really think like this, back then? Were my thoughts really, clearly formed? Or was it more like long, plum-colored light between our eyes, light shot twenty feet across pathways on a board-walk, locking me at one end and those grown-ups at the other?

Recognition. Did I think I could recognize them and look and drink my fill, so thirsty for role models, hints, any kind of mirror, without reciprocal familiarity from them? Women's symbol around my neck, women's symbols scribbled on my journal—animals stared like this. Are you a member of my species, my Latin classification, genus lesbo, or aren't you, then? A member of my pack? My turf? My kind? Shall I defend you in a conflict, share food, groom you? Am I one of your young?

They blinked first. Waving, the two women moved slowly down the midway, toward their car. When they had walked partway through the crowd, I saw one of them put her arm around the other. That gesture brought the *zing* out of my heart.

So, how long did it take from that day, back then, to the first time I kissed a girl? Just about twenty-two months. And how long ago had that first kiss been? Just about twenty-two years. Now I was back at the beach in Santa Cruz with my lover, looking for a place to hold her hand. Or hold her other parts. I loved her endlessly. When she suggested we go for a ride on the crowded carousel, the famous one that's featured in *The Sting*, I said, "Naw, babe, I already got the brass ring." When she tried to buy me a lottery card, I said, "Naw, I already won the jackpot." That kind of thing. But here we suddenly were at the Haunted House of my youth, and this time we were grown-ups holding hands.

And you bet, a seventeen-year-old girl sulking away from her family was gazing out at us. So I smiled back. She flinched and looked away, then stole another glance. We smiled and waved. Her jaw dropped.

History.

We got our tickets and squeezed our not insubstantial bodies into the little podlike cars. The bar came down across our knees and locked us in. The scary doors swung open for a three-minute ride through smelly vapor and fake zombies.

"Now," I said, and kissed my lover's mouth. I felt her resist, just briefly. The lights were out: total darkness. "No one's looking," I reassured, and her body relaxed, its heat rising across my forearms as I touched her soft breasts. A quick lurch to the left on the old

33

kiddie-car tracks sent our noses smack into each other. "Ow," we moaned, giggling.

A corpse rose casually out of a cardboard casket, and we heard seven-year-olds around us scream ecstatically in fear. I took the opportunity of sound to make my move, the one that always makes her moan. And moan she did. "What did you do to me!" she whispered.

Witches cackled all around us. I was cackling, too. "Loosen your shirt."

"No! The ride's almost over. We'll get caught."

"Come on, baby. You know you want to!" She did. She was ready and I knew it. I read her thighs like braille. I rode her like a surfer. I did the monster mash with my right hand. I stirred her witch's cauldron and raised hell.

The double doors slammed open, spilling our car into foggy Santa Cruz light. A teenage attendant cranked back the lever to stop our forward motion and threw up the bar, asking with rote friendliness, "Enjoy your ride, ladies?"

"Ohhhh," was all my girlfriend managed.

"You oughta try the carousel, it's pretty famous. It's the one featured in the movie *The Sting*, you know. And they filmed that vampire movie, *The Lost Boys*, here on the boardwalk too. If you go on the carousel you can—"

"—try to get the brass ring, yeah, I know," I finished his sentence, extricating myself from the ride car and hastily checking the seat for any lingering dampness. My lover looked at me, both shy and expectant. So I said it again, and I didn't care who heard it, and the seventeen-year-old girl of the new generation was still standing there, and recognized us. I took my lover's hand, and held it up, and explained to all and sundry, "I already got the brass ring." And walked away, not haunted anymore.

We were too absorbed in each other to notice the older dyke couple, weather-beaten faces, weather-beaten denim jackets, making out passionately on the bench that faces out to sea.

Chapter Ten

Morning Revelry

It's Saturday morning, seven fifty-nine. The alarm will be going off in a minute, sounding the beginning of a new day. Most days I would rise regretfully but happy. But today I want to linger in my carnal camp with my corporal lover. I turn to my side and mold my body against my strong GI, feeling the warmth of her back against my chest. My fingers gently stroll along her soft hip, not wanting to disturb her sleep but still taking pleasure from touching her. I rest my lips upon her shoulder and close my eyes, letting the stillness of the morning encase us. She stirs and signals with a low chuckle or a moan her request for me to proceed.

She wallows in a soft sleep, conscious of my movements but remaining still, letting my fingers maneuver along her magnificent terrain. Exploring my strong Amazon warrior's defined biceps and tight stomach from thousands of pushups and sit-ups, then cupping her soft warm breasts and entangling my fingers in the hairs of her mound, I sense both strength and suppleness in one being. I am aroused by my actions and in knowing I have those two worlds lying beside me. I have the commander—the embodiment of strength, courage, and virility when she slips on her camouflage pants and combat boots. Yet when I strip from her this armor of authority, she reveals the compassionate, sensitive heart of a woman. She is a woman with desires and passions, collapsing the trenches surrounding her heart so I may do her bidding.

Let me soothe your troubled soul, my comrade, who battles these two worlds within . . .

With her eyes still closed she slowly rolls over onto her back, letting my head rest upon her chest. I continue my morning play. My head fills with the beat of her heart—a steady war drum of power and fortitude as my hand is filled with her malleable mound below, dipping into her creamy pool generated from my finger frolic. I encounter my own wetness on my thigh and restrain my impulse to disturb my sleepy soldier. My platoon of fingers slithers along her thigh over her hard quadriceps, like loyal soldiers. They follow their commander's orders and survey the terrain. But there is no hostile land here. She is my ally, my lover, entreating me in the early morning hours to enter her headquarters. I oblige my lover, patrolling with my platoon the outskirts of her command center as I advance inward toward my target. Her excitement escalates as my fingers engage her swollen domain, and my hero stirs with her hips receding to my touch. I retreat and await further orders from my general. She whispers in her dreamy state, "Yes . . . I like that," as her hips move like a battleship upon the mighty ocean. Do I dare refuse my superior? My duty lies next to me and my orders are clear. My platoon cautiously penetrates deep within, slowly performing recon of their surroundings. I watch for signs of resistance to appear. Only the low moan of compliance and encouragement resounds in the morning quietness. My crackerjack platoon advances and retreats with precision and ease. Her mighty muscles contract around my forces as they gently push deeper, desiring to please their leader. My warrior, in her sexual slumber, urges my troops on, "Yes, don't stop . . ." With resilience and resolve they forge on, moving within, knowing the climax is close at hand. My champion, raising her flag in victory, awakens to my winning smile and proclaims, "Good morning."

Chapter Eleven

Butter Me Down

We were lying in bed exhausted. Worn out with lovemaking, our tongues and taste buds bruised, our eleven fingers (Max had an extra one, and that's why I was so weak now) lying limp at our sides. The radio was on, the TV was on, the CD we'd forgotten about kept replaying, and every sound and message was food related: commercials for restaurants, songs about ice cream, the food and wine guy drizzling chocolate on some rerun episode of *Queer Eye for the Straight Guy.*

"I'm panting with hunger," I said.

"I'm ravenous," said Max.

"We have to eat something besides each other," I moaned.

There was nothing in the kitchen. I've been known to boil water, and that's about it. The ancient Frigidaire held jars of pickles and mustard, sour cream and horseradish, the telltale signs of an undomesticated Jewish girl. The day looked promising beyond my windowsill, shafts of sunlight illuminating the hastily ripped-open packets of mint lube sitting there, creating a green-golden glow. "Why don't we go out for pancakes?" I asked Max.

She was inspecting her lucky eleventh finger. "You know what I'd like to do?" Max whispered. "I'd like to savor the spices I have right here, in you. Your carob eyes, your chocolate hair, your light brown skin like cinnamon, your ginger voice, your nutmeg laugh, your smoky taste like hazelnuts. Like chicory. Like cardamom." Max had recently returned from a research trip to the spice island of Zanzibar. There was a basket of those spices on my kitchen windowsill but nothing to eat in the fridge. Max was a poet and a tease, and talking about food when I was so hungry was her game; if I wanted to be taken out to breakfast I'd better play along. So I thought about what I was in the mood for, and turned my smiling eyes on Max.

Butter me down with yr wet blue eyes
Then slide yr syrup down my thighs
Banana wheatcake chocolate chip
Each forkful to your open lip
Remind me, soothing honey girl
To drink juice from yr sweetest curl
Let breakfast be the aftertaste
To feed our bodies, spent in haste
Of finding love. Eat me—I said it—
Every time I chose to spread it
Soft before you, butter fine
I'll lay my table so you'll dine
And spread it thick, not with a knife
But with small gestures, and big life
Butter me up, butter me wide
See what I look like inside
Remember that I had to wait
To be sure that you weren't straight

And then we had the dinner date
Where I gorged and licked your plate
I was so hungry. Famished. Pining.
Ready for some girlfriend dining

Max interrupted me with kisses. Her eyes looked like wet diamonds. Sometimes our wordplay could be coarse, but hell, we were smitten. We never left that room. Max thought for a minute, then finished the verse.

Sleeping close and sleeping late
Tells me to slow down, just to wait
And feel it. Roll in it. Relate.
It's not just an erotic dance. It's the wild girl's second chance,
To make a choice and settle in;
To let our pancake life begin.

I held her close. I felt her heart beating, tasted myself on her quiet smile.

And then we went out for pancakes. I mean, a dyke's gotta eat, right?

Chapter Twelve
Hope Rises and Hope Falls

Drucker Packaging Company was the largest company in the town of Sandalwood. More than one-third of its population worked for the Boss Man. The rest squeezed out a living through farming, opening small shops or service businesses. There was a street through the center of town named Main Street, of course, where everyone strolled past one another with no specific destination in mind.

I worked on the assembly line, boxing all sorts of merchandise. What we boxed depended upon the time of year and what orders old man Drucker could get. Today I'm stuffing novelty teddy bears clutching a red heart-shaped pillow between their little paws into boxes. Valentine's Day is coming, and we are banking on a huge demand for these little suckers. I also play on the company's bowling team. We kicked the shipping department's butt for the championship last year, and tonight they are looking to even the score. Can't say I blame them. We were pretty cocky after last year's victory. And things got pretty rowdy that night back at the Shady Tavern. I hightailed it outta there when the fight broke out. It also gave me cover to sneak out to my little hideaway just on the outskirts of town. I keep my interest in women pretty discreet. Folks around here aren't exactly politically correct. I would hate to be a topic of conversation at the town diner on Main Street. So I do my job quietly, bowl a few games and drink a few beers with my coworkers, and if I get the "itch" for some female companionship, I take a drive over to that other bar.

You don't need to be a rocket scientist to work on the assembly line. So I spend a lot of my time letting my mind take a mental drive back to that bar on the outskirts of town every now and then.

Hmmm . . . let's see . . . who will we replay during today's work shift, huh? How about Terry? Yeah, she was one hot lady. The way she hit that high note when my fingers found her sweet spot, oh baby! She was so easy to please. If I wanted a bit of a chuckle, I could think of Penny. She was the former point guard for the state university's basketball team. She always made me laugh when she used basketball terms as sex talk . . . *Baby, let me see your backdoor play . . . Oh yeah, I love your finger roll . . .* She had that incredible athlete's body. She would wrap those tight arms and tight thighs around me and never quit.

But for those days when life in this town became unbearable, I'd rewind Tricia. Women were whooping and catcalling behind me the night I left with Tricia. They were throwing hints my way like, "*Ya got yaself a live one there. I hope ya takin' vitamins!*" I didn't catch on to their taunts so I didn't see what was coming. Tricia was quiet when she came in that night. It was the first time I laid eyes on her, and she was real slow but determined to meet me. She made her way through the crowd and brushed up against me at the bar. Women made room for her, as if she had some power over them. I bought her a drink and we made some small talk. I was acting like the big-shot dyke in front of this petite blond femme. Little did I know she was a wild mustang with an insatiable hunger.

We went back to her place after our third drink. My head was clouded, but I craved this little beauty. We kissed in the middle of her bedroom and I felt the fire of her hunger cross the material plane and burn slowly within my belly. She urged me on, exposing her precious white breasts that I knelt to in awe as I feasted on them. We were desperate to satisfy our hunger, to fill this lust that took possession of our bodies. I raised her skirt, moving my face to feel the heat emanating from her mound, drawing me closer to dine upon her delicacy. My head was spinning in pure euphoria as I felt her hand push me away.

"No, please . . . let me . . ." I gasped.

Without uttering a sound she moved toward the bed as I scrambled to my feet, following the trail of her clothes. She was in charge of the scene—the director of what we were to produce.

She undressed me, brushing my hand away, causing my desire to rise with the absence of touch. She descended to the floor, kneeling as if she was a powerless mortal in front of a goddess. I felt the soft caress of her fingers on my legs and wavered to her touch. Her grip tightened and I felt that first wave of pleasure roll over my body as she teased me endlessly with her tongue.

We fell upon the bed and entangled our limbs, touching, kissing, stroking incessantly. Our hunger would not subside. We moved as one from room to room and desire to desire. Were those remarks my fair warning from past victims of nights of feeding her craving? Was this her love script in which many before me had been fellow actors and performers? I didn't care. I was experiencing a wellspring of lust and love that only she could tap. She had mined my shaft with her long fingers and her own wanting. She let me fill my soul with her boundless sexual delight, urging me on further, letting me explore every curve of her body, every erogenous realm. Our night came to an end with the first signs of dawn. But I am grateful to my beloved Tricia. She is my emancipator, my love warrior, breaking the walls of timidity that prevented me from feeding the voracious love running deep within me. I never saw her again.

"Yo, Hope! What's wrong, girl? You're sweating like a pig! You feelin' all right? You look like you're miles away."

I came back to my Sandalwood reality, finding my good friend Darlene standing next me and teddy bears scattered all over the floor. My mental journey to Tricia's place caused a traffic jam of boxes and bears.

"You must have something heavy on your mind, girlfriend. Somethin' botherin' you?"

I shook my head and blinked my eyes a few times to sober myself up from my mental love elixir. I turned and looked at Darlene just staring at me like I was a zombie. I smiled and said, "No, I'm not thinkin' 'bout much these days." But I was thinking, hope beckons.

Hope Beckons

Come to me my Love, into my dreams.
Let my pure light shine upon you,
Let my love sanctify your corporal being.

Come rest with me, my Beauty.
Let us stretch out beside peaceful waters,
And entangle our kindred spirits;
To become one with each other.

Come my Beloved and find comfort in my embrace.
I will gather you into the folds of my strength,
And soothe the fire burning beneath your breast.
With the balm descended from the Goddesses,
I will caress your worries away.

Come my Priestess of ancient times
And journey with me to the ethereal plane.

We will rise above life's endeavors,
By the heat of my desire for you.

Come my Divine Creation of love,
Let my kisses taste the sweetness of your lips
And fill my being with your delightful ways.
Move with me as moonlight upon the sea.

Come to me my Eternal Love, as we rise and fall.
In our ecstasy, I will satisfy your pleas;
Dipping my fingers into the stream of your life-force;
Fusing our love forever.

Come . . .

Chapter Thirteen
Venus Thigh-Trap

It began with the roller skates, I suppose. I used to roller-skate, when I was still in graduate school and preparing to defend my doctoral dissertation. Superstitious, I thought that if only I skated perfect circles every afternoon and never once fell down, I'd get my Ph.D. quickly with no complications. My skates were a magic charm against defeat. I skated in that park so routinely that a local television crew came out and filmed me in my sports bra. I received random obscene phone calls for weeks—one of them long distance. He actually called *collect.*

At thirty, I bought Rollerblades. I took my old, clumsy four-wheel roller skates to Lin Daniels' East Coast Lesbian Festival in 1991, canoed into the middle of the lake and threw my skates overboard. They're still there, resting and rusting deep at the bottom of those lesbian-summer-camp waters where I used to kayak nude. I'll always know they're there.

So now I was a hot young professor at an Ivy League school, I'd come home from my day job as a radical feminist scholar, leap into my in-line skates and take off, whizzing around the parking lot, relishing being over thirty with my tattoo turned up to the sky and my thighs controlling cross-overs and my mind racing, racing. It was the workout that I liked. I experimented with feeling sexy now that I was thirty and tried blading in a black spandex miniskirt and a T-shirt that said, "A century of women on top."

"You're brave, darlin', skatin' in a miniskirt," yelled a woman driving by in a car, and I went tumbling over onto the pavement and still have that scar on my knee.

"You make it look so easy," another woman whispered, though in truth I was a klutz and cautious, skating where there were walls, or parked cars, or lesbian bodies to grab onto. I skated and skated until my thighs were strong again after years of grad school studying, and I began to wonder if I'd ever meet somebody, a woman I could squeeze with my big thighs.

I lived in a residence hall called Scholar House, which had a wonderful slick, long hallway on the bottom floor that wrapped around from the piano lounge to the cafeteria to the laundry room, almost a mile of corridor. By June all the students had left for summer and no one was living there but me and a few housing staff. In utter disregard for house rules, I would take the elevator down late at night and skate up and down that long, silent hallway. I thought about the books I wanted to write, my mind a thousand miles away from my legs. Here on the marble floor there were no stones or pods or broken glass to avoid, and I could mentally write out my life, my politics, my next hell-raising essays on dyke culture, skating, thinking, motion, stroke, motion, stroke.

It took about three circuits of back and forth on that long hallway one night before I realized someone was watching me, a young woman I'd never seen before. She nodded at me in a firm and businesslike manner, then slid onto the piano bench in the lounge—no one ever played that piano during the school year, and I wondered why it stayed. But suddenly I was skating to the strains of the "Moonlight Sonata," then "Claire de Lune," two of my all-time favorite pieces, executed perfectly by the mysterious stranger.

I could not resist. I skidded to a halt.

I miscalculated. I toppled over onto my face.

She jumped off the piano bench, all concerned. "Are you all right?" Even in pain, my lip bleeding, I thought: look at those *fingers!*

She introduced herself. "I'm Ellie, on the math faculty. I thought—since the students have left, and no one's down here—that I could slip in and play this lovely piano. You don't mind?"

I finally stopped bleeding, blotting my lip with a corner of my T-shirt emblazoned with "This Is What a Feminist Looks Like." I was thinking, *this is what a fool looks like,* as I struggled to regain my lost cool. "Why would I mind? It's gorgeous. I'm not supposed to be down here myself."

"Well, I figure I'm not hurting the piano."

"And I have these soft wheels. I figure I'm not hurting the floor."

She glanced at her watch. "I have to go now, but perhaps we'll meet again some night." I watched her walk away, muscled legs below a swishing skirt, red hair tossed over broad shoulders. If this was a math professor, I'd better recalculate my stereotypes.

Every night we met like that, me skating energetically, lap after lap, and Ellie playing sonata after sonata, until we were both exhausted. The little side looks—my eyes straying to hers as I curved past the piano—grew nightly until the sexual tension was unbearable. Someone had to make the first move.

And that someone was not me, or Ellie, but the janitor, who without notifying anyone waxed the entire hall one day, and on my first lap I went spinning out of control and literally flew into Ellie's arms, knocking her off the bench, sending the piano cover crashing down. We lay there in a tangle of limbs, and the hall staff, night janitor, and security guard all came running from the front lobby, roused by our disaster.

We were in for it now.

"*What* are you doing with those *skates*?" yelled the janitor, outraged by my very visible skid marks. "Don't you know I worked all day to clean that floor?"

"*Who* gave you permission to play that piano?" scolded the security guard. "May I please see some ID?"

"You two might be faculty, but there are house rules we *all* have to obey," said the residence hall staff.

We lay there, two grown women with Ph.D.s, shamed and punished and disciplined like a couple of first-graders. There was nothing to do but limp away, defeated, get drunk on Slippery Nipples at the local women's bar, and make love like crazed bunnies all night long with our bodies quickly recreating harmony—her piano fingers, my Rollerblade thighs.

"Play me."

"Work out on me."

"Give me that virtuoso performance."

"Come around that corner really fast."

"In the key of *right now*."

"Your *best stroke forward*."

"Faster, louder, *fortissimo*."

"Slower. Brake gently. To the left."

"How'd you learn to play like that?"

"Where'd you get that speed?"

"Your fingers are worthy of Carnegie Hall—you must have practiced this before."

"You're a Venus thigh-trap—I don't ever want to get away."

In the early morning we woke up sore in every part of our bodies—bruised knees, throbbing heads, exhausted erogenous zones. We walked carefully to teach our classes, my Rollerblades in my bookbag, her sheet music in hers. At the entrance to the lecture hall, Ellie turned to me and said, looking at her watch, "I have to go now, but perhaps we'll meet again some night." We met every night that year, her fingers and my thighs.

Chapter Fourteen
Seven Stops in Queens

"Fifty-ninth Street, Lexington Avenue," shouted the garbled voice over the train's intercom. "Last stop in Manhattan."

I was reading the latest Patricia Cornwell mystery when she stood beside me on the crowded rush-hour train. The sweet smell of her perfume immediately made her presence known and made me lose my place on the page. It is amazing how the scent of a woman can instantaneously alert every nerve ending in one's body. The soft leaning of her thigh against mine awakened my leg to her nearness. The reflex of my arm to draw near hers was spontaneous. It took all of my willpower to keep my eyes on my book as the train jolted forward, and my body bumped into her.

"Excuse me, sorry," I muttered, looking up to find two dark endless pools staring back at me. I was entranced by her scent, trapped by the mystery of her gaze, and frozen in place by the slight elevation of her crimson lips.

"It is all right."

That accent. What was it? Russian? Polish? Definitely Slavic and powerful. Her eyes never left me as she uttered those words.

The train entered the tunnel as it crossed under the river, exiting the borough of Manhattan and entering Queens. The train's lights fluttered and dimmed. I could still see her soft white face and felt the warmth of her body as her fingers slowly slid down the pole we were clutching to keep our balance. Throngs of people pressed against us from all sides. It was a typical rush-hour crowd: pack them in and move them along. But tonight, I welcomed them enclosing us into our space. Her smile remained, acknowledging her move and the absence of mine to pull away.

What is happening here? What are we doing? Thoughts were spinning through my head as I did a quick check of the crowd. No one was noticing.

Desire overruled all my sensibility. She was bold, beautiful, and sensual. *I could never be her or be with her. If this moment is all I can have, this brief interlude with this woman, then so be it. It is better to have lust and lost than never to have lusted at all. I embrace the encounter.* I told her all this in my gaze and my submission. She acknowledged by stretching out her fingers, grazing my breast pressed against the pole, stopping at my protruding nipple. She delicately squeezed, sending waves of pleasure through me. My heart began to race with the train. Our eyes stared deeper into each other's as the train arrived at the first station in Queens.

"Queens Plaza," shouted the conductor as the doors flew open, and the crowd began to jockey in and out of the train car. She changed her position, releasing her possession of my breast.

Is she leaving me? Is that all? She can't. Not like this! Please come back!

People were rapidly coming and going. She had moved with the crowd, a strategy she created. She had a pleasure scheme, and I was the target. When she returned we were face to face. Her gaze told me we were not finished—she had more to do. The train began its motion with that initial jolt, giving her the opportunity to place her thigh between my legs. I closed my eyes as her leg pressed against me, sending pulsating waves of pleasure synchronized with the train's movement. *You are incredible! Yes, let me ride you, on and on and . . .* Beads of sweat were forming on my forehead as I feigned losing my balance so as to press harder against her strong thigh.

"Beebe Avenue," shouted the conductor, returning me to train reality. She didn't move this time. She let the people press against her as they exited and entered, enhancing my pleasure. *Was this really happening to me? Was I dreaming?*

The train continued its journey as I fought the orgasm that was building within. I was totally under her spell. I surrendered to her. I quietly pressed my pelvis against her, wanting more of her. She was pleased with my participation. Her smile revealed her praise and affirmation, saying to me, *yes my dear, that is it, yes . . .*

"Washington Avenue Station!" bellowed through the car. The crowd that had encompassed our love escapade was thinning. She moved again to my right side, extracting her thigh, removing our connection. I exhaled as the wave of pleasure subsided within me.

Were we done? Is she leaving me like this? Do I dare to speak to her? What does one say after having been sexually entertained by a stranger during their ride home from work?

I kept my face turned toward her but she was looking straight ahead as if nothing had transpired.

"Broadway," yelled the voice once again as the train came to a halt. More people exited and my Femme Nikita began to move out of my sight. I stood clutching the pole, disappointed, wasted, just staring out the window as the people rushed into the car. As the train resumed its trek, I could still smell the scent of her perfume. My grip tightened as I saw those beautiful fingers reach over my shoulder for the pole. I leaned back ever so discreetly to straddle her leg. We were in rhythm once again as the public faces surrounding us were blind to our train tryst. I could feel the strength of her leg as it nuzzled against me.

God! You are fantastic! I want you, I want more of you. I want to return the pleasure a thousandfold!

"Grand Avenue Station" blared over the intercom next, but my ride was still stationary. She bent her knee upward as the commuters filed out of the train, and a few climbed on.

How could we continue? We had to be noticeable.

I came to my senses long enough to do another quick surveillance of the occupied train. We were at the end of the car. From the corner of my eye I could see only a few seats behind me, and no one was giving much concern to the crowd standing in front of them. It was a typical New York attitude of indifference that fell upon every individual who rides the train. When the train exited the station, she moved her leg away.

I waited in anticipation for her return. She was baiting me, teasing me, waiting for my quiet plea to resume our game. I closed my eyes and deeply inhaled.

Please, Please, Please me, touch me! I looked to the side and saw the reflection of her face in the train's window. Her smile was still intact. Her eyes with their raised brows were conveying loudly, *Yes, you want more?* I nodded slightly. There was a bit of unclaimed territory in front of me, and she slowly moved to occupy it. Her back was to me with only the pole between us. She leaned her whole body against the pole. People encircled us with their backs turned, blocking the seated passengers' view. I felt a rush of warmth return as she began to slowly, ever so lightly stroke me with her finger from behind her back. I bit my bottom lip and clung to the pole with a death grip as she finished me off.

"Astoria Boulevard" resounded through my ears, forcing her to release me. In an instant she was exiting, no glances, no smiles, no good-bye, nothing. I stood in shock, perusing my fellow riders, looking for their reaction to our lust encounter during the course of our journey. I hung my head with a mix of relief and disappointment. We were entering the last station. How apropos! We had completed our "excursion" before the train's final run. Should I thank the train for allowing us to venture into a small moment of pleasure during a usually arduous sojourn? Shall I thank my fellow travelers for giving us this brief encounter to satisfy a hidden lust that was deep within us yet went unspoken?

"Ditmars Boulevard, last stop!" echoed through the car, rattling me out of my thoughts. I exited the train drained, yet content with what I allowed myself to have I broke the walls of inhibition that had kept me in a container of complacency. I walked down the platform with a lighter step and my head held high, proud of my own personal victory. I stopped dead in my tracks. There on the platform she stood, waiting at the exit gate. I approached her cautiously. *How did she get here? I saw her leave the train!* We were face to face. She smiled with those crimson lips and dark eyes. And as if she could read my mind she said, "There are other cars on this train, you know!"

Chapter Fifteen
If These Hairs Could Talk

It's silly to cry over a single pubic hair. But that's what Letty was doing in that steamy hotel bathroom, an hour before her best girl got married to some *guy*. Frank. His name was Frank. It was important to play it cool, be a diplomat, dredge up some semblance of etiquette from cotillion classes of yesteryear. He wasn't the *guy*, the *groom*, the *man*, or any of the rigidly distancing terms she'd applied all these weeks. His name was Frank. Letty wondered, though, if her ex Tara had been "frank" with Frank about her own past as the toast of Lesbianville, USA.

The honor of being a bridesmaid was dubious. The unbelievable expenses stacking up like burnt toast in her bankbook: ugly dress, inane shoes, flight to New York, sharing a hotel suite at the Wellington with three other Tara exes, wedding gift, time taken off work. And the emotional cost. That's why she was weeping in the bridesmaids' suite at the sight of Tara's red hair floating on the tile floor, other grumpy, frumpy dykes banging on the door: "Come on, Letty." "Get over it, Letty." "For fuck's sake, Letty, open up, I got a bladder full of hot piss here!"

They were an unusual bouquet of bridesmaids, all right, the four of them who'd loved Tara, pined for Tara, eaten Tara, in the ten years before he—Frank—came along. Letty was the longest, Gigi probably the most in love with Tara during the Northampton era but now quietly resigned. Delphy didn't give a shit—her only thought was who might be next. She lacked any gene of sentiment. And Kathleen? Who knew what *she* was thinking right now, eight months pregnant with that sperm donor pal of her brother's, building a home in the country with Gigi.

"Get *out* of there, Letty." Dyke knuckles on the door.

She sighed, stood up from the side of the tub and looked fleetingly into the mirror. Puffy eyes made ludicrous by the application of makeup—eyeliner, mascara. She'd used that eye mascara clamp leftover from some purse she once carried in high school. Even burly and tough Delphy had approved: "It's a *wedding*, you gotta clamp." Delphy had grudgingly conceded to shaving her legs, but only where it showed. She shaved up to the ankles and then quit. If a breeze came along to blow her skirt above mid-calf, all of the West Side would be treated to an early fur fashion show.

A shoulder crashed against the door, springing the lock, and Delphy flew into the bathroom, sending bottles of hotel shampoo and guest soaps flying. "Do you *mind* if I pee, hon?" she asked Letty, not unkindly, and Letty allowed herself to be coaxed out of the bathroom.

The wedding reception was predictable. Straight coworkers, relatives, mysterious Orthodox rabbis who turned out to be Tara's twin brothers, and other well-heeled guests sat at the round front tables closest to the dance floor, while Tara's dyke past was discreetly removed from the foreground by positioning all obvious homos at one table in the farthest corner. Letty, Delphy, Gigi, Kathleen with her giant belly, and several defeated-looking lesbians from a town in Arizona all sat together wondering what to say and whether the food was vegetarian or not.

"Look at these egg rolls—probably shrimp, right?"

"Doubt it—I think all the catering is kosher because of the twin rabbis."

"What about the dip? There's chunks in it."

"That's pureed artichoke. Tara always loved artichoke dip."

"I know that."

"Well, no offense. I didn't know if she liked it when she was with *you.*"

"What's that supposed to mean?"

A cadaverous-looking but elegantly dressed man with long sideburns glided up to their table. "Excuse me, but would any of you ladies care to dance?"

"No thank you," in alto unison.

Letty was thinking about the hair in the tub. About the long red hair on Tara's head, bobbed now and very chic under her wedding veil, but once so long and thick that after making love Letty might walk to class and in mid-seminar realize she had strands of her lover's hair standing out clearly on her green work shirt. She'd spend the rest of Philosophy 10 or Women's Studies 120 trying to pick off Tara's hairs, thinking, Mmm, if these hairs could talk!

She began to shiver in her thin bridesmaid's dress. A cool draft was chilling her. She stood up without regret. "I need a sweater, I'm not feeling well, I'll see you all back at the hotel." Outside, she quickly hailed a cab and flung herself into leathery refuge, barely whispering the address to the driver. They rode in silence.

In the deserted hotel suite, in the now red-hair-free bathtub, her own body submerged in cedar-scent bath gel foam, Letty felt the first throb of release and transcendence. It was over, that part of her life, her past, her gay youth. Tara had made her choice. His name was Frank. The question was what lay ahead for Letty.

Right now she just wanted to blot everything out, the mixed feelings for Tara, the bizarre static cling of a panty girdle under her bridesmaid dress, the heavy cream in the artichoke dip. She lit up a joint with moist fingers and took a drag, sinking farther into the tub, light ashes sizzling into the bubble foam.

The bathroom door suddenly flew open and, once again, Delphy skidded into view. "You didn't lock it this time, I see."

"No shit, Sherlock! What are you doing, barging in on my bath?"

"I came back to see if you were OK." Delphy looked with distaste at the joint dangling from Letty's lips. "That supposed to make you feel better?" She reached over and removed the soggy inch, stubbing it out on a washcloth. "Try this instead." From a folded paper plate, Delphy produced a slab of wedding cake, its femme frosting only slightly crushed.

That wedding cake was all it took to start Letty bawling. "She couldn't marry one of us, huh?"

"I know, babe. It hurts. But let's face it—the girl went both ways."

"Well, I don't! I feel betrayed. Geez, am I that radical? I was never a big separatist—like you—"

"Watch who you're calling big, honey baby." But Delphy smiled.

Letty regarded her with narrowed eyes. "What made you come back after me? I thought you'd be cruising for your next fling, as usual."

"With who, those Arizona exes? Naw. I got something better right here." She reached over and lightly touched Letty's cheek.

The gesture was so gentle, so unexpected, that Letty lay motionless in the tub like a piece of sculpture, not sure what to do.

Delphy did it for her. "Mind if I join you?" The rugby player had her bridesmaid dress off in an instant, partly shaven ankles revealed at last. She climbed into the tub, creating a tidal wave Water dripped over the inlaid floor, soaking their discarded wedding finery.

In the tub, their knees knocked. Their fingers wrinkled. Their asses slipped. They tangled quick as that.

"Jesus," moaned Letty.

"No men allowed," Delphy reminded her, reaching for the plate of wedding cake and smearing frosting across her broad shoulders. "Lick me?"

Chapter Sixteen
Hot Black Sweater

I hate blind dates! It is the Russian roulette of dating. It can shoot blanks, misfire right into your face, or get a loaded pistol sitting across the table from you. But sometimes, on that rare occasion, you get that "click" and all is well in the world.

This time, I got the "click." I was being hounded by my good friend, Miriam, for several weeks with statements like, "You two are so alike. You two were really made for each other. You two will have so much in common." I said yes to her just to get her off my case, and a bit of curiosity got the best of me. I wanted to find out who was the other one that made the "two." Miriam made all the arrangements. She was a sucker for romantic interludes and loved to create scenarios that she could later share with her friends. I could hear it now: *Oh, it was so romantic how they met.*

So I let her have her way and agreed to rendezvous with Natalie, my blind date, on Friday night at a little Italian place called Antonio's. How would we recognize each other? I asked Miriam. Of course, she arranged for each of us to carry a long-stemmed rose. I had red, Natalie's would be pink. As if all the rest of Antonio's patrons would be possessing roses that night, we would have to distinguish ourselves from them. Ugh: What was I getting myself into? But being a good, loyal, and horny friend, I subjected myself to all of Miriam's whims. I even allowed her to pick out my outfit for the date, which consisted of a simple ensemble of black dress pants, white silk blouse, and a collegiate-looking blazer. Miriam was tight-lipped about Natalie. All she kept saying to me was, "You'll see, you'll find out," whenever I probed for information. I just wanted some points clarified before I committed my Friday night to this fiasco. Such things as: Does she own a gun? Is she on heavy medication? And is the number of cats she owns under double digits? (Just a few minor details I find important.)

The big night finally arrived. Miriam was running around my apartment chasing her tail, getting me ready like a mother on her child's first day of school. I kept my cool. I had high hopes but low expectations. I was not entering into this tête-a-tête with eyes wide open. My high hopes were for other parts of the anatomy to be wide open, but that was being idealistic.

I made it to Antonio's on time and of course there was no other pathetic-looking, rose-clutching woman in the restaurant. So I got myself a table and a stiff drink. I read the menu a half dozen times, delayed the waiter, and kept the liquor flowing. I found talking to myself didn't help the situation either. *Are you that desperate that you are just going to sit here? Why do you put yourself through this torture? She's got some nerve standing you up when . . .*

The restaurant door opened, and there she stood in the soft light by the coat check room. My heart took a vacation and my jaw was somewhere down in the menu on the table. She delicately held a pink rose in her arms, cradling it like a child. She had a happy smile. Not a phony picture smile, but one that expressed true inner joy and happiness. She scanned the room with her light blue eyes that seemed to dance as they moved over the restaurant. She spotted me holding up the rose like I was bidding at an auction. *My heart be still, she is gorgeous!*

"Hi, I'm Natalie, you must be Chris."

"Yes, I am," I stammered, trying to retrieve my jaw from the table. She took her seat across from me and placed her rose on top of mine.

"I am sorry I am late. My client's deposition ran longer than I thought."

She's intelligent too! "You're a lawyer?"

"Yes. Didn't Miriam tell you?"

"Miriam left me in the dark, only revealing your name. But I am glad she did. It's a nice surprise."

My expectations were rising.

"Well she was a bit evasive when I asked about you as well. So I guess we were both left in the dark."

Man, would I like to be in the dark with her!

We ordered dinner and talked straight through dessert. Time passed, or perhaps it just disappeared altogether. Before we knew it, chairs were being upended, and we were the last occupied table.

"I think we need to get going," I said, smiling at the gorgeous breasts that lay hidden under her black sweater.

"I think so," she responded with a girlish giggle in her voice.

She was so fresh and alive, yet grounded and funny. She found everything interesting and listened to my stories with such enthusiasm. I found myself engrossed in all she said and how she said it. Nothing else existed. Nothing else mattered. She was polished without the snobbery. She was polite but not prudish, a welcome change from the motley crew I was surrounding myself with lately. She carried herself with dignity and very little "baggage." My heart was like a little girl skipping home after that first day of school.

"Would you like to go for a drink?" I offered outside the restaurant. I was on my best behavior. I didn't want to screw this up. My gut was signaling to me, *"Easy, girlfriend, keep it slow, she's a class act!"*

We strolled down the street, our hands brushing against each other until they finally met and gently clasped together. I turned and smiled into those blue eyes. They returned the smile as I felt her grip tightening and my feet stumbling over each other as she pulled me into the dark deserted alley. She had me pinned against the brick wall behind the dumpster. Before I could object, her mouth had found mine, and the warmth of her tongue melted my resistance. I relaxed the muscles in my arms, though still shocked by her unexpected play, revealing her "Ms. Hyde" sexual shadow side. She could feel my arms submit, so she released her hold only to move her fingers under my blazer, using her right thigh to hold me in place.

"Baby, I have wanted to do this to you all night." She moaned into my neck.

"Let's go to my place," I said, trying to regain control of the situation.

"Ooh, not yet, baby. I'm not done."

I heard the words *dignified*, *polite*, and *polished* swirling through my head, spewing from my mind as her finger swirled me below.

"Hmmm . . ." she moaned into my mouth as if the pleasure was all hers.

I grabbed on to that black sweater as I experienced the second coming right in that alley.

Whether it was the telepathic messages of emancipation I was sending her, or the fact that my legs were giving out, she finally released me from her two-finger force field. She smiled with victory as I gasped for air. We stood staring into each other's eyes. Mine were wide open.

She kissed me so tenderly upon my cheek and said, "Now, how's about that drink."

Click!

Chapter Seventeen

Warm-Up

She's always early to dance class. That way, she can watch the more advanced group finishing up. Crouched at the threshold amid the old *A Chorus Line* tote bags, the American Ballet Theatre tote bags, she breathes in the salty brown odor of the wooden loft floor, and traces with her eyes a trajectory of sunlight from its emerging point at the dirty window to where it highlights the golden fur of a forearm or neck. Body after body battles that intangible foe: the choreography. Bodies follow the arc of a turn, the hot slice of a leap, the glistening pathway of combinations. Vertebrae curve beneath vertebrae, hair whips the air, rib cages pull against the containing embrace of a leotard.

She's watching the young bodies dance themes of desire, themes of rejection. Classic themes, irrespective of the dancer's personal experience or sexual history. At the same time, each dancer exhibits subtle choices of meaning in the steps, bringing tender individuality. She feels herself responding to the sensual tension in these bodies around her, and hurriedly takes her place at the barre for her own dance class, only half afraid. She thinks, last night at the bar, next morning at the barre, ha, ha, as the older girls from the advanced technique class stalk off the dance floor in a sweat. There's a studied elegance in the way they sling on their shoulder bags, snap the tabs off cans of diet soda. Energy in its prime.

Her 10:10 dance workshop begins. Though her focus is supposed to be on the head and shoulders of the student in front of her at the barre, she steals continual glances across the room at Selene, "her" dancer, the one she's fallen in love with, the hippie princess, lean and long of limb, pale and sparkling as Perrier, body casual, dignified, fragile and irrelevant all at once. The whole campus wants her, it's almost cliché to want her, yet Selene acts blissfully unaware.

She leaves her yearning unexpressed, the better to bottle it up like savored kitchen ingredients: cinnamon, honey. She weighs Selene's careless beauty and cat's eyes against her own lesbian virginity; she's ignorant of lovemaking, discouraged, can't seduce royalty first time out of the box. She'll just have to wait. And wait. And wait.

Her very brain stutters with embarrassment at the thought of asking Selene "out." To where? To what? She's not even old enough to drink legally. She doesn't even have her own car. She's living with her *parents*. At night, in the bathtub, she furiously debates with herself: what untested reserve of arousal has been tapped by this dancer, Selene? She knows she's ready to leave adolescence behind, like a used Cinderella slipper, childhood magic replaced with grown-up sex, if only that new magic could happen naturally, adult magic as tempting and frightening as all first ballet classes, all final mysteries.

Thousands of middle-class girls spend their awkward adolescent years in one dance studio or another, kept away from boys by dancing safe romantic fantasies of love written centuries earlier. But in her case, it's different; she isn't interested in boys to begin with.

She leans her hot neck against the cool white porcelain of the tub, looks at the sheen of Pears soap on her knees. The heat that summer is malicious, unbearable, the dance studio not air-conditioned. But there are shadows, green from campus trees.

One day, she's made Selene's partner for no reason. No reason at all. The dance instructor paired everyone at random for the morning warm-up. That was all. She's stupefied. It's a muggy day like many others. She pushes back damp wisps of her hair, watches Selene peel off striped legwarmers and fling them nonchalantly to one side. Selene is hers for fifteen minutes, even standing in simple first position devastatingly sultry, hands at loose rest. Selene smiles, stretches, poses, stares. She's ready.

"Hand on your partner's shoulder," says their teacher, and tentatively she places her damp palm on Selene's bicep. Selene's black shirt sleeve is turned up elegantly, Selene's finely boned, finely veined hand lands on her own shoulder. They execute pliés in a state of seeming calm. Then they half turn and their eyes lock.

Their fingers, gripping shoulders, are warm. Calf muscles tense and rounded. Ribs pressing against flesh, flesh against shirt and leotard. Down, up, pause; down, up, pause. "Second position, please, turned out, ladies." The crackle of knees. They begin the next set of exercises, watching each other—perfect rhythm, perfect timing. Her lips are parted, her heart is pounding—Selene gazes back at her soberly, unflinchingly attentive.

They release, fall away momentarily, await the teacher's next command. The voice floats, disembodied, across the studio space: "Use all parts of the body and improvise a small duet."

Selene stands on one long foot, thoughtful, withdrawn, and then says, "Just follow me, kid."

Kid. That hurts. Or does it? It doesn't hurt for long. Because Selene says, "Like this," and puts an arm around her waist and actually dips her. "Like ballroom," says Selene; and then, conspiratorially, "I love ballroom."

They practice. They swoop around on that stained wooden floor, their toes gripping the planks, as they extend and reach, roll and rise, sweep arms across bodies, turn and face each other again. She follows Selene's feline curves, feeling herself sturdy but graceless. *I'm out of it. I can't keep up.* A head turn, a rolldown. "That's good," Selene says, catching her breath at the end. "So, do you want to go with that?"

"Yeah. Sure. Whatever. Cool."

"You," says Selene, wiping her face on a towel, "are too much. I see you in the library all the time. The three-o-one section," she adds wickedly. She seems to know that's women's studies, lesbian studies. "What's your name, anyway? Bergen?"

"Morgan."

"Of course."

The eye contact is fantastic, unbearable. Out of nowhere she suddenly blurts, "I've always wanted to dance with you."

Fuck! Shit! Did she really say that? Here? Oh, man.

Selene isn't surprised. She looks at Morgan evenly, then extends her hand. "So dance."

Nobody is watching them, anyway. They're supposed to be touching, anyway. The dance instructor said so. They're supposed to be warming up their bodies. Perhaps not this warm, this kind of warm, this kind of sweat.

"It's your tuition," whispers Selene. "It's your move."

David, at the piano, accompanies them with music.

She reaches for Selene's elegant neck and pulls the dancer to her, cradles her head on Selene's shuolder for an instant, her left hand in the small of Selene's back, her right hand pressing against Selene's breastbone, the inch between their faces a pocket of secrecy. Then she hears it. The three little words.

"You're so hot," Selene whispers.

"I'm hot for you," Morgan hears herself say.

"Then dip me."

She does.

The sun eats its way through the dirty window to sparkle in their mutual release of sweat.

What comes later, later that year, between them, is pure improvisation.

Chapter Eighteen
Fourth Coming

"I'm outta here!" I screamed as I grabbed my packed bags and headed for the door. There was nothing she could say that would make me turn around and go back to her. Even if she was the last dyke on earth, I'd stay on my side of the world with my trusty vibrator and a lifetime supply of batteries and just ignore her. When was I ever going to learn! Fool me once, shame on you, fool me twice, shame on me. Well, this was twice, so I am gone. How could I be so foolish to believe she could be with me and solely with me? I guess she proved me wrong when I walked in on her and Collette groping each other on the balcony at Collette's birthday party. And then she tried to sell me her excuse.

"It was nothin' baby. Collette had too much to drink, and she was all over me. I couldn't help it. It wasn't what it looked liked."

Yeah, well, it looked pretty mutual from where I was standing.

I heard this line before and bought it. But not now, not this time. It was over for me and Kara, and I felt it in my heart as well as knew it in my head.

I got a ticket to Las Vegas and was heading out of town to exorcise all of my Kara demons. A few days in Vegas, and I would feel as good as new again. Sometimes one needs to go off to a place of solitude and refuge in order to clear one's mind. The desert seemed like a good choice for me, though technically there is a city in the middle of it. I sat staring out the plane's window as we sat on the runway for an hour, just replaying the past year with Kara. Yeah, sure, there were good times had by all. Our weekend at the shore in the little rundown beach house Kara rented for a song and a dance. Just the two of us, a six-pack of Diet Pepsi, a bag of tortilla chips and a bottle of lubricant—the bare necessities. She was a wild, free spirit and somehow I thought I could tame her with my love. I was so wrong. Why would I want to? It was her wild side that drew me to her like a moth to the flame. I had let my own passion for life and love—my élan as the French call it—to fizzle out. She had restored me, resurrected me from my drone existence. I thought I could handle her "excursions" with other women, but I was wrong. The heart is a fragile vessel and though one can convince oneself it is all in the name of fun and freedom, one still feels the pangs of hurt, envy, and jealousy. We are human and not immune to free love's repercussions. *Man, I can get really deep looking out the window!*

My flight landed into ninety-degree heat and a packed airport. I got my luggage, hailed a cab, and started my retreat for the brokenhearted. The strip was hopping—tourisst dodging traffic, neon signs offering the best deals or the biggest jackpots, hotels showing off their headline performers, sending the perennial subliminal message: *Spend! Spend! Spend!* I got to my room at the Bellagio with very few detours. My retreat was a bit on the luxury side, but pain is worth it. I took a long hot shower, trying to wash away the last twelve hours of anger and resentment still clinging to me. I had a plan: a good, expensive dinner, a trip around the casino, and then back to the room for a good night's sleep. Tomorrow is another day, right?

I headed out styling in my fresh-pressed jeans and jacket. I had to pass through the casino en route to the restaurant. *Maybe a few hands of cards will ease the pain.* The joint was jumpin' with all sorts of characters. The hustle was on. As they say in Vegas, *We won't cheat ya, but we will beat ya.* So I was cautious, wanting to keep most of my money firmly in my pocket instead of theirs. I found a five-dollar minimum blackjack table and parked my butt in a chair between a Tex-Mex fellow and a Dolly Parton wannabe. I was in good company. I pulled a Marlboro from my jacket and placed it between my lips. Before I could reach for my lighter, a small flame cupped by some very long but beautiful fingers was flickering in front of my eyes. I turned to see who owned the flame and the fingers.

"Can I get you a drink?"

She had the darkest eyes—mysterious, powerful eyes. One could look into them for a whole lifetime and never reach their core. Her hair was pulled back neatly, but it extended down to her tight waist where her long, shapely legs began. The cigarette fell from my lip, causing me to burn my finger on the flame and knock down my pile of chips attempting to catch it.

"Uh, yes, yes you can. I'll have bourbon—neat," I said coolly.

"Yes, ma'am," she said with a twang as if she was impressed by my choice of beverage.

I watched her in that tight black skirt strut her merchandise toward the bar. My gears were oiled and my engines were started. *Houston, we have liftoff. Ooh baby that is one sexy lady!*

I turned back to find the dealer with disdain written on his face and blackjack with my cards. I took my winnings and headed for the bar.

Should I head her off at the pass or just pull up next to her and let my engine idle for a while? Hmmm . . . choices . . . choices.

I found her placing my order, so I quietly moved beside her.

"I decided to have that drink standing."

She turned slowly, neither startled nor surprised by my presence. It was as if she knew I would follow that walk of hers. I found those dark eyes pulling me into her like magnets. They were tractor beams pulling at my heart and other places further south, forcing me to gaze deeper, making me disappear into her dark pools. There were only the two of us. The noise of the casino, the lights, and the movements of people slowed to a dream state. I could see nothing but her eyes, her soft smile, and those long fingers holding my bourbon.

"I like a woman who takes her pleasure standing," she murmured.

I felt my knees buckle and heard explosions of desire within me, releasing alerts. *I want you, here, in the casino, on the bar, on the floor, at the blackjack table, anywhere . . . I want you!* But I kept my cool, gave her a little bit of a smile not to let her think her line was wasted on me.

"Well maybe we can stand together and share a few pleasures tonight."

"Maaaybe," she said in that sexy southern twang.

Shivers rolled up and down my spine as she handed me the bourbon, and her fingers brushed against the back of my hand. I threw back the drink, picked up the pen lying on her serving tray, and wrote my room number on her order pad.

"Here's a tip for your gracious hospitality." I spoke into her eyes and started my own strut down the aisle toward the hotel elevator.

As I took the security card from my jacket and stood in front of my door, I heard the "*ding*" from the elevator and its doors opened. Out stepped my dark-eyed mystery woman, slowly moving my way. I pushed open the door and entered as if I didn't notice her, but made sure it didn't close right behind me. I wanted her, I needed her. I hated Kara for her own extracurricular activities, for the way she led me to believe I was her main squeeze. I wanted to clear away the last remnants of her from my mind and evict her from the space she occupied in my heart.

I threw my jacket on the bed and headed for the wet bar, knowing my jackpot had followed me into the room.

"So, what's your pleasure?" I asked while fixing myself a drink.

She pulled lightly on my shoulder. I turned right into the gaze of her ebony pools. I was locked into their secrecy, traveling deeper into the dark abyss beyond the point of return to reality.

"This is my pleasure," she whispered as she placed her lips softly against my neck. My eyes closed as the breath escaped from my lungs. Her hands fell upon my rib cage and held me against the bar. Our mouths found each other as her fingers began to undo my shirt buttons. She cupped my breasts with those long fingers, gently squeezing them, teasing my nipples with her thumbs. I was in agony and ecstasy all at once. I reached for her, wanting to reciprocate the sexual havoc she was causing within me. She pushed my hands away, placing them on the edge of the counter and holding them there with her own.

"Let me, darlin'," she whispered into my throat as she made her way down my chest, finding my breasts excitedly awaiting her kisses. My mind was spinning, lost in the whirlwind of desire, trying to signal, "*Faster! Faster!*" But she was slow and deliberate, savoring her tongue's stroll along my breast and down my stomach. I felt a rush of cool air as she freed me from my jeans. My head fell back anticipating her tongue's arrival. Sparkles of light passed in front of my eyes as she engaged. Rockets' red glare swirled above me as her tongue swirled below. Illuminations of emerald greens and electric blues burst before my eyes. Roman candles streaked across the room in flickers of gold and silver. I exploded with the boom of a cherry bomb as she launched into her finale. With a burst of radiance and a firecracker thunder in my ears, I cried out to my enigmatic lover waitressing me down under. *Aaah Yes! Yes! Ooh yeah!*

I released my grip on the counter with sweat trickling down my forehead; I opened my eyes to her smiling face, very pleased with her doings.

"Whoever said timing is everything was right," she chuckled.

My mind was still swirling like a whirlpool. "Huh? What? Oh yeah . . . sure."

71

"Outside, baby . . . the fireworks . . . outside your window."

"Oh yeah . . . them," I muttered, trying to comprehend what she was saying.

She kissed my mouth with the lightness of a feather and then gave me that smile with her dark, beautiful eyes.

"Happy Fourth of July, darlin'."

Chapter Nineteen
Tank Top Tomboy

That night I was sitting at my usual place in the bar, trying to sketch faces on bar napkins. Sketching relaxed me, gave me something to do with my hands. Everything was cool, icebox cool, until, at a nearby table, some young hottie in a tank top lit her girlfriend's cigarette and threw down the used match with this subtle little flourish. She was so cute it hurt me to watch. Another tank top tomboy! I had to bite down on my toothpick, hard, and look away.

I'd loved a city kid like that, oh, that city kid, that girl. That cool one. Babette. She dumped me. Recently. Yeah, it was painful. How was it painful? Let me count the ways. How did it suck? With indescribable suckdom. But the good memories washed over me, like a wet poem, my tank top tomboy. I shifted the pen in my hand and dreamily sketched the face I remembered.

I had already brooded all that winter. By now I was going stir-crazy, March being two months from January and two months from May, the first real spring we'd get here. I'd been thinking that if I could just find a decent support bra I could start jogging again and jog Babette out of my mind. I knew I had to get out of the house, but I'd only gone as far as the bar. That's why I was just sitting on my old bar stool, mentally digging through the layers of how she'd dissed me, like our relationship was this archaeological mindfuck.

Here's what I wanted to say to Babette. Oh, Babette, you cool kid sprawling in your honest cotton-shirted grime, boy, I never had a chance. I wasn't from your neighborhood, where everything had pockets: coarse pants, softball gloves, subway corners, airshafts between women's bars, where delis sat at the edge of high-rises feeding siren music to the pavement. All-night groceries with strong meats, girly calendars, an angry wilderness of empty lots and broken family hearts. You cool kid with your games of urban poise and pose, your tough talk, lusty chuckle, rage, some fear, locked knees, love of junk food, stylin' dress. Babe, I never had a chance. I was a mile behind the curve. But listen, pal, I dream of you still, inhaling perfume from my naked torso, your long smile in my short neck, in my wide breasts. If I'd just shut up, or said more, or clawed my way into your story, or learned your rules, talk big, talk fast, talk cool and bored, unflappable, trade insults, name bullshit, spew bragging tales and never give an inch. I was agog at your tough stance, your terms. I slept in your torn tank top that night when, drunk, forgiving, friendly, soft, you walked me home, put me to bed, and stayed. You made love like a champ. I kept that tank top, wore it like a scarf around my neck for its perfume, which it still seems to breathe sometimes. It conjures you. I rode that chance to be with you till you got out. We only rode that chance around the block. I recognized you needed someone else. Someone small, or someone big, not me at all.

That's what I wanted to say, but I'm no poet and much better at drawing faces. So I sketched Babette and then did ugly things out of lonesomeness, like flicking cigarette ash on the sketch. A hand came down on my shoulder. "That's a good way to set a napkin on fire. You want to be careful with my countertop, OK?"

It was Jan, the bartender. She knew me. Now she eyed me in a pitying way. "Ah, jeez. Still mourning Babs?"

"Maybe. So what if I am?"

"All tank top and no brains, that kid. If she had brains she'd still be with you." Jan swept away spilled ash, beer bottle sweat, and my rumpled napkin sketch with one expert flick of a hand towel. This got my attention. Jan gave compliments about as often as a rabbi writes to Santa. Why now? She'd seen me moody before and never poured me a shot on the house then, as she was doing now.

"It's about time for my break," explained Jan, as two more bartenders came on shift, and she put the shot glass in my left hand and pulled me toward the back of the room by my right hand, past the pool table and past the jukebox that never had any songs by women artists on it. LADIES and LADIES, said the signs over the two bathrooms, so we went into the LADIES that always smelled great because in a silly catfight on New Year's Eve, some hippie girl smashed a bottle of sandalwood oil on the floor.

Inhaling that sandalwood oil and that vodka shot had me breathing through my nose again, which was a good thing because my mouth suddenly seemed full of Jan's lips and tongue. "I can't keep waiting to catch you between tomboys," she moaned.

"Isn't that what Rhett said to Scarlet?"

"Not hardly." Jan had short graying hair and snappy black eyes, and a broad leather belt with a gorgeous turquoise buckle that I coveted. She liked to play rough, and she knew I didn't but now as she threatened to take off the belt and spank my fanny until I had some sense, I started to grin. "No beatings, just eatings, that's my rule, Miss Janet."

"Rule or proposition?" Her fingers, so swift and knowledgeable from years of mixing drinks and jabbing in swizzle sticks and dispensing change, had my skirt pulled up and my Victoria's Secret silks pulled down and the bathroom door bolted all in a matter of seconds. Pretty soon my preference of being eaten, not beaten was being respected in a very real and immediate way. Whoa. There.

Jan was tomboy enough, and hot enough, and I had just one question, which my mind formed weakly as waves of pleasure burst out of my body. "Jan," I stammered. "Your jacket. Take off your jacket."

She wrenched it off and threw it on the old and sandalwood-scented tiles.

I saw what I wanted and, for the first time since January, let out a laugh of glee. The rippling muscles of Jan's well-defined back showed off her tight lavender tank top at its best.

Chapter Twenty
The Chuckling Nipple

"Don't worry, I'll be there at ten o'clock, I promise." I hung up with Shelly and shook the aggravation out of my head. I hate when she becomes my social director and plans these "night out on the town" excursions with me. This time we were doing the cabaret thing—dinner and a show. Reminds me of when I broke up with Kara and took off to Vegas except no waitress this time. That was a weekend for the books. Yeah, she stayed after the first set of fire-works, but I bid her adieu on Monday with a weak promise that someday I would ride back into her town.

Shelly has really been good to me since Kara. She had tried to play matchmaker on several occasions, but no luck. This time I stipulated no matchmaking tonight, just a night out for the two of us. She crossed her heart to me. We were meeting at Jester's, a great women's establishment—very classy and very sassy. Shelly was waiting at the entrance when I arrived.

"Hey, you made it!" she exclaimed.

"Of course, did you think I would stand you up?" I said defensively.

"C'mon, let's go get a good table." She smiled.

After a few drinks and a hearty dinner I was ready for the entertainment. It was the best that I have felt in a long time. My stomach was full, and my heart was light, released from the anger and resentment I clung to for these past six months. The lights dimmed, and the emcee for the night appeared on stage.

"Hey, everyone. How y'all doin' tonight? Well, we got ourselves a great show for you. We have lots of great talent, some returning to our stage by popular demand and some really up-and-coming stars making their debut with us. So let's get this show started with one of our new comedians. Please give a big welcome to Ryan Stiers."

The place howled as this young babe came walking out onto the stage. We had a good table, front and center, so I had an up-close and personal view of our young comedian. She was a looker and I was looking at her tight black jeans, her sparkling blue eyes, and her T-shirt with no indication of a bra, which allowed her little friends to wake up and say hello to me in the front row. My eyes could not look away from her breasts. They were such a beautiful sight. Her round delicate orbs with their hard nipples were calling to me. I imagined them minus the shirt, light-skinned with a tan line right at the top of her breast, beige and pink colors blending together surrounding her nipple; keeping it safe and secure until it is visited by a lover's hand.

Perhaps it awaited the tender touch of the thumb, the gentle squeeze of thumb and forefinger. Ahh, how delightful that such simple stimulation can lead to such firm results. It is a wonder how a wee bit of flesh resting quietly on the left and the right side of a woman can rise from its soft slumber, emerge with greatness saying, *Look at me! I will bring you sensational feelings. I have made women cry for more when I appear. I have made women roar for me over the centuries. My response to your titillation will leave you to want more and more of me. Yes, I have this power.*

And how many various times and places are we drawn to encounter our petite friends? While holding our lover in bed, our hand cannot help but lay itself upon her breast and know she will greet you, acknowledge your presence. Or maybe in the early morning when your lover is showering, pampering her friends, we feel the sexual tug pulling us to the shower. Our mouth savoring the mixture of flesh and water as our little friend chuckles, knowing it has again accomplished its mission, detouring us from our doldrums existence to stir the desire lying within and lust for that moment again once it is over. Yes, it is the crown of women's majesty, compelling us to kneel to this splendid jewel and adore.

My young comedian's "girls" were still saluting the crowd, and I smiled as they stood at attention under the white hot spotlight. *You are calling to me, but I cannot have you. Not now, not here. But perhaps in time I will greet you with the gentlest of touches, and you will show your greatness, your mighty form and chuckle as I submit to the pleasure you bestow.*

"Hey, you look like you're in fantasyland," observed Shelly. Shelly's words jolted me out of my gaze and reverie.

"You thinking about Kara," she inquired.

"Shel, you're not even close . . . but she"—I pointed to our entertainer on stage—"would be a closer guess."

"I should have known," Shelly said, hitting the side of her head with the palm of her hand.

And we both let out a good chuckle.

Chapter Twenty-one
Embassy Trash

Friends, it's a weird kind of sophisticated fun living in the Embassy Row area of Washington, D.C. Surrounded by embassies, my apartment building never lacks for entertaining moments in the hood. Sometimes it's a protest—usually Falun Gong supporters demonstrating at the Chinese embassy. Sometimes it's the entire embassy staff of a tropical or desert country taking group photos in drifts of snow after a winter blizzard. A sudden increase in police cars tells me that trouble's brewing, perhaps an assassination attempt on a diplomat, who now requires an extra security detail. I'll never forget the tension on the night of September 11, when embassies burned their lights long past midnight readying their responses and their plans, and almost every restaurant in D.C. shut down, and all the embassies sent out for Chinese food—for me the horror of 9/11 is mixed in my mind with the scent of egg rolls being delivered to embassies on bikes.

Diplomats' wives—or mistresses—walk in pairs, arguing in Russian or Khmer. Men in magnificent robes fold themselves into sedan limos driven by chauffeurs in fezzes. One night I knocked on the front door of the Laotiau embassy and told a startled attaché, "Your limo's lights are on. What if your kid needs to go to the doctor and your battery's dead?"

Oh, sure, there are drawbacks to living among the powerful. Some bozo with full diplomatic immunity slammed into my car one day, and do you think I ever saw a penny for bodywork repair? Nope. So like any academic on a budget I covered up the scrape with Wite-Out.

But best of all is the trash. Trash left at the curb on pickup days, trash left in my own building recycling room by low-level embassy staff who get housed in nearby studio apartments like mine instead of in the embassies themselves. These low-level guys move in and out pretty fast, the turnover speaks to the stress of an international posting. When they leave, they leave all the furniture they were set up with: leather-topped bar stools, wicker wing chairs, glass-framed art, and whatever "American" souvenirs they've bought on their own and can't cram on the plane back to Oppress-istan. So over the years, walking along the sidewalks and rooting through the giveaway pile in my basement, I've furnished my whole pad, even got a surfboard once, bookshelves, pottery, a pretty decent vase, a lacquer stool, and once or twice an unopened bottle of cognac or wine when the trash goes out after a gala and the good stuff gets swept into the empties pile. Fun times, man, especially the year my salary got cut back. Did I tell you about the file cabinet? Some guy got sent back to Haiti so fast he left his possessions at the curb for trash pickup, and when I dragged home the very excellent office furniture, his credit cards and Playboy card were still in the top file drawer. I sent them back.

Wouldn't you love to go through the stuff they *don't* put out at the curb? I mean the shredded documents and spy material that goes in the Dumpster I can't reach just behind the Chinese embassy. But I've never dared to Dumpster-dive for documents.

81

So this is the backdrop, where I live, and it's normal by now, just the environment. It's a different kind of neighborhood, I know. I can Rollerblade right by Donald Rumsfeld's house, no big deal, I went to junior high with his daughter, Marcy, back in '76—but here's where the story gets eerie.

One day, I was walking past the embassies, just thinking about ice cream, when I saw a woman sitting out on the curb, like she's been put there, put out with the embassy trash. She was crying.

I stopped in my tracks. "Are you OK?"

The woman looked to be about thirty, with red highlights in probably dark brown hair, little gold earrings, a very sexy silk dress and good shoes, but makeup running down her face. "I don't know where to go," she sobbed.

I sat down on the curb. "Are you with the embassy?" I nodded back at the silent stone building, its flag down, the ambassador not in residence today.

"I had to get out before he threw me out," she sighed.

I'd heard about the diplomats who brought into the U.S. as "help" virtually enslaved servants who could be abused and unpaid with little repercussion from our government. If they escape, it's usually without papers or money or any other options. But was this woman a housekeeper, a cook? I hated to stereotype, but she was outfitted more like a mistress.

"If he found out," she seemed to be explaining to me, "they would kill me."

Whoa. Did I want to be involved here? But I'd carried home a lot of great, cool embassy trash from this curb. Maybe it was time to give back. Could I help?

"Are you . . . is *he* your boss?" I gently probed.

She looked at me with disdain. "No boss. I work for the wife. I dress her."

Wow. An actual lady-in-waiting to an ambassador's wife. She must have become the ambassador's mistress, and if the wife found out there'd be hell to pay. So now she was out on the curb like embassy trash.

82

"I love her," she said. "I cannot make scandal."

"Were you . . . dating the ambassador?" I whispered, trying to understand.

"I loved *her*," wept the lady-in-waiting, and suddenly I realized she must have become lovers with the *ambassador's wife*. It was a lesbian scandal the embassy couldn't afford; it couldn't afford the scandal of the ambassador looking emasculated, cuckolded, did I really know these words? They rarely applied in my world.

"I love a woman, too," I told the distraught lady and awkwardly patted her hand. My fingers touched emeralds. A gift from the forbidden secret partner?

"Ah. Then you know," she nodded at me. "You know what it is to want a woman's scent, her skin, her hand knocking at your bedroom door in the night, or taking you in her own bed, that when you want that love, anything is possible, you will risk anything, everything for that love. That kiss. That breath on your cheek."

I really wasn't prepared for what happened next. A door slammed, followed by an ear-piercing whistle: "George, *now!*" I turned to see behind us in the circular embassy driveway a uniformed chauffeur hurling two Gucci bags into the limo and then revving the enormous black car to life. The limo peeled out past us, did a quick U-turn up at the corne,r and then pointed almost in our faces. A gloved hand shot out of a back window, and that same throaty voice commanded: "Nina, *now!*"

Nina—seated beside me—rose to her feet as if pulled up by that hand. "What are you doing, my lady?" she cried. "Have you gone mad?"

"Get in. It's now or never. George is driving us to the airport," the voice explained. "I have your passport and the jewelry. We're going to Canada."

"You said you wouldn't leave him."

"I was a fool."

"How do I know you won't leave me?"

"Because I'd rather die than be without you."

Nina looked at me with huge eyes, streaked with makeup but

glowing with love and relief. "And you, you love a woman?" she asked me.

"I sure do."

"May you be happy," Nina blessed me, and slipped one of the emeralds from her hand into mine. She ran to the side door of the limo and quickly climbed in.

"Get us *out* of here, George," shouted the ambassador's ex-wife, as the limo headed down Connecticut Avenue. I caught a brief glimpse of two heads in the backseat, bent at that angle that says kissing, long cinemascope kissing, noses crushed.

The ambassador was recalled a few weeks later, and they put his unwanted things out at the curb: bad art, old furniture, a twirly chair I thought my office needed. Like I said, I've taken a lot of things away from the high turnover rate of the embassy staff in my neighborhood. I've seen a lot of things I haven't told. Once, I got an emerald at the curb.

Chapter Twenty-two
Byte Me

I had three days to finish revising my thesis paper. This isn't happening, but I had to give it my best shot. I hit my local grocery store to stock up on supplies and was ready to hunker down Saturday and Sunday in my apartment with me, my computer, and this lousy paper. I spent the better part of the morning with my graduate advisor, Dr. Jane Anderson. It was the equivalent of having teeth pulled without the anesthesia—not my favorite oral procedure. I sat in her office listening to her condescending remarks, scolding me like a teenager for not meeting her professional standards.

"I assume you plan on using more accurate sources and more current research? Is this the actual paper or is there more you are not allowing me to review?" My favorite was: "Ms. Carey, did you have your next-door neighbor's ten-year-old proofread this paper for you?"

She was Genghis Khan in a navy blue suit. But it was a really hot looking suit. She had killer legs and a pair of pleasingly plump boobs that made my mouth water on sight. When I had to conference with her, I had to take deep breaths while that female voice within me guided my impulsivity: *Easy, tiger, you are here for academics; be a professional, not Marlene Dietrich!*

From the moment I first laid eyes on her I felt that pang inside of me. I hadn't experienced an attraction this strong, this intense in a long time. I was like a schoolgirl with a crush on her teacher. *Let me bring you an apple and stay after school for detention yeah, baby!* I'd walk into her office and have sweaty palms, the heat rising from the base of my throat, and I'd start stuttering and stumbling all over the place. But Dr. Anderson, Dr. Jane Anderson, was as cool as cookies 'n' cream ice cream dripping down a cone on a hot July afternoon. She wasn't always insensitive or arrogant. She had a very warm and friendly side to her. She would chat about things she liked, movies she saw, but never mentioned a husband or boyfriend. Interesting, huh? I didn't detect a ring on her finger, either. Make another mental note. Sometimes she would glide right up beside me while we were reading a journal article together. I'd feel her knee press against mine, her sweet perfume invading my senses, and I'd have to close my eyes to fight off the rush of sexual adrenaline rising within me. On one occasion, I sat right across from her with only her desk stopping me from giving her a lap dance. She was wearing this red silk sweater with no bra. My Lord! It was Niagara Falls between my legs that day. While we discussed my thesis topic, a series of sex scenarios ran wildly through my head.

Do you think she's into leather? I wonder if she owns a vibrator. What kind do you think she likes? The metal/plastic ones or is she into rubber? You think she had sex last night? You think she's ever done a threesome? *Stop*, I would scream in my head, a smile plastered on my face. Once while in midsentence I had this incredible fantasy: She is sitting on the edge of her desk, her legs crossed and her hands resting by her sides. I come running into the room and just ravish the woman;

pushing her down onto the desk, kissing her mouth with a g-force while my fingers find her G-spot. She wraps those luscious legs around my waist, breathlessly ordering me, "*Yes, right there, yes, yeah, slower, baby, that's it . . . you're incredible . . . ah yes . . .*"

"Tess, are you OK?" She then brought me back to reality.

"Oh . . . yes . . . yes, I'm fine. What were you saying?" And I would shake away the moment in my head.

"Your face is flushed," she observed.

"I guess it got a little hot in here," I would answer.

I can see her smile. She had a beautiful contagious smile. A smile that began in her eyes and then the corners of her mouth would creep upward. There were many times I felt this tension between us—a sexual tension. A moment of self-consciousness if we were standing too close to each other or looked too long into each other's eyes. I would try with all of my mental strength to send the message to her, "*It's OK, I feel it too. Let it happen. Let's make it happen.*" But nothing would happen. We would clear our throats and look at our papers and just go back to work. Speaking of work . . . this paper . . . what am I going to do with this thing?

Ding dong! "Thank God, the door. Maybe it's someone who can give me a good excuse not to do this paper tonight," I said aloud.

"Dr. Anderson," I exclaimed as I stood with my mouth open, clutching the doorknob.

"Yes, it's me," she said skittishly.

"Well, this is a surprise . . . I'm sorry, I was just starting revisions . . . I didn't expect . . . I'm sorry. I'm just a bit surprised to see you!" I was now clutching the whole door with my entire body.

"I hoped I could talk to you. Can I come in?"

"Sure, of course . . . I'm sorry . . . come in."

She walked right in and headed into the pseudo-living room which, at the moment, really had that "lived in" look.

"Sorry about the mess. I wasn't expecting . . ."

"It's fine . . . really. I just wanted to say I felt terrible after I spoke to you this morning. To be honest with you, I had a few things on my mind, and I guess I just let go when I saw you . . . and . . . I didn't mean to be so cruel toward you." She was struggling with this act of reconciliation. She looked at her feet, my walls, the sofa, everything but me. I was somewhat shell-shocked by this whole scenario, but I let her have her moment trying desperately to find the words, hoping she'd say the words I had been waiting to hear for a whole semester.

"I really want you . . . I mean I want your work to be a success," she continued. "And you have a fine body . . . I mean body of research . . . and I am sure we can get it pubic hair . . . I mean published here, after you finish with my ass. I mean my class."

"Dr. Anderson." I spoke in a soft voice and she stopped her fumbling soliloquy of honesty. We looked at each other. That long stare into each other's eyes that neither one of us wanted to end. I whispered, "Jane," as I moved slowly toward her. "It's OK . . . me, too," I whispered with my lips just a breath away from hers.

"Really?" she asked, fighting back the emotions that were on the brink of exploding within her.

"Most definitely." I softly kissed those lips that I spent endless nights desiring. I kissed that mouth that I wanted to devour over and over again with each visit to her office.

She acknowledged my kisses with her own, releasing the months of sexual constriction that had kept us apart but yearning. She held me in her arms, pressing her body firmly against mine. I felt her strength, her passion, her ass . . . it was gorgeous. My mouth fell into her neck as we both gasped for air. I thought of my paper.

What! Not now?

It was sitting on the computer desk. I saw my two worlds, personal and professional, enmesh with this embrace. My priority was to satisfy my longing for her and only her. There was more important editing to be done.

We needed to revise our relationship, and this embrace was the beginning. I researched her inclinations and tapped into her source, her wellspring of love and desire. That voice within, the voice of female energy, spoke loudly as I made love to this woman.

Let my fingers dance across her magnificently formed keyboard—backspace, shift, italics her fancy. Let me make bold sweeping strokes in her love window. I will delete your inhibitions as I download to your hard drive. She was inspiring to kiss, to caress. A work product par excellence. Yeah baby! *Open up your file. Let me spell-check your work. IM me, sugar. Let me be your attachment. No margins, no spam, no icons in our way. I will browse and surf your sites. With one right click I will maximize our performance to a gigabyte frenzy. Come on, come on, hit enter and let me upload you.*

Our work was done as we lay limply in each other's arms with legs entwined and beads of sweat rolling down the back of our necks. I looked once again into those gorgeous eyes.

"Dr. Anderson," I said, amused.

"Yes, Tess."

"Does this mean I get an A?"

"Sweetie, tonight you get an A-plus."

Second revision initiated.

Chapter Twenty-three
Coffee-mate Mule

"You're flying down Friday night?" I was on the phone with Jenny, my long-distance girlfriend. It was her turn to visit in my city, and I could barely contain my glee. Friday night! I twisted the phone cord this way and that—nope, *this* preherstoric homo still gets along just fine without a cordless phone, a cell phone, or a palm pilot. We made the usual preliminary plans to meet at the airport and were about to go kiss-kiss and hang up when I remembered something important. "And you'll bring me a bottle of Coffee-mate, right?"

Her sexy voice grew cold. "Denise, what am I to you—just a Coffee-mate mule?"

She had me there.

I don't know how I got hooked, frankly. I'm not the addictive type, no other bad habits at all, booze and drugs at a nondependent minimum, and I never *touched* coffee or even good tea until I was well over thirty. I was the kind of kid who spent her allowance on books, not candy, and I had a health-food mama who made sure we drank milk and orange juice, not Coke or Pepsi. My early woman lovers expressed bewilderment at my healthful and, to their sensibilities, juvenile beverage habits. "I wish you drank coffee or tea so I could bring it to you in bed!" was how one of them put it. But now here I was at forty with a Coffee-mate monkey on my back. I guess it all started with that one babe I dated who dared to bring me coffee flavored with amaretto creamer, knowing I liked almonds.

No, I can't blame this one on the lesbian community. I'm a victim of clever corporate ad themes and well-timed trends. As a nondrinking poet type, I applauded the resurgence of coffeehouses in the early nineties, the open-mic vibe, the beret-wearing beatnik tabletop groove. I went for the poetry, never planning to sip coffee; I sipped hot milk steamers with a bit of Torani flavor. Torani almond, Torani hazelnut, Torani cinnamon. I was on my way to becoming a Torani whore when Cappio came out, that iced coffee in a bottle. I did like coffee-flavored milkshakes, and early one spring when I had a huge stack of papers to grade, I tried chilling a Cappio in the freezer to make a frozen coffee sludge at home. You can see how I was a sitting duck for the Starbucks craze that began sweeping the nation almost the next week. And if I liked a *cold* mocha, thanks to the sweet tentacles of Cappio, bumping up to the demonic teat of hot sweet coffee drinks was almost inevitable, especially after that babe in Colorado tricked me with morning amaretto. The next thing I knew I had amaretto-flavored creamer in my apartment because I had noticed the building management put out a free, fresh pot of courtesy coffee in my lobby *every day*. And finally, I found my heroin of choice. *Cinnamon vanilla crème*. I knew it wasn't the best thing for me. I, like every other American hooked on sweet coffee servings, had stumbled upon some sort of vestigial brain center triggered by what's really just breast milk for grown-ups. Oh 'mate! Sweet 'mate!

But now I had a girlfriend who drank coffee, brought me coffee in bed, made me coffee at her place or mine, or walked down to Starbucks when I was still asleep and showed up at my place with vacuum-sealed bags of gourmet-ground Kona, and wired on caffeine, we made love like compressed coiled springs flying out in your face. *Oh yeah, oh yeah, right there, oh God, oh Jesus, don't stop! Oh, that gives me the chills, oh, that way, no, a little to the left, yes, yes, oh, my God, your tongue. That's it, stop, I'm done, I can't take any more, is there any more coffee left?*

So here was the problem: It's hard to find the cinnamon Coffee-mate, the pink bottle. Real easy to find the hazelnut in the gold bottle or Irish crème in the green bottle, but the cinnamon vanilla is somehow elusive and often unavailable in my neighborhood. But Jenny's neighborhood? Her grocery's lousy with it! So am I such a raving fruitcake to suggest, casually, that she pack in a bottle when she flies down to see me? I don't think so.

I'm at the gate, just behind the security barrier. No one but me knows the deal is going down. She's holding. She's my mule, that one, big gorgeous Jenny with her sportcoat hiding the stuff, the drop going down right there at the airport and no cop's gonna stop it. She comes out of the gate area, and I fly into her arms, and her body's hot against me, her thighs, her big soft breasts, the neck I like to bite and the hard nipples rising to my welcome, and all weekend long we're going to make love with the air conditioner on and the CD player blasting the Indigo Girls and now Jenny's handing me a cool damp double-wrapped plastic bag, and it's Coffee-mate in my hand, and I'm heading home with both my girls, my lover and my addiction, and I'm going to eat Jenny and drink coffee, and everyone on the subway wonders why I look so happy, and only Jenny knows.

Chapter Twenty-four
Number One Value Meal

It was a beautiful, sunny day, a clear blue sky with a wind blowing through the trees. The park was alive with the sounds, smells, and sights of various people. Children's shouts and laughter echoed from the playground as teenagers' radios resounded in the background. Couples sat on park benches gazing at each other, sunbathers laid their blankets on the freshly cut grass while others walked along the river's edge watching speedboats bounce off the wake of the mighty city ferries rolling down the river.

Jessica took her usual spot—a bench between the joggers' track and the park's mini meadow. It was her Sunday constitutional, and she hoped it was the usual routine for the blond-hair jogger she spotted running last week. She was a real sight for sore eyes and an aching heart. A little bit of eye candy, perhaps? Baby, she was more like the whole sweet shop. Jessica placed her sketchbook and charcoal pencil on her lap and began to let her artistic eye wander over her surroundings. An old man with his dog, a mother and child playing in the grass, but neither seemed to catch her attention. Jessica's stomach did a flip and her heart skipped a beat as she spotted her jogger enter the track. She watched her lean her hands against the track's fence and stretch those legs that were as long as a cold winter's night. Blondie then spread her legs and bent over to touch her toes, giving Jessica a full view of her backside.

Hmmm, baby, I could do a few laps around that track, Jessica remarked to herself.

Before she knew it, her charcoal pencil began to glide along the page. Her eyes branded every detail into her mind as her pencil brought the image to fruition. Blondie moved slowly onto the track and began a slow jog, pumping her arms and rotating her head to loosen her neck. Her blue nylon shorts cut right at mid-thigh, while her white T-shirt fell just below her navel. She began to accelerate and so did Jessica's pulse. Jessica's hand moved quickly, urging her on. *Catch her! Catch her! Catch her essence. Catch her tight muscular frame moving with grace and agility. Catch the sweat trickling down the back of her neck as she turned at the quarter mile mark. Catch her erect nipples as they protrude more and more with each completed lap. Catch the outline of her thigh muscles as they strain with every stride. Keep going! Keep going! Don't stop! Yes, yes, I'm almost there!*

Jessica's breath became rapid as her hand zigzagged across the page. Her eyes jetted from subject to paper, from beauty to paper, from goddess to paper. *Get the details! Get her long fingers. Oh those long fingers! How I wish they were touching me, caressing me, in me.* Her long blond hair, pulled tightly into a ponytail, flapped between her shoulder blades. Jessica closed her eyes to fend off the image soaring through her mind of those blond strands grazing against her breast as Blondie lay above her, gently kissing her mouth.

"*Oh God, please stop!*" Jessica whispered.

She opened her eyes to the frightful sight of her luscious lady's legs stumbling on the track propelling her face-first to the ground. Jessica sprang from her bench in a flash, throwing her sketchbook into the dirt. She was over the waist-high fence and at her fallen angel's side instantly.

"Are you OK?" she said, touching her fingers to her beauty's elbow.

"Uh, I think so."

Her voice! It is music to my ears!

"Your knee is bleeding," Jessica declared.

"I guess it is," Blondie retorted. She gathered herself and rose from the asphalt. Jessica tried to play Florence Nightingale without seeming too desperate.

"Here, lean on me, and we'll go sit on the grass."

Blondie threw her arm over her shoulder, and Jessica caught herself before she hit the turf from the touch of her runner's arm. Together they slowly made their way to the small grassy knoll off to the side of the track. Blondie lowered herself onto the grass and glanced up at Jessica.

"Where did you come from?" Blondie inquired.

"Huh? Oh, me? I was just . . . uh . . . sitting . . . actually sketching, I mean, I was sitting and sketching . . . you . . . I mean, I was sitting and sketching and I saw you . . . I mean I saw you fall . . . and when I thought you might be hurt . . . I . . . ."

Blondie's lips parted, revealing the smile that could melt an iceberg.

"You're pretty funny." She chuckled.

"Uh, I'm sorry. I didn't mean to make fun of you or uh . . . anything . . . I . . . ."

Blondie laughed softly, "And you're pretty cute, too!"

"Really?" Jessica's voice revealed a new octave she didn't know she had in her.

"Especially when you're fumbling over your words like me fumbling over my feet. Have a seat. I'm Kate."

"I'm Jessica." She took Kate's hand and held it as if she was holding a sacred icon.

95

Kate let her hand rest in Jessica's while her eyes rested on Jessica's glowing smile.

"You know, if you smile any wider, your face is gonna split in two."

"What? Oh, I'm sorry. It's just . . . um . . . I'm used to staring."

"Uh, come again?" Kate remarked.

"I mean . . . I paint, draw, sketch, and I stare to get details for my work. It's an occupational hazard."

"Oh, I see. You're an artist."

"A starving one, I'm afraid. Say, we need to get that knee fixed up."

"Well, how about you fix a runner's knee, and I'll fix a starving artist a meal."

Jessica got up first to assist Kate to her feet. She held out one hand, then the other, taking both of Kate's. She rose with ease right into Jessica's arms. They stood face to face, breast to breast, thigh to thigh. *"A perfect fit!"* Jessica thought to herself, revealing her observation with a broad smile.

"You're smiling again." Kate laughed. "My car is in the parking lot," she added. They began their slow trek with Kate maintaining her balance by clutching Jessica's shoulder as Jessica wrapped her arm around Kate's waist. They stopped briefly to gather Jessica's sketchbook.

"I'd like to see what you were drawing while I was running and falling all over."

"You don't need to see it. It's pretty familiar to you."

Kate looked a bit puzzled as she slid into the driver's seat, but she shook it off. She was feeling that all too familiar stirring within her. That swirling arousal that begins between the legs and ascends through the stomach to the heart, ready to erupt like a volcano now triggered by a natural force. Jessica was that force, that energy, that stimulus. She reached across to open the glove compartment, leaning her right hand on Jessica's thigh.

"I have something in here you can use."

Jessica felt a rush as Kate's hand squeezed her thigh.

"Here, you can fix my knee and I'll fix you a meal."

Jessica moved toward Kate to dab at her knee. Kate's hand moved toward the seat lever, forcing Jessica to fall back against the cushion. Jessica could taste the salty sweat above Kate's lip. She moaned with pleasure, cheering on her athlete. Kate's hand ran Jessica's course with a marathon pace, making her way along her curves, her soft terrain, making her way to the finish line below. Jessica pulled away, gasping and startled by Blondie's advances as well as her own. She looked into Kate's eyes, matching the smile reflecting back at her.

"I thought we were going to your place so you can fix me a meal," Jessica uttered.

Kate chuckled and whispered into Jessica's ear. "Baby, this is my number one value meal."

Chapter Twenty-five
Skywriter

It was so lonely on the night shift at the airfield. I wanted you, I thought of you. I know I said I'd let you sleep. I broke my rule and telephoned. I woke you up.

Now both of us were sleepy and apart. My vision was aroused, drawing portraits of your half-furled sleepiness, your tucked legs, your head cupped in a pillow, your mouth half open and your teeth nudging the air. The still room, gurgling its noises, the goldfish swimming in the tank, the rubber plant growing up toward the light, the humming air conditioner, the sudden madness of my phone call thrusting you awake on flapping feet. I could see your hand on the black phone cord, your bent knees creaking, the sweatshirt pulled hastily over your head.

I didn't mean to wake you. But somehow it made the dawn of morning palatable, palpable, tangible, leafy and tender as the gardenia waxes, soft with the clinging fuzz of blankets, quilts, dreams cast aside with a long rosy arm, cast aside like the sheet peeling off last night. I should have been with you last night. I had to work the night shift. I thought of you all night. I had to call, too early, woke you up.

So, maybe you'll call me back. Your hair a jumble, your wrists grazing the butter dish, the toast, the sugar bowl, the paper. You'll yawn into the table, rub your knuckles through your hair, and sigh at me because I woke you up. Your day began as my night shift was ending.

I can see you rising like a little island. Facing me, the lapping ocean: need you, miss you. You'll wash your face, blinking, dazed and fresh, walk to pour yourself a cup of tea. What are you gonna do with me, huh? I grabbed you from a dream. A dream of us.

All summer it was like this because I had to watch the planes, the code yellow alert. The pilots could be bad guys. But none were. The airfield unimportant, small, unused. I wanted summer nights in bed beside your body, to fly the plane that was your sex, your life force. Take off slow and rise and tilt your wings. I had my pilot's license in my wallet, had your photo tucked behind the crease. I yearned to touch you where you creased and fly you sky-ward. I sat alone, unarmed, and watched for trouble.

I had to call, to hear that you were there.

Maybe it was the seventh time I woke you. Seven lucky times I'd made you mad. "I have to *sleep*," you moaned, although you wanted me. You worked all day in the hot sun, lifeguard at the pool, a different kind of security job, watching over lives. You watched swimmers, I watched planes. But if I woke you up and made you sleepy, you'd be a sleepy lifeguard—bad news. My bad. And if I felt this way, missing you, guilty, I'd forget to watch for trouble, too. My bad. So.

Once a week they let me fly a plane, just to keep the older engines running. I went off shift and climbed into my choice. Into the clearing and up over the field, twenty minutes of freedom, toward our house.

It was noisy, living so close to the airfield, but it was the only house we could afford, and after a while you got used to the noise, the background buzz, and there wasn't much of it, just lessons and cargo, and of course there was my job. So I had my mark laid out, and timed it to you leaving for work. I knew you'd walk out early, because I woke you up.

Cheryl stood on the front lawn, her still-damp bathing suit chafing under overall cutoffs, keys to the Honda in her right hand. Sue had waked her up early again. She rubbed sleep out of her eyes, sipped at the strong tea in her travel mug, shifted the pool maintenance schedule tucked into her left armpit. The buzz of circling planes from Sue's airfield throbbed in the halls of her mind. Damn that airfield. The plane seemed to be closer. She looked up.

There in the blue, the sky-frame blue above their yard, was the ancient skywriting plane, the one Sue longed to take out for a spin and never could because it wasn't working. Someone must have fixed it. Sue'd be envious, probably begging, unless—was that her lover, waving from the cockpit? Was the plane diving diagonally, now, on purpose?

Plumes of skywriter smoke puffed down and swooping lines spelled out the message: LOVE YOU BABY.

The letters, smoky cursive, hung in morning air.

The plane turned and headed back to land inside the airfield.

Cheryl, smiling, laughing at that sky. *You woke me up.*

Chapter Twenty-six
Something in My Drawers

"I'll tell you, I enjoy competition the same as the next person," said Ms. Chesnick, who was my third interviewee this morning. "But I am frustrated with going through the whole process, you know what I mean? There's the early rounds, then the round robin, the trials, until the final match arrives. Geez, a woman can go crazy with all this competition."

"So you compete in a sport?" I asked politely, though a bit confused by the whole conversation.

"Sports, who, me? Naw, I'm talking about dating in the bar scene."

"Well. Thank you for coming in today, Ms. Chesnick. We'll be in touch."

"Yeah, I hope to hear from you. I really would like to work with you. If you know what I mean?"

She added a wink and a smile and I felt the nausea rise in my stomach. I took a long breath as I flopped back in my chair.

No more. Please, God, no more like Ms. Chesnick. That makes three this morning. There has to be someone out there that can handle a simple public relations project for a concert. Someone who isn't just one step from being institutionalized, someone who's got both their oars in the water, whose elevator goes to the top floor, you get the picture?

I shrugged Chesnick out of my thoughts, took a gulp of my now cold morning coffee and hit the intercom button.

"Beth, will you send in the next candidate, please," I requested of my secretary.

A few seconds later, the door opened and in walks this cool, tall drink of water. She had the whole package on the outside and my insides were drinking the whole glass.

"Ms. Cleary, I am Susan Wellington. It's a pleasure to meet you." She had golden blond hair that floated around her shoulders. Her coffee-colored suit conformed to her shapely body, revealing little to the eye but speaking volumes to other parts of the anatomy. She sat on the edge of her chair with her long legs crossed, causing her skirt to rise and letting me peek at the gorgeous thigh in front of my desk. She undid the button on her double-breasted jacket, allowing her double-breasted chest to work its magic on me.

Well, well, well. Keep your cool, girlfriend. Don't you go falling in the well for Wellington.

Beef Wellington . . . Duke of Wellington . . . she can dip into my well anytime . . . Stop! Get control of yourself and talk to the lady.

"Thank you. Please, sit down. I see by your résumé you have had extensive experience coordinating social functions and fundraisers. It is quite impressive," I stated quite professionally, though tiny beads of sweat were starting to form on my forehead.

"Thank you," she responded confidently and added, "I always try to please my employer."

"I am sure you left them very satisfied." I said instinctively.

Please . . . pleasing . . . satisfy . . . satisfying . . . pleasure . . . what are you saying?

102

A small grin appeared on her face with my remark as I fumbled with the papers on my desk, trying desperately to show some decorum as she continued her pitch.

"Though my time with many of my former employers was short term, I always met their expectations and never left . . . how should I put this . . . never left them wanting . . . for someone else to finish the job." Her tongue lingered over the "wanting," sending shivers up my neck.

I was shocked by my reaction to this woman. Yes, of course, she was gorgeous and sexy and from the tone of her voice, willing. But it was more of a surprise to find myself being seduced and reduced to a ball of hormones, desiring her with no regard, letting my own desire take control of me. I was infatuated by her beauty and completely horny simultaneously. Such is the quandary of an older woman when given the attention of such a magnificent-looking younger babe. Ugh! The agony of the heart! Well, she wasn't that much younger . . .

I hit the intercom button. "Beth, would you bring in some coffee for us?"

"So tell me about some of your women . . . I mean your work with women's issues." I was squeezing my thighs together, trying to fend off the onslaught of wetness that was accumulating below.

"Well, one project I am very proud of was my fund-raiser for displaced homemakers. I was able to raise one million dollars to help women gain job skills training to reenter the game."

"The game?" I inquired.

"Yes, I am sure you understand the 'game,' the job market." She smirked as she lowered her leg to cross the other.

Beth entered with a tray of coffee, fresh fruit, and muffins. I thought it was a bit over the top, but I had a feeling Beth was experiencing an increase of her pheromone production this morning. She bumped into the coffee table due to having her eyes glued to my lovely interviewee.

"Thank you, Beth, that will be all. Please hold all my calls, will you?" Beth's feet were nailed to the rug.

"Yes, Ms. Cleary. I will make sure you are not disturbed."

Too late for that, I already am, and it's growing by the minute.

"I am sorry for the interruption." I regained my composure while picturing Beth making a beeline for the women's bathroom for a private moment. My sumptuous blond goddess was playing with the gold necklace that fell so innocently onto her chest. The button on her white silk blouse was undone at some point during my conversation with Beth. Liquid production was now in double-time mode between my legs.

I believe there comes a time in everyone's life when they are faced with a certain set of circumstances that cannot be understood with a rational explanation and the individual just has to say, what the fuck! This I believed, was one of those situations.

"Perhaps we would be more comfortable on the sofa," I said with a flirtatious smile of my own. I slowly raised myself from my seat, keeping my eyes on her gold chain and her long manicured fingers. Lady Wellington followed my lead and positioned herself in the middle of the sofa, allowing our legs to brush against each other.

"How do you take your coffee?" I asked, letting my own vibes emanate toward my young apprentice.

"Light and sweet," she said in her seductive tone.

I began to fix her coffee when I felt her fingers on the back of my neck lightly caressing under my hair.

"I like many things light and sweet," she whispered in my ear, finishing her sentence with her tongue grazing my lobe as an exclamation. I sat motionless, letting my blond beauty play.

"Would you like to see some of my skills for this job?" she asked, enticing me to play with her. I turned my face toward my lovely charge, finding creamy soft lips waiting for reply.

"I think I need to explain some of the criteria included in this position." I kissed her with the sweetness and my fingers touched her chest with the lightness that was to her liking. She moaned with approval, crumbling under my touch and onto the sofa. I followed her down into the leather, pushing her leg against the back of the sofa and letting the other remain firmly on the floor. My head was spinning with anticipation of what my hands would discover as I moved them along her silk stockinged legs and found their tops mid-thigh. I leaned in to taste her sweet lips once again as my fingers engaged her own wetness and gently squeezed my succulent peach, causing her hips to ascend off the sofa.

"Perhaps I need to explore your talents further," I suggested, already knowing the response.

"Yes, please continue," she whispered breathlessly as she raised her skirt to her waist, allowing me extensive access to her qualifications. I glanced down at her luscious asset wrapped in black silk panties and immediately began my own hands-on training.

"Your job performance is outstanding," I murmured into her ear as my fingers bypassed her panties. "Something might open up for you very soon," I asserted as my fingers inserted.

"I also like to jump right into the action," she stated between breaths as her hand lowered the zipper on my trousers and began her own exploration of my company benefits. I buried my tongue in the back of her throat, maintaining my restraint of trade, trying to ward off the hostile takeover she initiated with her maneuver. She felt my submission and moved in for the kill, pushing me back on the sofa. She climbed on top, giving her the advantage in these negotiations. We stared into each other's eyes, feeling each other out, yet going with our instincts.

"I believe we can seal this deal right now," she claimed.

The pounding of my heart and the small voice within me screaming, "*more, more,*" made my decision. I smiled into those beautiful baby blues.

"I think you will find what I have to offer you in my drawers, and all its perks, quite satisfying." My young executive let out a chuckle while she shimmied my pants down my leg.

"Ms. Cleary, I'm sure I will." She smiled back.

Hired!

Chapter Twenty-seven
Thrown Out of Bed

Ann-Marie was amused by her new girlfriend's total nervousness about a simple trip to Los Angeles. Why the ridiculous fear of California? Why the ongoing tension about so many things that "might go wrong"? Patty Johnson was a tough litigator in court. Her power suits sure didn't require that extra padding in the shoulders—she carried her broad, impressive body with ease and took up space in public places as if to challenge, *What are YOU looking at?* Back east, as "left coast" Californians say, Patty was confidence served on a platter. But not, apparently, as a traveler. Oh, well.

From the second she'd landed at LAX for her visit with Ann-Marie, Patty cringed and whined. She was terrified of the freeway, though Ann-Marie handled her small Volkswagen blithely amid the speeding Porsches and beach-bound convertibles with aggressive license plates like ISUEM4U. Patty kept the car window on her own side carefully power-locked, scrutinizing every car around them for incipient drive-by snipers, while Ann-Marie had her own window down and her hair flying blond in the wind. Patty sniffed at that air suspiciously, looking through the airline's courtesy *Los Angeles Times* for a pollution index. Most of all, she seemed panicky about possible earthquakes. What if? What if? What if there was an earthquake during their trip to Disneyland and they were hurled off the Matterhorn? What if the earthquake hit while Ann-Marie was driving?

"Look, there's nothing to it." Ann-Marie spoke reassuringly through a mouthful of lunch at the In and Out Burger. "I grew up here, I lived through all the earthquakes, I know exactly what to do. Just go stand in a doorway or if you have a good sturdy table, you can crouch under that. You shut off the gas if you have time, to reduce leaks and risk of fire. And expect little aftershocks, small tremors after the big one." She smirked. "Like with an orgasm."

Patty's pale face was a mask of anxiety. "Please, don't even use that phrase *the big one*."

"And do you know what's really cool?" Ann-Marie forged on, beginning to enjoy her role as the butch UCLA scientist protecting the eastern lady lawyer. "Dogs and coyotes know when a tremor is about to start. You can hear their howls across the valleys, all at once, like a psychic orchestra warming up. I taped it once."

"You never said anything about *coyotes*. How big? I didn't bring my pepper spray. They wouldn't allow it on the plane. What about rabies? Are you telling me that if an earthquake hits, you're just going to start *tape recording* it?"

Ann-Marie sighed, wondering again if this weekend fling had been a good idea. They barely knew each other. Patty had seemed so *together* at the medical ethics conference where they met: passionate about feminism and law, willing to sign Ann-Marie's petition on medical marijuana for AIDS patients. Perhaps she was a court and classroom genius who otherwise led a hermetically sealed life.

All around them were anorexic movie stars picking at salads. That was one reason Ann-Marie responded so sensually to Patty's big, curvy good looks. They'd give it a try.

"Honey," said Ann-Marie, "this is Hollywood—you can avoid nature. But the pull of the ocean and the tectonic push of the land are real and beautiful. Beautiful to me. I'm sorry if you feel put upon."

Patty knew she'd been a pain in the ass this first hour and now attempted to seem like a good sport. "Well, in Girl Scouts they teach you to make these little mats called sit-upons. But in my troop we made put-upons."

"Oh, not bad, babe," laughed Ann-Marie.

After that things picked up. Patty allowed her hand to be held across the gearshift. And whatever the air pollution level was that afternoon, it didn't prevent Patty from inhaling sufficient oxygen to tell her life story—including the source of her present-day phobias—during their long drive to Anaheim. Coyotes, gangbangers, and natural disasters were undetectable as they checked into their hotel near Disneyland and prepared for big-time fun.

Ann-Marie, a native Angeleno, had been to the Magic Kingdom almost every year since she was born, but seeing Patty's undisguised delight brought out her playful sense of delirium as though Sleeping Beauty's castle were a new experience. They spent a twelve-hour day and several hundred dollars trying every ride, food novelty, and gift item, posing with Minnie Mouse for lesbian-suggestive photos. The theme park was packed with gay and lesbian tourists that day and the safe camaraderie added buoyancy to their visit. Ann-Marie expected Patty to collapse with exhaustion that night but instead found a whole new "ride" beginning as soon as they unlocked their room and hit the bed.

"Fantasyland," whispered Patty.

"You're not tired?"

"Baby, I'm wired."

"Then I'm inspired."

"As I desired."

They made love in the giant Minnie Mouse–shaped bed. Ann-Marie found the sexual rhythm she'd enjoyed at their first meeting, that night at the conference in Atlanta when Patty invited her up and then went down. Up, down, east, west, who cared? Whee! The delicacy of the lawyer's flesh, her new Goofy hat thrown over the bedpost, her whininess was forgiven. What an animal! Her mouth moved low on Ann-Marie.

And so, lying under Patty, mere seconds away from coming, Ann-Marie was in the unique position to see the light fixture slowly swaying over their heads. She knew what that meant! Patty, moving back and forth, couldn't see the chandelier swing—or their coffee mugs starting to dance spookily across the bureau. As the bed finally began to shake, Patty sat up proudly. "You come like an earthquake," she said.

Sound waves, motion, and the crashing of small objects all hit at once. "*Earthquake!*" screamed Patty. "Aiee! Aiee! Aiee!"

"Hold on to me, baby," yelled Ann-Marie over the ominous rumbling. She threw her arms around her lover and pulled the well-padded quilt over their heads as chunks of plaster and dust drifted down from the ceiling. At the same time she couldn't help but notice that the motion of the bed and Patty's death-grip were creating definite sensations between her legs.

"*Jesus!*" moaned Ann-Marie.

"Oh, my God, if you're starting to pray it must mean this is the *big one!*" Patty sobbed.

"It is!" Ann-Marie cried jubilantly, as their luggage flew across the room and water glasses smashed in the bathroom. "It is! It is! It is!"

Seconds later, the quake reached its end. A spent Ann-Marie shifted position and gasped for air. Patty peeped out fearfully from under the quilt and saw that no real damage had occurred. The lights flickered out, then back on with a buzz. Guests on other floors were babbling with excitement.

In the far, far distance, dogs and coyotes howled.

Patty looked down at Ann-Marie in amazement and then scowled. "You knew it was an earthquake! Weren't we supposed to move to a doorway? Why didn't you push me off?"

Ann-Marie, still in the throes of the longest orgasm of her life, could only respond weakly: "Babe, what can I say. I'd *never* throw you out of bed."

Chapter Twenty-eight
Preview of Coming Attractions

I arrived one minute before seven. Emma greeted me at the door and kissed me before she closed it.

"Hmm, thank God for Fridays," I said in response to her gesture.

"So, you ready to go?"

"Just let me get a sweater, and we'll be on our way."

I stood on the porch with a big grin on my face. I was going out with my girl on a Friday night date. All was right in the world. I worked all week at the counseling center helping a slew of adolescents trying to get their life back on track, and now I was helping myself to a good time with a beautiful, intelligent woman. Emma was still a bit closeted when it came to being seen in public holding hands or kissing. But me, well, I guess you can say I was "out" pretty far with a rainbow flag sticker on my motorcycle. Emma was now on the porch with me.

"Should we take my bike?" I inquired. She turned around and gave me this hesitant look.

"It was just a suggestion. Emma, maybe I should put the bike in your garage."

We both stood on the porch for a moment, considering the ramifications of my bike always parked in front of her house. Especially after her boss showed up one night while I was visiting.

"That's a good idea," she acknowledged.

I hated the fact that we always had to remember small details, always had to stay one step ahead, calculating, thinking. We just couldn't be. What if Hennessey, her boss, showed up and saw the bike—and the neighbors keep seeing me arrive at night and leave in the morning.

Hey, I didn't care if the eyewitness news van showed up for an interview. Just let us be! I was screaming in my head again. I got into the car with those thoughts changing both the expression on my face and my mood. Emma could see something was wrong. We drove down the thruway in silence. I couldn't shake what I was feeling. I tried looking out the window to admire the sunset over the Manhattan skyline.

"It's a beautiful night," I commented.

"Yes, it is." Emma was watching the road and me at the same time. "Janet, you OK?"

I mentally shook away these thoughts and turned to face her with my back partially against the door. I reached for her hand lying on the shift.

"I'm fine now."

Touching her, looking at her, could change my mood instantly.

"Good. Now tell me where we're going before we end up lost in some desolate place."

Now there's a suggestion!

I directed her to the theater, and we sat in the car momentarily. My mood was still hanging in the air.

"I'm sorry, Emma. I'm just getting a bit frustrated with this cloak-and-dagger crap. So we are seen together, so what. Can't they just believe we're friends?"

She looked at me with a raised eyebrow and a you-got-to-be-kidding look.

"OK, I know we are more than friends, obviously. But they don't know that!"

She still had that look. She didn't say a word.

"OK, so they find out we are . . . lovers." The word stuck in the back of my throat. I hadn't used it before to describe our relationship. "So they find out . . ." I had a fiery look on my face as I met her eyes. "So what."

"Not yet, Janet, OK? Give it time, give us time . . . give me time."

I softened my expression as my chin dropped down. She picked it up with the tip of her fingers and smiled into my eyes.

"It'll be OK," she reassured me.

"That's my line." I returned the smile.

She leaned over and laid a gentle kiss on my lips. "Let's go to the movies, I'm buying."

"OK, but the popcorn is on me."

"I don't eat popcorn at the movies."

"What do you mean you don't eat popcorn! It's an American tradition. It's like eating a hot dog at a ballgame, or cotton candy at a circus, or pork at a southern barbeque! You can't do one without the other!"

"Where do you come up with these things," she exclaimed.

I loved joking with her. We were so connected we could joke and make fun of each other.

I bought a small popcorn.

The theater was quite empty since the film we chose had been out for a while. The crowds were going to see the latest Tom Cruise film. We weren't interested. It was nice to sit near her in the dark. I wished the armrest wasn't there so that, you know. I ate my popcorn and quietly offered it to Emma every so often. She turned me down with a look of disgust every time. I smiled, enjoying playing with her pet peeve. Halfway through the espionage/murder/boy-gets-girl movie, Emma leaned over and whispered in my ear.

"Can I have some popcorn?"

I looked at her in surprise. "Sure."

I offered her the bag and she took the whole thing and placed it on the seat next to her. She lifted the armrest up, placing it to the back of the seat, just like the ones on planes.

They move!

Emma adjusted herself in the seat, inching her way closer to me. I didn't know whether to just watch the movie, watch her, or watch the audience. I tried to do all three, but she had placed her hand on my right thigh, and I almost ejected from my seat. Her eyes never left the screen as her hand massaged down to my knee, up to the inside of my leg and back down. I did a quick surveillance of the perimeter. There was no one in our row, and no one sitting behind me to my left or to Emma's right. We had approximately three rows to ourselves.

I took a deep breath and closed my eyes for a moment, trying to steady myself. Her hand was causing a sexual catastrophe inside of me. I wanted her to kiss me. I wanted to join in on the fun. I wanted to raise all of the armrests and go to town on her right there. Instead, I encouraged her. I bent my leg up and rested my ankle across my left knee, moving my right knee closer to her. She acknowledged my signal by moving her fingers closer to my center and brushing briefly against my crotch.

Oh Lord, I am going to die!

Emma continued her hand movement down my thigh and back between my legs. I became aware that my left hand was in a death grip on the other armrest. I leaned over and whispered into Emma's ear, "Someone might see us."

"So what," was her response as she looked straight into my eyes.

A verbal boomerang landed right between my eyes.

She didn't have to go this far to prove her point! Well . . .

I released my grip and relaxed my head against the headrest—as well as the rest of my body.

As the action on the screen picked up, so did the action in our seats. Emma moved her hand up to my shirt, unbuttoned two buttons and slipped inside. The back of her hand grazed against my breast, causing my nipple to protrude through my bra. She discovered its appearance and gently squeezed it with her thumb and forefinger. She leaned over and whispered, "I like this part the best."

Her double entendre seasoned the moment. I lowered my leg because it was falling asleep and shifted myself a bit closer to her. I reached with my hand to touch her leg, but she brushed me off and placed it to my side. She was still squeezing me, sending SOS signals down below. I tried to control my outward reaction, stifling my moans, reducing my breathing. Emma wouldn't let up. She retrieved her hand from my shirt and moved again to my pants. She attempted to lower the zipper, and perhaps it was instinct or desire, but I helped her. She leaned over and whispered, "I think this is the exciting part," as her fingers massaged me through my panties. I found myself lowering in the chair and my legs slightly farther apart.

"Emma," I whispered, "I will do a lap dance on you right here and now if you don't stop."

Her fingers moved faster against me as she whispered, "I think this is the climax."

My eyes closed, and I pressed my mouth against her shoulder to stifle my cry as I came.

The movie ended and I adjusted my clothing and zipped up before the lights came up. Emma stood in the row, reading the credits.

"That was a good movie," she exclaimed. She reached over to the seat next to her. "You want your popcorn back?" She had that devious smile on her face.

Actually, I wanted revenge, but not here, so I kept my cool. "Very funny. We could have been arrested for lewd behavior." I acted annoyed.

"I didn't find it lewd." She smirked.

We exited from our theater of love. We drove back to Riverside. I couldn't even discuss the movie because of our play in the seats. But then again, I missed half of the plot at the end. Pulling the car into the driveway and cutting the engine, Emma turned to find me looking at her with my own devious smile.

"You think you're pretty slick, dontcha," I remarked.

Emma nodded in the affirmative, very pleased with herself.

I leaned over and kissed those luscious lips I had desired the whole ride home.

"Well, you can consider that just a coming attraction, baby. The main event starts inside." She whispered, "A five-star performance."

"Amazing."

Chapter Twenty-nine
Enough Cream Cheese

Summer had barely started and it was already the worst year for storm-related flight delays and cancellations, according to that day's *Washington Post*. As if Frieda didn't know it—she was having a bad, bad day.

All flights were presently grounded because of a nasty storm cell that sat right above Chicago's O'Hare Airport, and stranded passengers pawed through the terminal like enraged buffalo, snorting and stomping. Nothing was landing, nothing taking off. "We continue to experience delays," blared the P.A. system at every airline desk. Dark rain pounded the glass windows. Frieda's journey had barely begun. She was now safely in Chicago, true, but there was a long second flight to San Francisco she was supposed to be on. She had missed her connection, and the next available flight wasn't going anywhere as long as the heavens continued to rumble and split and pour. Worst of all, as airlines no longer served free meals on most economy flights, Frieda had had neither breakfast nor lunch. Now she would be forced to pass the long hours either resisting the expensive airport food choices or caving in and spending her travel budget on eight-dollar slices of pizza. Damn it! She checked the monitor one more time. No, her flight west wouldn't be leaving for at least three hours, probably closer to four. She started down the long hallway, heading for the food court in the other terminal, but was quickly stopped by a uniformed security agent.

"Ma'am, you can't leave that backpack at your gate. All unattended items will be treated as a possible security threat."

Now her heavy carry-on knapsack was digging in against her bra straps as she trudged alongside similarly aimless and hungry travelers. Frieda sighed and surveyed her options in the food court. No fast-food burgers today; her mind was still numb with horror from seeing the documentary film *Super Size Me*. Really, the most economical and meat-free choice seemed to be a bagel. A big bagel, thick with cream cheese . . . ah, that sounded *sooo* good. She could fit it into her backpack and pull it out later on the flight to San Francisco, invoking envy among passengers who hadn't thought ahead to bring their own food. Cheered, Frieda told the cute young deli cashier, "I'll have a sesame bagel with cream cheese."

Using long plastic tongs, the cashier pulled out a bagel and placed it in a brown paper bag. Then she reached into a below-counter refrigerated compartment and pulled out a tiny round container of cream cheese, about the size of a silver dollar. "Here you go. Enjoy your snack."

Frieda thought she would burst into tears. *This* was the cream cheese? She had fully expected her bagel to be sliced and then piled high with *shmear*—as in her New York neighborhood deli, as at every family brunch of her life, as God had intended cream cheese to be served, in sculpted, soaring, inch-thick waves.

"Please," she choked. "May I have two little cream cheese tins?

You see, I'm really hungry, and this is *dinner*. For me, this just isn't ... I mean, it doesn't seem like enough cream cheese to cover even a half of a bagel."

The deli server, whose orange name tag had RACHEL printed on it, nodded sympathetically and reached for another tiny cream cheese tub. Frieda looked at it and started to cry.

Rachel's eyes widened. "Wow, I'm so sorry! Would you like a third?"

"It's not you," sobbed Frieda. "It's paying so much for a flight and not getting any dinner. It's being stranded here for hours and not being able to afford a decent meal. It's going out west to attend my ex-lover's *commitment ceremony* when I could have spent my travel dollars on an Olivia cruise. It's schlepping around this heavy backpack full of wedding gifts she doesn't deserve after fucking the UPS woman on our new IKEA couch. It's the final insult, having to cut and spread my own bagel and *shmear* after paying for it and *not getting enough cream cheese!*"

Rachel was reaching into the paper bag, neatly slicing the bagel, peeling off the tops of cream cheese tins and piling frothy whipped cream cheese high on Frieda's lonely little dinner. Abruptly, the deli girl threw off her apron, locked the cash register and came out from around the counter. "Tell Al I'm going on break," she yelled over her shoulder, steering Frieda out of the food court.

"No—" Frieda was protesting, embarrassed. "You don't have to—"

Rachel locked eyes with her. "Listen, sister. You're right. I'm a nice Jewish girl like you and I stand here all day dispensing insufficient cream cheese. It's an insult to our people. Plus, my ex cheated on me, too. She tossed with the PTA mom who only two years ago had arranged for me to be expelled from our high school. We both deserve something stronger than a bagel. Come this way."

Frieda was astonished to be led through a mysterious doorway and into what appeared to be an employee's lounge, now deserted. A coffeepot perked to one side, empty fast-food bags and used napkins littered the tabletop. Rachel pulled a key from her hip pocket and opened a locker, removing what looked like an authentic "Peanuts" lunch box.

"You be Marcy, I'll be Peppermint Patty," she joked.

"I always loved them," agreed Frieda.

Rachel flicked open the lunch box and removed a bottle of cinnamon schnapps and two corned beef sandwiches dripping with coleslaw and Russian dressing. "Let's pour some of this kosher hooch into that fresh coffee," she suggested, and within seconds Frieda was tucking into the greatest airport lunch of her life. As she ate, Rachel talked openly about herself: how she'd been the notorious queer at her local high school, expelled for seducing a cheerleader, forced to take a deli-counter job while trying to finish her GED, living with cheerleader Sue until Sue experimentally tried to change the viewpoint of their PTA-mom nemesis.

"I miss the kissing," Rachel sighed. "I have no diploma, no lover, and, in my dead-end airport job, I disappoint women all day, never giving them enough cream cheese. Until Sue cheated, and I had to move back in with my mom, at least I went home to good kissing."

Impulsively, Frieda leaned in and kissed her. Rachel's eyes widened.

"I'm sorry," Frieda stammered. "Maybe that was rash. But you've been so sweet to me. I'm so full and happy right now."

Rachel stood up and, glancing at her watch, appeared to reach a decision. "I'm on break for ten more minutes," she announced and strode over to the door, locking the bolt and removing her shirt in one impressively coordinated motion.

Then she stretched out on the employee lounge sofa. "Everything else is grounded," she advised. "But babe, *this* plane is ready for boarding."

Frieda smiled. "No security check? Don't you even want to see my ID?"

"I do recommend that you remove your shoes and belt."

Frieda tentatively did so. "Listen, do you do this often?"

119

"Am I a frequent flyer? No, hon. Let's just say this is an unexpected stop."

"For me, too." But Frieda felt the grin steal over her face. Ten minutes, huh? That wouldn't be enough, after so long without . . . "I fly back from San Francisco two days from now and change planes at O'Hare again. Will you be working at the deli Monday night?"

"I'm here every night. Oh, and I get two half-hour breaks. If I knew you were coming I could combine them and take the whole hour."

"But can you get this lounge for an entire hour? What about other employees on break?"

"If I pay them off they'll lie low. I've taken bribes to stay away for others' liaisons. It's finally my turn! So you want to be sure you'll see me again before jumping in at all? Ah. Sentimental."

"Yes, I am," Frieda agreed, adding her bra and undershirt to the pile of her belt and shoes, and climbing aboard for a most unscheduled flight, not knowing what pleased her more—the thought of the return stop in two days, showing up at her ex's wedding with a hickey, or, finally, whenever she wanted it as a traveler through Chicago, enough cream cheese on her bagel.

It was turning out to be a pretty smooth ride, after all.

Chapter Thirty
Bonfire

I walked aimlessly along the white sandy beach. The sky was full of sunset colors, crimson reds and soft oranges. My bare feet played with the sand and were caressed by the ocean foam. I became lost in my thoughts, lost in the emptiness that occupied my heart. I wandered on, no destination, no purpose now that she was gone. I gazed out into the horizon, letting the gentle ocean breeze pass over me, wanting its comfort like mother's arms. How could this come to an end? How did it happen? Over and over I played the tape in my head—rewind, forward, play the conversation, the accusations, the blame until, finally, eject. She left. The tape is now blank. No one left to point the finger at or to pinpoint the cause. Our time is over. We gave it a good run when we were together. We had some good times, moments that still bring me to tears when I feel their intensity. I loved her, I truly did. And yes, I still do. I let things get in the way. Petty flaws and weaknesses like holes in Swiss cheese, never seeing the whole product, the goodness and quality of her whole self. Will I ever return to my old self? I hope not. The old self caused the loss. Now, I must learn from this and move on. Yeah, sure it's easier said than done. Where is she now? Does she feel this pain, this persistent ache in her heart as I do?

I stood facing the ocean's eternity with all my strength, my anguish, my pride, my anger, my tears. With my arms outstretched, beckoning for her, I cried aloud for all the heavens to hear, "*Noooooooooooooo! Don't leave me!!*"

I dropped to my knees, letting my tears wash over my face, surrendering to my heartache.

"Hey, are you all right?" My torment was invaded by a female voice. "Are you hurt?" I felt a hand touch my shoulder, and I jumped from its contact.

"Huh." I looked up toward the twilight sky into the face of an angel.

"You want me to get help?" she asked in a concerned tone.

"No, no. I'll be all right," I muttered, somewhat embarrassed by my condition.

Where did she come from? I could have sworn I was alone.

"Look, why don't you come sit with me over by the dunes. I have a fire going and you can get warm there."

I hadn't noticed that I was shivering from the combination of the cool night breeze and my emotional outburst. She took my arm and slowly lifted me to my feet. I walked unsteadily toward the bonfire burning in the near distance.

"You gave me a scare," she remarked as she lowered herself next to me in the sand. I sat Indian style with my arms wrapped around my knees, staring into the golden flames shooting up from the wood.

"Here, this will warm your insides."

I took her offering silently, wondering what thoughts were running through her head. Did she see a deranged woman who could be considered ready for the loony bin?

122

"What's your name?" she asked lightheartedly.

"Dana," I mumbled.

"I'm Carrie. Nice to meet you." She spoke as if we were meeting for the first time at a mutual friend's potluck dinner. We sat in silence, which seemed an eternity. From the corner of my eye I could see her outline. She was an older woman, maybe in her fifties. Her short brown hair and plaid flannel shirt and jeans gave the impression she might be a member of the sisterhood. She had a gentle smile on her face, and her hands were strong, but one could see a soft quality about them as she carefully poked the firewood with her stick.

"You got heartache?" she asked directly.

That took me by surprise. How could she have known that?

"Uh, yeah. I guess you can say so," I responded sullenly.

"Some people around here tell me I'm a pretty good listener. They like to tell me their story, because they know it don't go no further than me."

I thought about this. Can I trust her? Can I start to explain to a complete stranger what I am feeling, my relationship problems or the termination of said relationship?

"What's her name?" she went on asking as if she could read my mind.

I turned to look at my beach companion with my mouth and eyes wide open. She just kept poking at the fire.

"Maggie . . . her name is Maggie."

"Been together long?" she inquired further.

"About five years."

"Helluva thing. You give that time to one person and then it's over," she declared.

"I guess so." I was astounded by her nonchalant manner, how she probed with her questions but with care in her voice.

"Well, you must have had some good times, right?"

"Yes, we did," I replied slowly as I envisioned those good times.

Maggie and I had met at work. We were coworkers working late hours on a project with lots of time to talk and to get to know each other. We hit it off from the start, and I wasn't surprised when

123

she asked me out to dinner after the project was completed. We would sit and laugh for hours. And when we finally gave in to our desire for each other, our passion flourished. I loved our lovemaking. We moved over each other like the soft waves on a moonlit beach. We mirrored our strokes and caresses, knowing each other's pleasures, reciprocating the delight we were taking from each other. She would lay her body on top of mine, and I would feel the warmth of her skin. The security I felt in her arms when I would let her hold me. I opened my heart to her declaration of love as she moved her hands slowly along my body, transforming her words into action, soothing me, keeping me safe from the world's tribulations. I lived for those moments when we left our daily stresses outside the bedroom door and tended to the care of each other's intrepid spirit.

I would gaze at her voluptuous body in the soft candlelight, arousing every inch with my touch. She would moan into the pillow as she let me into that secret place within where only true lovers gain admission.

"You are so beautiful," I would whisper tenderly, professing my own love for her as I held her supple body in my arms. We ignited each other's youthful spirit, the passion and impulsivity of our twenties. We danced out of sync and sang off key, but we didn't care. We had each other and fueled our fire for life and love. But now the fire was extinguished. What happened? Where did we go wrong? How could we let such a love slip away like sand through open fingers? Yes, we. Both of us were guilty of our transgressions. We played judge and jury with each other's faults and then pronounced a death sentence on our relationship. We exaggerated the negative elements so as to be right while ignoring the goodness and love that was always there waiting to be reclaimed.

"You really loved her, didn't you." Carrie's words drew my mind back to the fire.

"Yes, I did. I guess I still do." I pondered this realization.

"Can you fix it?" Carrie inquired.

"No, she's gone." I began to sulk and felt the feelings begin to well up inside as I faced this reality again.

"Well, you know. There's a saying," she said while still poking the fire. "When love's involved, anything is possible." She stopped poking the fire and turned to look straight into my eyes.

"With you, I'm getting the feeling it's possible. And when I get the feeling, it's usually right on. But you might have to go and get it, if it means that much to you." She held her gaze that seemed to travel deep into my heart. A calm fell over me, letting a warm sensation fill my body. Her eyes spoke to me, saying, *It's going to be all right.* This prophet, this soothsayer, was reassuring me, giving me that hope.

I stood up, not letting my eyes leave her, momentarily looking at the smile on her face.

"Thank you," I said. I hadn't a clue why I was grateful, but I felt compelled to say so. Somehow my heartache had subsided and I felt I could go on. She was magical in her simplicity.

"No problem, anytime. You take care now." She gave a wink with the smile. I turned and began my trek down the beach. The tape returned to play in my head, but it was a song of relief. I heard our laughter, and the giggles we let out under the covers in bed. I smiled at my mental reverie. I was remembering our love, the simple acts of kindness we performed for each other. It was OK to remember. I remembered our first kiss and how I nearly fell off the sofa in my awkward attempt. I chuckled to myself. I remembered how I would sneak quickly into the bathroom just to watch her shower and when pulled by my desire, I would join her. Memories flooded my mind. I cried tears of joy and sadness simultaneously. I closed my eyes briefly and summed up all of my mental and spiritual energy. *God, Maggie, can I see you just one more time? I want to make it right. We can make it work, I know we can. Please come back,* I silently prayed.

I walked over the dunes toward my parked car. My heart skipped a beat as my swollen bloodshot eyes spotted my love standing on the driver's side.

"Hey, I thought I would find you here," she exclaimed.

"Maggie!" I shouted for the whole world to hear. I ran into her arms, letting all the drama erase from my mind, body and soul. She held me tightly, whispering into my hair, "I can't let you go."

"Don't let go, Maggie . . ."

"I won't ever again," she declared as she held my face in her hands, kissing the tears of joy streaking down my face. We stood smiling into each other's eyes, touching, chuckling, and apologizing for our wrongs.

"Dana, you are too important to me to let this stuff get in the way."

"Yeah, you're right," I responded "We can make this happen. Anything is possible when love is involved, right?" I added.

Maggie had a shocked look on her face as if my words were a profound revelation. But they were only the words of my mysterious bonfire buddy, Carrie.

"What? What did I say?" I asked apprehensively.

"You just said the exact words I heard from this lady I was talking to in the town bar. I sat in there sulking after I left you," she explained.

"Maggie, you're kidding me. I was just talking to a woman by the dunes who said those words to me."

We both stared at one another and then turned to look toward the beach. Our jaws fell to our chests as we watched our love angels walking hand in hand along the shore. They waved as they strolled past our sight. Maggie and I looked at each other in utter perplexity.

"How could that have happened? Coincidence . . . you think?" Maggie said aloud.

"Babe, anything is possible, right?" I said happily as I hugged my beautiful lover and waved good-bye to our cupids.

Chapter Thirty-one
War Bonds

Rosie had me riveted to the couch. We'd been WAC-ing off all afternoon. No one in the boardinghouse seemed to notice or care. The other broads were exhausted from their round-the-clock shifts at the defense plant. You could hear their snores from every room and, in the kitchen, Marsha was using up all the sugar coupons rattling pots and pans for an after-dinner cookie fest with her gal Selma. Our place at 250 Garfield Lane was a houseful of liars and cover-up artists—we all said we had a boyfriend Over There, a feller at war, but nobody got any letters and there weren't any pictures of studs in uniforms in any photo frames I ever saw. We were girl-chasing girls and that was all right because we were all together at Garfield, working defense and loving in the free time.

Bix was really the house butch. On line at the plant, she made bullets. And it was rumored that she had hidden one defense bullet in each tip of her bullet-shaped bra. "No man will ever get fresh with me and live," she'd growl over dinner, and we'd all stare at our chipped nails or the chipped beef on the chipped plates. She hated having to wear that uniform bra, but with those enormous boobs she had no choice. Behind her back, we called her the Western Front—she was from Oregon. We didn't know what happened in Bix's past to make her hate men like that, but she had our respect.

Tobi was Bix's femme, assistant secretary to Bix's female super-intendent at the plant, and oh my God, the jealousy that led to! It rocked the ceiling fan, their fights. The I'm-so-sorry-baby sex that followed also caused paint chips to flake off my wall.

Rosie and I were already a couple before we came to the city and landed defense jobs, but of course we acted regular at work, which was a scream since everyone else on the line was a bigger dyke than we were. Denise, Lotta, Marsha and Selma rounded out our boardinghouse buffet. It was like musical chairs with dykes. One would go on shift just as her partner was coming home, the one coming home exhausted and the one heading out jacked up on hot coffee, and somehow they'd meet in the bathroom for a five-minute afternooner and knock all the towels and hosiery off the shower rack. Two others might have the same work hours for a stretch of weeks and would be asleep curled up together at odd hours of day or night. The sexual energy that ran the house saved Uncle Sam some pretty good electricity money. No one ever sat around under a table lamp reading or sewing at night. We didn't need to turn up the gas heat, what with our own body heat. We fig-ured we were damn good citizens, building ships and saving elec-tricity and all rooming together like that so married families could have the good housing, and our bosses sure knew we weren't likely to get pregnant and miss work.

So there I was, getting a pretty good riveting and settling in for a second invasion, too. Rosie had the map to my sweet spots and moved with the competence of a general. Her fingers were like ten little troops. She was bivouaced in my trenches. That was how we talked in bed, with a kind of wartime dirtiness. It got me off fast—and I always ended up feeling strangely patriotic afterward.

The doorbell rang and Rosie had to pull out of the South Pacific pretty fast. She threw on a skirt over the men's boxer shorts she liked and, running her fingers under the taps, belted out, "Who is it?" We didn't care what the ministers back in our home towns thought of us, but we all needed to look decent if the block captains paid a call. We needed that boardinghouse.

"Ah, hell—it's only Hazel," yelled Marsha, scooping cookies off the oven tray and heading to the door. Hazel was the war bonds dame, probably the biggest lezzo in town, though of course any guy who called her that to her face had either his teeth or his nuts rearranged. "Come on in, the cookies are hot off the sheet," Marsha beckoned.

Seeing it was just Hazel, Rosie took her skirt off and walked comfortably into the parlor in her boxers and Girl Scout shirt. "Sell a lot of bonds today?"

"You betcha. Hey, where's that honey of yours?"

I popped my head in. "Just freshening up."

"You're fresh enough," said Rosie, with a smack on my bottom.

I could feel old Hazel's hazel eyes burning cinnamon circles on my retreating buns. "If I had a little femme like that, Rose, I'd take in knitting and never leave the house."

"Yeah, you would, because she's got a job on the plant line, and you'd like to watch her at work."

"She's the cutest on the block, that one."

"Well, you'd know, Hazel. How many houses you been in this month, selling bonds?"

"Houses, or gals' sitting rooms and bedrooms?" Hazel munched a cookie as she ticked off on her fingers how many working girls she'd tried to make time with that month. She ran out of hands before the cookie was half gone.

"You're a wench." Marsha squealed with delight.

The screen door banged open and Selma rolled in. "Shush!" warned Rosie; "Bix and Tobi and Denise and Lotta are all asleep upstairs."

Selma stopped short at the sight of Hazel. "I already told you, I

129

bought defense stamps at work—I can't afford no bonds this time. Will you stop being so pesky?"

"All right. All right," said Hazel, looming to her feet and lingering over the cookie tray for one more minute. "I'm outta here. Be good. Don't do anything I wouldn't do!" Her bass-throated cackle could be heard for several minutes as she headed down the block.

I was thinking about how we were our own war bonds. Bonded together, I mean. We had bonds as women and bonds as gay-girl women and bonds as working women, and as housemates and lovers, and friends. More bonding was what I wanted out of the evening, myself. I went back to the attic bedroom and spread out on the cot for Rosie.

Maybe it sounds mean that we were so happy, with so many people dying in the war. Maybe it was wrong to feel so good.

All I know is being loved by Rosie was better than anything. Once, when we were hot into it, somehow I lost a blouse right in our bed. It just never surfaced again. Don't ask me where it went.

"Ah," said Rosie, surveying my bush. "A Victory Garden. Coming along nicely."

"It's more like a jungle now." I frowned, embarrassed, wanting a trim. With all of us in the house and one bathroom, personal hygiene was short and sweet.

She was on her knees beside the bed. "Jungle patrol, then. No enemy ambushes?"

"None. You can lay down your arms."

She laid her arms around me.

That was peacetime, see? That was how we had peace in the middle of it all. Thing is, there wasn't a soul in our families we could tell. We didn't try to explain. We lied, lied, lied about fake boyfriends. But years later, it got easier, and obviously we were still together, Rosie and me, like married. When my nieces and nephews were learning about the war, and asked us if we'd had war bonds, Rosie dared to tell them, "Sure did, kids. We bonded every night."

Chapter Thirty-two
Juice Box

Oh love, how I seek thee! How I hunger for thee to quench the thirst of my desires. Play on the strings of my heart the music of passion, of longing for my true love.

Hmmm. Now, this is hot! I turn and survey my aisle in the bookstore for any inquisitive eyes. I am alone. Ain't it the truth. I am alone and have been flying solo for three months now. I have substituted reading about love for the real thing. I know I need to get "the juices" flowing again. What is a middle-aged professional dyke to do? Go "clubbing" where everyone is multi-pierced and multi-amorous? Not my scene. I read on, creating the scenes in my head. I will experience flickering fantasy while standing in the Gay/Lesbian section.

She comes to me in the shadows of the night amid the sweet-smelling orchids, eucalyptus, and honeysuckles. An outline of her hourglass-shaped figure moves toward me. I exhale, making space within me for her love to possess. My senses keenly awaiting her scent to intoxicate my being, her touch to arouse my mortality and transcend this earthly state . . .

Baby, it's getting hot in here! I do a quick perusal of my surroundings and spot a brunette at the end of my aisle. Is she watching me? Her eyes are fixed on a paperback she is leafing through. A small smile curls her lips upward, but I surmise it's the book that interests her. I take a deep breath and return to my scene.

. . . The heat of her breath warms the blood racing through my veins. I close my eyes and with parted lips I move closer, yearning for the taste of her kisses. Our lips meet in the darkness, a conduit for pleasure. I recoil slightly when her fingers graze my breast. It has been a while since I have been fully aroused by another woman. And though I crave her caresses, they are estranged to me . . .

I shift my weight from left leg to right and feel my own juices begin to emerge between my legs. I clear my throat and unintentionally throw a glance toward my aisle buddy. She catches my eye, nods with the same impish smile and returns her emerald eyes to the book at hand. I feel the heat ascend my neck as I fumble to find my place on the page. Where was I . . .

With lips against her soft cheek, I whispered "Vanessa" into her ear as I felt her firm touch against the small of my back and her free-floating fingers found their way along my jeans. I mirrored her actions, reciprocating the sexual delight she was giving me. She moaned into my shoulder an affirmation of my handiwork and whispered, Please, Cally, please. I knew what she wanted . . .

My legs begin to slowly buckle so I lean against the bookshelf. My eyes discreetly glance at the brunette babe and she, too, is leaning against the shelves in my direction. We are human bookends in aisle four. But my eyes this time are frozen in their gaze. She is lovely to look at. The curves of her hips, her long silky hair: she's a sight for lonely eyes. And they take all of her in. My body is at rest letting my eyes have their fill, and I am lost in thought, creating my own fantasy. The cry of the store clerk, "You'll find the book in the New Age section," jolts me back to reality. I return to my book but not before I notice her smile still implanted upon her full rosy lips.

With the moon casting beams of light upon her golden hair, I kneel before the altar of My Desire, My Goddess, and My Love. She is all that I wanted. I taste the sweet nectar pouring from her sacred chalice. I pay homage to her inner sanctum. Our spirits are one in ecstasy . . .

I stand in the aisle staring at the last page, locked into that word—*ecstasy.* Does anyone really get to experience ecstasy? It is only a word, an ideal, a concept that never comes to fruition but is dreamed and desired by so many. I toss the book on the shelf. *It's just a fantasy, it's not the real thing,* I tell myself.

I throw a timid glance down the aisle, but my brunette buddy is gone. "Yeah, bet she's heading home for some ecstasy," I murmur.

The crowd in the bookstore is starting to thin. It's Friday night, and it seems like everyone has someplace to be, right? Well, not me, no ma'am. I am little Miss Independent working woman, no attachments, no obligations. Yeah, and no woman, too! I head toward the exit, feeling the tinge of dejection wrestle within me as well as the uncomfortable moisture from my reading session. The streets are abuzz, lights flashing, horns blowing in traffic, people scampering left and right. I turn my back to the nightlife and begin my trek home, disconnected from the scene.

All is quiet in my little neighborhood. Everyone is nestling safely behind their doors. Only a lonely soul lingers under the elm tree in front of Mrs. McKinley's house. I get a gut feeling and I go on alert. I put my head down and walk with a purpose. No eye contact, no strolling past, I just mind my business and get home. I pass the person without even giving a glance or a "good evening" to them.

"Nice story, wasn't it?" The voice comes from the shadows of the tree.

I stand motionless for a few seconds and then turn to find my brunette buddy leaning against the tree. I'm speechless with thoughts and questions whirling around in my head. *Who is she? How did she find me? What is she doing here?*

"Yeah, it was pretty good," I stammer, still shocked by her presence.

My fellow bookend comes out from the shadows, heading in my direction.

"But you know, for me, there is nothing like the real thing." She takes my hand in hers and pulls me slowly back under the tree. All my will, my resistance, the questions in my head vanish with the touch of her hand and her lips kissing mine. Time stands still, but my world is rocked by the scent of her perfume and her fingers running along my spine. I am lost in her mouth, lost in the darkness that surrounds us.

She pulls me closer, leaning her body against the mighty tree. I lean mine against her tight form, leaning my thigh between her legs. She moans with pleasure from my doing so.

She is a mystery to me. In my mind she is a stranger, no name, no address, no occupation. Yet, in my heart she kisses me like an old lover, her sweet fingers gently moving along my breast as if they had been there before, as if we had made love a hundred times before. It is safe, and sexy, and genuine. Who is she? I don't care. I will follow my heart and leave the analysis in the darkness of the tree.

She pushes me slightly away. I stand amazed by my actions and feeling the results between my legs. I stare into her emerald pools.

Is that all? Is she leaving?

She smiles again, that impish smirk.

"Now, that really gets the juices flowing," she murmurs. I return the smile and begin my own play as I take her by the hand and lead her up the stairs to my door. I kiss her again in the light to be sure nothing has changed. It hasn't. And I smile my own satisfaction of our play.

Maybe ecstasy isn't just a dream.

Chapter Thirty-three
The Bad Girl Bathroom

The mean girls met there between classes to smoke and apply eyeliner. It was strictly off-limits to studious types like Amy and me. We knew we'd be teased, harassed, hassled, spit on, sneered at, because everyone knew we were straight-A students—and queer. No one had found a way to kick us out of Eastern since we broke no rules. Occasionally we dared to hold hands in the hall, but by the time anyone complained we'd be in opposite wings of the high school. We had absolutely no classes together, just lunch—and bathroom breaks. But even that was risky. Have you ever had a cafeteria tray loaded with green Jell-O, Salisbury steak, Tater Tots and slaw dumped over your head by a bad girl? So why would we even go into a bad girl bathroom?

We went because Amy had heard from her big sister, who was one year ahead and sometimes sympathetic to us, that there was something we needed to see in the last stall on the left. OK, then. We flipped a coin and I went in first—after math. Stoners usually didn't go into that bathroom until after third period.

I tiptoed in, trembling in my blue and yellow Stockholm Adidas. You could smell the cigarettes and hair spray and the sweat of the seventh-graders who'd been beaten up by bad girls. No one was in front of the mirror, but I heard someone taking a pee in the first stall. I moved into the last stall really fast. When I closed the door, I saw it: a double women's symbol written in what looked like blood.

It was probably just red nail polish, I told myself, trembling, pants down, scared.

Two more minutes passed before Amy came in, tapping on the stall door with her short-bitten nails.

"Ellen? What—"

She never finished, because the bathroom door slammed open, and Cherry Harlan waltzed in, her breasts flopping in her gauze Levi's shirt with the strawberry-shaped roach clip that everyone could see in the front pocket. I knew it was her because of her perfume, Love's Baby Soft.

"Well, well," she hissed, and Amy's high-top sneakers shifted away from the stall. "If it isn't the queerling! Why don't you use the bathroom in the nurse's office so normal people don't get your lezzo cooties?"

"If you're normal, I'm glad I found the alternative," Amy was bold enough to say, but then I heard her squeal in pain as Cherry yanked out a piece of her hair. I came flying out of that bathroom with my trigonometry book up over my head like an anvil and whacked Cherry on the back of her neck with all my strength. She whirled around and slammed me across the face with her fake tortoiseshell hairbrush. By gym I'd have a black eye.

"Come on, Ellen, let's GO," Amy panted, grabbing my hand, and we split. But as you can imagine we had our trouble with the mean girls all spring, and even though we avoided that bathroom, they laid in wait for us around corners and at the bus stops, stealing our lunches or writing graffiti about us on our lockers or just shoving us into the ground. We didn't dare complain about being bullied. Did any queers complain in 1976?

But who had drawn the lesbian symbol in that last stall on the left?

It was twenty years later and Amy and I had long since broken up when I read in the paper that they were tearing down our old high school to build a newer, better one. Something made me drive by and look at the wrecking ball and strike up a casual conversation with a construction worker on site.

"You're one of the old students," he suggested, and I nodded. It was almost five on a Friday night, and the teamster gave me an even look. "Tell you what—this whole deal comes down on Monday. You want to walk around, take a look, pick up a souvenir brick? I'll give you five minutes. Here, take this hard hat." He waved me up the hill.

I had a fun moment when I realized I could park in the old space marked PRINCIPAL. Tense and curious as a lion cub, I prowled into the halls, dusty now with crumbled walls and open insulation, dangling wires, and rods.

In the third-floor hallway I hesitated, then went in. The bad girl bathroom. Would the double women's symbol still be there? No, certainly not after twenty years. Hell, it was probably wiped off with some industrial varnish that summer after we graduated— me, Amy, Cherry, and her posse of mean girls. I looked in the stall and saw the smooth, blank doorskin.

I pulled out my cell phone and made the call. Incredibly, Amy answered. Like me, she had stayed in the area, stayed gay, too, though we had different partners now, of course. I'd seen her last at Christmas in the mall, where she ran a sporting goods store.

"Amy? Guess where I'm calling from. Say, can you get away for an hour after dark?"

Good old Amy didn't ask any questions after all these years. After I had exited the school site, returned the hard hat, and made a pretense of driving away, I pulled into the nearby Roy Rogers and had a quick takeout supper. As soon as dusk fell, I heard Amy's SUV pull into the parking lot.

We hugged, as always. She still looked great: athletic but nerdy, same old elbows and knees. She was born to sell sports gear. I beckoned her into my car.

I knew what we were about to do was trespassing, but no one was around as I urged my car up the hill, lights off, into the school parking lot. The poised pile drivers and crew trucks clustered together in shadowy angles, spelling doom to our memories: half the school had already been crushed and exposed like broken dentures, the dingy halls an upper plate of teeth.

Amy had a screwdriver and a flashlight. "How much old asbestos are we willing to sift through or inhale?" she asked.

"That's the sort of thing only a grown-up would ask. If we were still sixteen we'd already be inside taking away treasure or looking in the guidance office for our permanent records."

Timidly, we crept into the building. Ballpoint pens, soda cans, and acrid cinderblocks littered the halls we'd once walked in as a couple. Amy, growing bolder, led the way with her penlight to the third floor. The screwdriver came out of her pocket and she nodded at me: "Will you do the honors?"

I leaned my weight into the flathead, turning, ridiculously aware of how short the bathroom door seemed. The sign chinked off unexpectedly in my hand. The screwdriver fell with an echoing scrape, and I caught in my hands the sign in hard brown plastic: a simple word, GIRLS.

"This is for you," I said.

We tiptoed into the bathroom and Amy headed straight for the last stall on the left. "The symbol's gone," I assured her.

"No, it's not," she told me, frowning now.

I stepped up and peered over her shoulder. There it was again, as fresh as it had looked in 1975—blood-red nail polish drawing an entwined double women's symbol. I touched the red lines: dry. *How was this possible? The door was blank and clean when I looked at it an hour ago!*

"Maybe you looked in the wrong stall," Amy whispered, the flashlight trembling in her hand.

"I swear to God, it was *not there* when I came in just now. This is *totally* spooky. It's like it came back because *we* came back."

Amy turned and looked at me. "Do you think there's something we're supposed to do? A magic thing, to put some closure on the era? After all, a lot of gay kids got beat up in this bathroom. Not just us. But some mean girl, or one who ran with that crowd, was obviously a dyke and made that mark. I wonder if she survived."

"You think it's the mark of a dead girl? A lesbian ghost? From our past?" Now I really needed one of these old bathroom toilets.

"We have unfinished business here," Amy reflected, and added, "I really think we're supposed to do some sort of ritual here to help that spirit rest. Otherwise the new high school will be just as harsh for gay kids."

I don't go in for all that moon-circle incense stuff myself. But suddenly we were holding hands, like old times. In the moonlight Amy looked sixteen again. When she said, "I won't tell Pam if you don't tell your girlfriend," I knew what she had in mind. It was the kiss I had missed all these years, the kiss and the touch and the sigh I remembered, the scent of her hair, her warm mouth, her coconut lip balm.

We made love on that cold bathroom floor and let our bodies make a pattern in the dust. We made our women's symbol on the tile. We went at it like we used to on her parents' rec room sofa when no one was at home, and we used words and suggestions we'd learned from other women since those days. At one point I bumped into the flashlight and screwdriver where she'd thrown them down.

"Ow," I said, and Amy chuckled

"Look," Amy said, "you're going to have the same black eye you got from Cherry Harlan that day."

"But it comes from love, not hate, this time," I pointed out. "We'd better get out of here. How will we explain how we look to our partners?"

139

"I don't know. I don't care." Amy brushed dirt from her breasts and looked around for her T-shirt. "Do you want to look at the bathroom door again and see if it's changed?"

I did not. Too spooky. Instead, I took my Sharpie from my jean jacket pocket and tenderly inscribed our initials on the bathroom mirror. "It's enough now," I told Amy. "You take the door sign that says GIRLS. I just want the one downstairs that says FACULTY LOUNGE."

We didn't get caught by the cops for trespassing, so we never made a dent in our "permanent records" as good girls, straight-A girls, queer or no. Our lovers never knew, and we never developed asbestos-related asthma, or met any lesbian ghosts in other bathrooms. I made up some excuse for the second black eye of my life, and Amy began driving around town with the plastic GIRLS sign in the license plate holder of her SUV. Me, I keep the FACULTY LOUNGE sign in my office—I'm a professor now, and no one has to know it's from my high school. The funny thing is, I always avoid the last stall on the left in any restroom. I wear a double women's symbol, though.

Chapter Thirty-four
She Rubbed Me the Wrong Way

I was heading for the coffee shop for my caffeine fix. It was my constitutional on Monday mornings. But today would be my last fix from this one.

"Hey, Harley, how's it going?" Barbara asked from behind the counter.

"It's going all right," I responded reluctantly.

"Yeah? Well, you look like you had a pretty busy weekend from where I'm standing."

"Yeah, it was a busy weekend—a lot of work to do."

"A lot of action, you mean. I saw you leave the lounge. Did you meet up with the real looker later on? She looked like she needed one of your own personal tune-ups."

"That's pretty funny, Barbara—you got me there." Barbara loved poking fun at me, mixing my love life with my trade. I'm a bike engineer, which translates to I fix bikes. Hogs, Hondas, you name it, I fix it. Man, I get one of those babies between my legs and I am gone. Yeah, and I love riding bikes, too.

Saturday night I was cruising along the boulevard just enjoying the sky and the ride. It was a cool fall night so I was styling with my leather jacket and jeans and a Hog underneath me, scoping the scene for some pretty babe to replace my bike later on. I met up with Barbara outside the Peppermint Lounge. She was hanging with her crew, Betty and Brenda, better known as the "Killer B's." It's somewhat of a throwback name from the sixties but they loved the identity and the reputation that came with it. They would brag about how any one of them could "sting" a woman and render her helpless with their sweet honey of love. Ooh, baby!

"Hey, Harley, what's shakin'?" Barbara shouted from the side-walk. Barbara loved calling me Harley on account of the bikes and all. But my real name is Thea, short for Theadora. I prefer Thea, and sometimes I even preferred Harley.

"Not much, Barbara. Catch anyone with your stinger tonight?"

"Not yet. But the night is young and the place is full of potential. C'mon, check it out for yourself."

I backed my bike into a spot on the corner and joined the "B's" in front of the bar. The place was hopping. Women standing in their little cliques—there were the factory girls in their plaid flannel and boots, and the college group trying to look like they are regulars, but the piercing is a dead giveaway.

"So it's worth paying the cover at the door?" I asked.

"Sure is, babe. There are some nice ripe tomatoes in there just waiting to be plucked by a butch like you," Barbara remarked.

"I'm not a butch!" I said defensively.

"Yeah, sure you're not. You just like fixing bikes, playing softball, drinking beer from a bottle, and women in tight miniskirts, though you wouldn't be caught dead in one yourself." The "B's" all laughed.

"OK, so I am a bit rough around the edges. That doesn't mean I'm not sensitive inside. I like to cook, and I like to shop, too."

"Honey, you cook hot dogs and you shop at Home Depot. That doesn't count." Barbara wasn't backing down and I was definitely losing this argument. But I still didn't see myself fitting the "butch" persona, whatever that is. I loved treating women with the utmost care and was truly sensitive to their needs. I never liked "rough play" or role play for that matter, and you wouldn't find me wearing a tie or having a buzz cut. I considered myself a balance of both worlds—a yin/yang of queer world.

"So who's inside?" I segued.

"Same girls you know, but there seem to be a lot of new faces in town. There is this one babe . . . man, is she spinning my wheels. But she is definitely out of my league. But you . . . now I can see you winning her over with your butch charm."

"*I'm not a* . . . forget it." I surrendered the argument and headed for the door, leaving the "B's" chuckling at my expense.

"Hey, Thea, what's up?" a chorus of my softball buddies cheered. They were just hanging at the bar doing shooters and knocking back beers. I took a quick look around the room as Janet handed me a longneck.

"So Barbara was right, the place is hopping," I mentioned.

"Yeah, and you gotta check out the cute babe by the pool table. She is custom-made for you, Thea." Janet gave a small punch into my arm.

I got curious. What's all this talk about this one babe? How hot could she be? What made her so special? I grabbed my beer and started to stroll back toward the pool table. I stood discreetly behind the jukebox. She was bent over taking aim at the eight ball in the corner pocket. Her legs were a perfect pair of hourglasses that traveled straight to an ass that was as tight and hard as the tires on my bike. But there was something familiar about that ass and those legs. She finished her shot, making the corner pocket, and straightened up to take her winnings off the table top.

"Thanks for a good game," she said to the factory plaid girl she just whipped.

I stood frozen in my place—frozen in time. I recognized that

143

voice, those legs, and that ass. *It can't be her,* I said to myself. But it was true. It was Nikki. She walked into my life three years ago and walked out after a year and a promise that we would live together and love each other forever. I left town and landed up in Lancaster, wanting to leave her and the memories behind. But she is just too hard to forget. She branded her love in my mind and etched her soul on my heart. We had passion. We'd make love with the intensity and drive of a V-8 engine. In my mind, I retained all of her pleasures. How she was aroused when I caressed her long legs, dragging my nails along her thigh, teasing her, stroking her slowly waiting for her to moan in affirmation. I would feel her body respond to my kisses, and my own desire would swell within me. She became my driving force, my reason to get up in the morning and to come home from work, knowing I would see her. I would smile with anticipation of our nights of undressing each other, feeling her body rise as I kissed her breast, tasting the salty beads of sweat upon my tongue. She would watch me shower and then join me when her own desire overwhelmed her.

We would picnic in secluded places. She would stretch out on the blanket, undo a few buttons and a zipper and in her sweet seductive voice say, "Come here." I would heed her call to make love like the call of the birds in the trees. She would guide my hand to her secret places, touching her tenderly as she buried her head into my shoulder, holding her close as she trembled in ecstasy.

And in a blink of an eye it was over.

"We must end this," she said. "We're not going to last. We have to move on," she declared.

"To whom? To where? To what?" I asked.

It was over and she was gone. I was gone, never to look back. Now, she was in my town, in my bar and back in my head. I should have known. In life, some things just don't come to an end or go away. They are only put on pause inside of us until a better time, a better place, different circumstances, or when you think your heart can handle it. With Nikki, back then was better. I turned and walked toward the door, stopping to deposit my empty on the bar.

144

"So, whaddaya think," Janet asked, anticipating an affirmative answer from me.

"Not my type," I said with a straight face and walked out of the bar and out of Lancaster. And in my mind I put Nikki on pause once again.

Chapter Thirty-five
Queens English

I was barefoot and topless in the kitchen in Queens when I realized I'd left an earring in the batting cage on 38th Street. I was an absent-minded femme, all right, and Jo knew it, but as she would say in her excellent Queens English, I was her Best Yet. I was her Top Tomato. I was King Penny. I always Traded Fair. These were discount stores, groceries and fruit stands on Ditmars where we went shopping for fresh pineapple, you understand—not that I was a particularly good chef. Jo always said I was mainly capable of serving "honeymoon salad"—Lettuce Alone. But looking over her shoulder toward the borough of Brooklyn, Jo would add she sure was glad I wasn't no Flatbush.

So now I'd have to go back to the batting cage and brave more hot stares from brawny young men who wanted to know why a femme dyke had to practice her swing, anyway, and I'd have to feel around on the floor full of spit gobs for my spouting whale earring. It seemed I'd left pieces of myself all over New York this week. A shirt I thought I'd wrapped securely around my waist rubbed off in the crowds at the Our Lady of Mt. Carmel festival in Green Point, and I'd left a pen in the New York Public Library and a really good mango lip balm in the ladies' room at Madison Square Garden during intermission of the WNBA game. But mainly, I'd left my heart in Queens, and Jo knew it. I would sit at the breakfast table while she ranted at the political news, and the rhythm of her voice was like surfing on syllables. I'd listen and dream and watch her soft lips forming tough talk and all I wanted was to slide the woman onto that kitchen floor and make honeymoon salad.

"Oh, yeah," she'd say. "You getting frisky with me?" My imagination would veer off to vaudeville: I was Frisky Witt, dance hall babe of the borough. I'd start to laugh to myself and she'd look at me, head to one side, and say "It ain't the chucklin' I'm worryin' about."

Our bodies were neighborhoods. Our language didn't matter. "I don't have an accent, everybody else does," she told me before our first date, and that settled my hash, but now she had me barefoot and aroused in that Queens kitchen.

I slipped behind her and whispered, "How ya doin'."

"My little zeppole," she purred, and we would have done it on the floor, except her car alarm went off. "*This* ain't happening any time soon," Jo sighed, and went to the window to see who had accidentally backed into her on the boulevard. A man was waving anxiously up at Jo's window: "No problem, no problem!"

"You do *not* wanna be messing with me tonight, you moron," Jo shouted down.

The most romantic of languages. Actually they knew each other by sight and would be on friendly terms again by morning. This was the gentleman who had cleared his front stoop of snow, that winter, by sweeping it onto Jo's car hood.

My modus operandi during these little mini-dramas on the block was to offer everyone cookies. That was the Southerner in me. I was an alien with my Carolina friendliness, startling Jo from the day we met by introducing myself so chirpily: "*Hi*! I'm *Pam!*" Now she teased me for saying "y'all" just as I teased her for saying "I already axed you." I'd sing, "Nothing could be finer than to be in your vagina in the morning," and we'd crack up together. But I knew my place in Queens. My place was on her face.

Mmm, that sounds frisky, indeed. But now there was the troubling question of my earring at the cage.

"Fuggetabout it," she exhorted. "I'll get you another pair." She touched my ears tenderly with her warm lips. My scalp tingled.

For spoken language in its many affectionate accents begins between mouth and ear. The sound of a voice speaking words of love, the familiar octave of a lover, that was part of Jo's kitchen. I rolled in her speech as a cat rolls on its back in pooled sunlight, exposed, grateful, desiring only that moment. She came up behind me and slid the chill wet belly of her soda can along my forearm and I drooped like a coconut palm. Man, I wanted her to hold me and turn my bones to jelly. To jam. Grab any metaphor of damp, sweet, wiggling delicious.

"Put your full weight on my heart," I whispered, barefoot and missing one earring. "I can take it." Slowly we lowered ourselves onto that kitchen floor. I could smell the coffee brewing, the arousal steaming.

Desire's a trickster, riding unannounced up to the door in traveler's clothes. You never know when a first kiss will turn into a small emerging nation where you live. I trusted that wayward shiver that said, *you have been touched.*

Jo was touching me through my shirt now and warming me to jelly, October winds blasting through the streets of Queens below, and car alarms going off from lightning. It was just before winter and plenty of long and jubilant evenings to come. And come. And whatever plan I'd had to go out later, go back to the batting cage, was reduced to the bare inches between our eyes. Jo's voice: "Ah, babe." My queen and her Queens English. "What did you do to me?"

On the floor in Queens, a kitchen floor, a barefoot femme, feeling beneath my back the rumble of the TV program in the apartment downstairs coming up through my spine. I think it was "Law and Order." In that kitchen, lawlessness, disorder, obedience to a higher calling, her kisses speaking English on my tongue.

Chapter Thirty-six

Leave It to Cleavage

(A welcome home story)

Baby, where are you? I am here longing for a moment with you. But you are away fighting the cause, advocating for those who cannot speak for themselves. You are out walking the walk for justice and equality. You are my strong, radical superwoman for the underprivileged. But here I sit selfishly waiting to have you near me, waiting to lie beside your muscular frame and caress with my fingers the soft curves of your hips, the delicate flesh of your supple breast oozing in cleavage. I long to savor the sweetness of your kisses and drink the nectar of your sacred fruit. I am waiting, as never before, for your tender touch upon my body, your lips softly kissing my shoulder as you change my inner world with your love. My brave woman, taking on the plight of the oppressed with your strength and wisdom. Yet I know your sensitivity and softness when we lie in bed in the silence with only the streetlight penetrating our darkness as you penetrate me. I am a desert flower dried up from your absence waiting for your return so your love can rain down on me.

"Hey, I'm back!" That sweet familiar voice came from the front door. "Where are you?"

"I'm in the bedroom. I'm coming out." I ran to the door to find Dana standing with her suitcase by her side and a wide smile on her face.

"Welcome home, baby. I missed you," I declared, running into her arms.

"Did you, now. Well, I missed you too, sweetie," she replied while placing kisses up and down my neck.

"I left the conference a half day earlier and caught an afternoon flight home just so I could be with you."

"Oh, baby, you are the best! I was hoping to have a bit of a welcome celebration ready for you, but I'm glad you are here."

"Well, we can still have a 'celebration,' can't we," she asked with a raised eyebrow and a mischievous smile.

"Hmm . . . yes, I guess we can," I remarked. "This *is* America and we *can* do what we want." We both chuckled. "Well, at least behind closed doors," I added and landed a real wet one on her lips.

"Sweetie, let me get my bags inside, these grungy clothes off, and a hot shower; then I am all yours." Dana headed for the bedroom, and I began to scheme our celebration.

To be honest, I never minded when Dana went away on one of her causes. Her time away was sometimes difficult for me to bear. No conversation at the dinner table, shopping alone, but mostly sleeping and waking in an empty bed, that was the hard part. But the "welcome home" time is always so delicious. Better than "make up" time after an argument, one pays particular attention to the person. It is getting reacquainted with their partner. Details are important, starting with the surroundings and then moving to the details of the person. For me, I love a romantic setting, so I had to work fast.

I could hear the shower running as I popped open a nice bottle of Chablis and arranged strawberries, grapes, small wedges of cheese and chocolate on a serving platter. I carefully carried them into the bedroom. I put k.d. lang on the stereo and lit all the candles in the room.

Hmm . . . the mood is right. Now all I need is the woman.

I am a true romantic, enjoying my work and letting the atmosphere surround me. I felt my desire for Dana that had been dormant for the past five days rise within me, ignited by the soft candlelight and my anticipation.

I made my way to the bathroom. I did a quick check of myself in the mirror and spritzed a bit of her favorite perfume on my hair. I grabbed the towel as she shut off the water. She stood naked in front of me as I wrapped the towel around her warm, wet body and held her from behind, feeling the shower's heat permeate from her shoulders, inhaling her fresh scented hair. She was sumptuous, a ripened peach ready to be eaten.

"Your welcome home party awaits you, my dear," I whispered as I softly bit my sweet peach's neck. Her head fell back against my shoulder.

"Ooh . . . you are too good to me," she moaned.

"Never too good to you," I responded, as I moved my hands along the sides of her frame; feeling her hips and legs through the wet towel. I quickly removed my shirt and shorts.

"C'mon, baby," I said as I took her by the hands and led her to our little romantic sanctuary.

Our eyes never left each other. Her face beamed with love and excitement. She let out a short giggle like a little schoolgirl waiting for a surprise. I kissed her in the doorway; leaning her against the woodwork. She moaned in my mouth as I slowly removed her towel, letting it fall to the floor. I kissed her neck, giving her a view of my petite romantic picnic over my shoulder.

"Hmmm . . . sweetie, what have we here," she exclaimed.

I pulled her toward the bed, and we lay side by side with the platter between us. "Just a few things to titillate the palate," I stated.

"Titillate away!"

I picked up a small piece of cheese and slowly placed it on the tip of her tongue. She moaned with delight as she washed it down with the Chablis.

"Hmmm . . . that is *soooo* good," she exclaimed.

"This is one of my favorites," I said as I placed a strawberry in my mouth and kissed her, letting its juices drizzle along my lips, flavoring our lips together.

"Hmm . . . yummy," she commented. "But this is my favorite." She smiled as she placed a piece of chocolate between her teeth and leaned over. Our mouths filled with luscious dark chocolate, our lips clinging to each other, preventing it from escaping. I became lost in her chocolate-flavored tongue, wanting more nibbles of her. I was fighting the impulse to terminate the picnic. As we finished our third piece of chocolate, my eyes scanned this beautiful woman lying with me. She was a marvel at forty, always having an appetite for more than just chocolate in the bedroom. Her strong thighs, her beautiful supple breasts with exquisite cleavage that made my heart skip a beat. I loved her inside and out and wanted to express this love in so many different ways. My "welcome home" was just one of the ways.

I reached across and grazed my fingers along her lovely cleavage—a deep crevice of soft, sensuous flesh. Our eyes were fixed with a loving gaze as I moved our love platter to the floor, but not before removing one more strawberry.

"But this," I said, "this is my all-time favorite." I held up the strawberry for her view.

"Oh yeah? What is it?" she asked.

I moved closer as she lowered her head to the pillow, and placed the strawberry between her breasts. I gently pulled them together, creating my own voluptuous vise for my fruit.

"Ahh, yes, leave it to cleavage to do the job," she proclaimed.

"Welcome home, baby."

Chapter Thirty-seven
Microclimates

The central coast of California: Open any local newspaper, and you'll find humor in the repetitive forecast, "Morning fog giving way to some sun." It's like that daily, but you can drive through microclimates, be caught in a mile of fog coming out of San Francisco, be in sunlight for hours when surfers are shivering elsewhere, see owls in the dawn if you drive up Highway One. The ocean sprays over the road, the cliffs fall into the Pacific, the roadside fruit and vegetable stalls take a windy battering and end up advertising not artichokes but "TCHKES."

My parents had their courtship on this road, their early marriage, picnics at Bean Hollow and Pescadero and a starter apartment in Redwood City when my mom was still too young to drink. They had me, the mermaid daughter who haunts beaches for beach glass, who reads the shadows of foot-marked beach sand like a medium reading tea leaves. But I've had my courtships, too, on Highway One. Driven down to Carmel, that pretty village for pretty millionaires, stood there at the corner of Uptight & Pretentious and laughed into my lover's easy shoulder, driven the seventeen-mile loop through Pebble Beach and found a mood ring in the sand, driven up to San Francisco and negotiated hills and kisses and long soaks at Osento Bathhouse, driven with the sunroof open and Two Nice Girls tapes blasting.

But once, maneuvering down that coastline, I thought I saw a mermaid off the cliffs, down in one of the narrow coves near no particular pull-over, and I had to fight the urge to stop and park and plunge down in that inlet. Just a trick of fog and sun, just a play of light on the artichoke fields, and yet—why not? Why not, in that Bay Area so known for women's culture, a mermaid tribe below?

I'd be a mermaid's girlfriend then, and walk looking for beach glass, but find her. Every morning, after swimming, I'd plait my dreams into her lush tail. Each evening, after running on the beach, I'd count the crescents of the white moon bobbing between the shadows of her resting eyes.

Mermaid girl, sucking at the richness of the air through ribcage gills, her flesh gathered beckoning like anemone, floating toward me over murky slabs of cliffstone and driftwood, flickering past the buried husks of foundered ships, making herself treasure to my pirate's hands. I can swim like a fish—the legacy of my California childhood, each day riding waves with my father's tutelage, knowing just when to surface, when to roll, how to pace breathing, let fierce power curve overheard. I'd help my mermaid girl avoid deadly fishermen's nets tangling down to capture her. I'd sift the sands through my fingers and let the fool's gold twinkle on my palms to win her over. I'd learn to pet the starfish, her companions, little tidal pool warriors, to pluck them from her shoulder blades and replace them with my kisses, soft sucking sounds and undersea sensations.

I will secretly awaken her someday, I thought. But it would be dangerous. What romance isn't? There are furled undertows out beyond those breakers, even a starfish can be ripped from rest, cruel eddies, swiftly changing tides. I've seen the surf at Mavericks. I've felt the slap of jellyfish stinging at my legs, lain on a towel packed in meat tenderizer, the best sting remedy, feeling stupid, landlubber, human, stranger, intruder. Rocks bite at my feet, seaweed chokes around my neck, the great white sharks are out there, like drawn guns. Far beyond the dangers and the human stumbling blocks, my mermaid girlfriend glides. Why reel her in? As though I'm hooking prey? It's best to keep it fantasy. And yet. A mermaid would mean *really* going down. How long can I hold my breath? Should I reveal my secrets? Wouldn't it be—cold? I do love women's warmness. Inside and out.

And down the coast I go, amusing myself. These thoughts, my surfing heritage, passing pretty miles on Highway One.

Chapter Thirty-eight
Almost There Car Service

What does Murphy's Law say? If one thing goes wrong, then everything will? Or is it if it's not one thing, it's another? Something like that. All I know is that many things went wrong that night, but in the end it was all good.

It started when my girlfriend for the past six months gave me an ultimatum during a romantic candlelight dinner I planned for our anniversary. I should have known then that things weren't going to go the way I planned. I should have stayed home, crept into bed and hid under the covers for the next six months. Abbey was, how should I put it, "high maintenance" to the nth power. God help the waiter who put a lemon in her drink or forgot to put the salad dressing on the side. It could be the beginning of Armageddon. Yeah, meaning, "Amma getting none tonight!" Well, for this night, that was about right. She wanted me to move in with her, which meant relocating my job as a dental technician, selling my condo that I bought only six months ago when I met her, and the cherry on top of this whole scenario would be getting rid of my cat, since she is allergic to Sally. But I sat and listened attentively with my look of concern and understanding plastered on my face, nodding at appropriate moments while thinking to myself, *I gotta get outta here! Quick, walk calmly to the nearest emergency exit, don't panic, you'll get out safely. My God! Please make her stop!*

There was a break in the action. Abbey had finished her relationship speech, laying out her demands and conditions that were not open to negotiations or arbitration. I held my breath, reached across the table and gently placed my hand in hers. With a loving smile that took all of my willpower to muster, I said, "Sweetie . . ."

"Yes, baby," she said with great anticipation.

"I'm outta here!" I firmly stated. I threw a couple of bills on the table. "Have a nice life." And I began to make my exit.

I hit the street without looking back at the table. I exhaled and felt six months of aggravation leave my body instantly. *I am free! Free at last! Yippee!*

I headed toward my car. It began to rain, which I took as a sign of my world being cleansed of Abbey. I started my ride home heading onto the expressway.

Bam!

"Oh, what now," I clamored. I had a flat. I pulled over to the shoulder and sat contemplating my options as the rain cascaded down my windshield.

OK, I just broke up with my girlfriend, I got a flat tire, I'm more than ten miles from home, and it's raining cats and dogs outside. Great night, huh? What else can go wrong?

I dug through my knapsack for my cell phone. I'll give Shirley a call. She'll come to my rescue. I found her number in my address book and hit the call button.

What! No signal! Unbelievable! Can it get any worse? I put my seat back, closed my eyes and sat listening to the rain while replaying the night's events.

Why me? I'm a good person. I help my fellow human beings. I recycle.

Why are these things happening to me? Can't I get a break? Three girl-friends in a year and a half and all psychos. It just isn't fair!

A knock on the passenger window startled me out of my pathetic reverie. I sat staring at the hooded face staring back at me. *Who the hell is this?*

"You need some help?" the hooded stranger yelled through the window.

Either it was reflex or out of desperation, I lowered the window.

"Hey, you look like you can use a hand."

"Yeah, I guess I do," I said helplessly. My tough butch persona went right out that window. I would have dressed up in a ballroom gown, stilettos and all, just to get home.

"Can I give you a lift somewhere?" asked the stranger.

Decision time. *Is she my guardian angel or the latest serial killer in the area?*

"Sure, that would be great," I responded.

I exited the car, locked it up, and we both ran to her SUV parked a few yards behind me. I jumped in the passenger seat as my savior jumped behind the wheel.

"Phew! Thank you so much. I really appreciate this."

"No problem, my pleasure," she said.

She had these incredible blue eyes that were surrounded by the sunshine of her sandy blond hair. She was fresh and alive even in this dreary storm. With all that had happened to me tonight I still could smile—she made me smile. That was her power, her magnetism.

"I'm Ellen," she said.

"Scooter . . ." I stuttered. "It's a nickname . . . I fix bikes." I always felt I needed to explain my name.

"So, Scooter, where can I take you?"

To heaven and back, sunshine! "Uh, you can drop me at the nearest gas station, and I can get a tow truck to come back here."

"Babe, there ain't a gas station with a tow truck within ten miles of here."

She called me babe!

"Yeah, you're right." I got disgruntled again.

"You live nearby?" she asked.

"Yeah, I'm just the next exit off the expressway, if it isn't too much trouble."

"No problem. Just guide me along the way." And she smiled more sunshine my way.

I sat trying to catch glimpses of her profile, her soft white skin, her full rosy lips that kept a smile on her beautiful face. I stared at her full breast slightly exposed under her zippered sweatshirt, and her long thighs encased in her blue jeans. She was statuesque in build, an athlete perhaps, maybe volleyball, or a swimmer. My mind was filled with all sorts of speculations.

"A rough night?" she inquired.

"Yeah, car trouble is a bitch," I stated.

"Seems like more than car trouble," she said with a know-it-all look.

"Does it show?" I said.

"I know that look. I had it a month ago."

I raised my eyes in disbelief as she kept glancing between me and the road.

"You meet the woman of your dreams, so you think. Only to find out she's a kleptomaniac or something. It's not pretty."

Her hand started to pat my thigh. "Don't worry, it'll get better," she reassured me. Her hand sent waves of unexpected excitement that I haven't felt in months. I reached out and prevented her from removing it. She turned quickly and just gave me that sunshine smile. She relaxed her fingers on my leg and began a slow massage. No words were spoken, but there was a mutual understanding. I leaned my head against the headrest, keeping my eyes on her, wanting her fingers to spread her sunshine all over me.

"Where do I go from here?" she asked.

"Turn right at the light," I instructed, "and move this a little bit to the center." And I moved her hand between my legs without any resistance. She began stroking me like fine fingers on a feline. I could feel the warmth emanating from her hand penetrate my jeans, seeping into me, relaxing me, my body aching for more of her touch. She was excited by our play yet showing restraint, darting her eyes from the road to me and back to the road.

"What now," she asked, keeping one hand on the wheel and the other on me.

"Turn left and head up the hill," I barely answered.

"Just like this hill?" And she moved her hand inside my shirt, squeezing me, fondling my breast with her toasty fingers. We reached the top of the hill and began to descend. So did her hand.

"We almost there?" she asked in this low sensuous voice, knowing she was not only driving the car but creating a turbocharged sensation within me.

"Oh, yeah, we are very close," I responded, as her fingers maneuvered like a well-oiled diesel engine, driving me to pleasureland and back.

"Yeah, right there on the left side," I uttered to the van's ceiling. The car veered to the left curb as her middle finger moved slightly to the left, causing me to let out a small cry. My body jerked under her driving fingers, forward, reverse, forward . . . *Don't stop now, keep driving me, sunshine. Shift, baby, into high gear, and steer into my core. Inject me with your high octane. Spin my wheels with the flicker of your fingers. Yeah, right there . . . left, now right . . . keep it steady . . . oh yes . . . bring me home, baby, to your finish line . . . I am there . . .*

Ellen leaned over me. Her eyes sparkled with contentment. I sat staring into those eyes, not wanting to break away. The rain pelted the van as the windows fogged from our body heat.

"Thank you for the lift," trickled off my lips.

She was beaming with delight from her doing. "Well, I think you owe me 'a lift,' hmm?" she said with a raised eyebrow. She proceeded to move the both of us to the back of her van.

Drivers, start your engines!

Murphy was wrong. Things do get better.

Chapter Thirty-nine
A Power Trip

It's a freezing winter night and all I can see from the icicled windowsill is the radio tower silhouetted against the low mountains, blinking, blinking. Calling me to you. All the other lights are out across the valley. I could get in my car and drive up over the mountain to your tumbled yard and press into your waiting hand this piece of writing: here, I want you. But I can't go to you. The car won't start, the roads are out, the phone line's down, the power's out. And the pilot light's blown out in my apartment stove—not even cocoa is a possibility for me, this night. I can't walk across town and up into the hills in my worn snow boots to find you on foot. It's 1987, no one has e-mail yet. With the electricity out, I can't play back your voice on my answering machine, the message saying firmly, "I just want to be *friends*."

Loving you has become a political act, an act of will, a stance of prayer. After all this waiting I still want you as much as before. And

I want to start at the top of your head and work my way down to the arch of your feet. I want to place one hand on the back of your neck, the peach fuzz there, and one hand between your breasts, and slowly feel the pulses between our skins. I want to lower you very gently onto some soft/firm surface, bed, beach, field, rug, futon, and look at you for three hours long. I want your fingers on my arm. I want you absolutely. I want you to tell me that you want me, too. I want to run my index finger over the wondrous bridge of your nose. I want to eat out of the light in your eyes and drink out of the white in your teeth. I want to feel you kissing me deeply all around me, the crown of my head, the palms of my hands, the insides of my knees. Tell me you want me. Tell me you love me. Brush your fingers through my hair. I want to kiss you from your throat to your forehead and listen in the still room for the sounds of these good kisses. I want to feel you break into a hot sweat. I want your hard bicep under my hand. I will lean over and kiss you and you will blush with arousal and pull me down alongside you. Then we will entwine our limbs, soft parts, hands, and exchange our tongues for twenty-seven minutes. I will part your lips and hear you sigh. Slide down me like an arrow, feel the ocean burn between our legs. Outside are many backdrops: dark sky, city park, backyard, desert, bare beach, small town, winter. Press your mouth against my neck. Kiss me so the flesh of our mouths meets and our noses touch. Pull back and look at me. Trace your nails across my wrists. Give me chills. Make me shudder. Sing to me. Pull my hair very very gently and let it slide through your ten fingers. Brush yourself against me like a cat. Wrap me in your robe. And now, I say, now curl into my beating heart.

I'm writing this by candlelight. The power's out. My typewriter won't go. The phone, the stove, the fridge, the light, the stereo, buried in quilts, in woolen socks, long underwear, a stocking cap, and gloves with fingers cut so I can write. Late-night battery-powered radio my only comfort, though I suspect the late-night battery-powered vibrator will be a comfort, too. The radio says, be patient, the power crews are working overtime. My vibrator says, be patient, reminding me that in due time you may want to be more than friends.

What a power trip, itself, to think that I could bring you just by wanting you, through an act of will. I'm settled in the bed with starlight streaming in, the windows iced and gorgeous, my own breath puffing ghostgirls in the air. After all this wanting I'm as hungry as a bear, though hibernating still. When the power comes back on, then I'll dash forth from this bearcave and re-animate. I'll call you, I'll drive over to you, I'll make cocoa on the stove, fill the apartment with the heat of my desire, cook sweet bread I'll present to you, to win your heart. I will. But now, too shivering. Angry. *No TV!*

Falling into dreamless sleep, wanting, wanting, tired from replaying that one fantasy image over and over like a worn record album until it skips, scratches, catches, is no good. I'm two hours into slumber when the power grid blares on. The lights pop on, the stove cooks up, the heater blares, the TV blabs to life. The whole town flicks awake with winter energy. I roll off the bed and stumble to make cocoa, and that's when my answering machine goes off, almost in midsentence, and it's your voice obviously recorded earlier last evening just before the power died: "I'm thinking about you." Pause. "I'm on my way over."

On your way over! When did you call? Where are you now? What happened? Are you crazy, in that snow? I couldn't get to *you*. My mind now has you crashed into some ditch and the cocoa's boiling over when your fists knock at my door.

I let you in, a bundle of chilled wool. "It took me *two fucking hours* to get over the hill into town," you gasp, breathing on your frozen mitten-covered fingers. I force cocoa on you, turn on my extra space heater, massage your hands and feet.

"I had to see you," you say. And I am speechless. Somehow, I willed you over, to my bed. To my kitchen chair, at least. Your eyes take in the bed, the disarray, the pages I'd been writing you, the pushed-aside vibrator. "What were you working on?" you ask, and I say, "Only this."

Chapter Forty
You Wanna Pizza This?

Bridgeport was a quaint little seaside town in its unique way, with its small shops, colorful fishing boats in the harbor and townsfolk that have been here for generations.

"It ain't no trip to Paris," I heard one tourist declare about our town. Another exclaimed, "Not much to write home about." Well, it was home for me. I lived here most of my life except when I was away at college and when I studied abroad at Cambridge for my doctorate as well as studying the female anatomy. There is a long list of lovers from my "studying" period. Yeah, there was many a late night filled with long sessions of "intellectual intercourse."

There was Amelia, who could sit for hours with me drinking coffee, dissecting the problems of the world, spewing philosophical abstractions and arguments left and right. And when the conversation got really heated, she would just get up, rip off her shirt

165

and begin a lap dance on me. I loved getting her all hot and bothered with such "deep thoughts." I loved having her expose her defenses to me as my hand invaded her sovereignty while she whispered foreign policy strategies in my ear. Yeah, she had a great mind but a greater body that didn't know how to say no.

Patrice was quite the opposite. She was a tall, reserved blonde with a dignified walk and a stoic expression. But underneath that cool persona was a firecracker just waiting to ignite, and I held the match. We would sit in the library across the table from each other, and I would catch her gazing at me over our pile of books. I would smile with a knowing grin and she'd drop her glasses and head into the stacks with me right behind her. Somewhere between the Art History and Ancient Civilizations sections I would have my own sexual excavation of her glorious hidden treasures. She would toss out Sapphic verses into the air with the same fluidity and pace as my tongue's exploration of her beautiful site. Ah! Women, wisdom, and words—a wondrous way to win at the game of love!

But this recipe wouldn't take when it came to Toni. She wasn't the type that could be swooned by intellectual foreplay. She was a realist, a blue-collar babe with matching blue eyes. She came to Bridgeport one day, and I have never been the same. I was heading home from teaching at the local college in early September when I first noticed a new addition to our small town. There was a banner hanging from the old Miller's Tavern, "Grand Opening of Toni's Restaurant."

It was late, I was hungry so I thought I would check it out. The owner hadn't renovated much of the tavern, keeping the dark wood paneling on the walls and some of the red leather booths in the back. I slid into one of them as she showed up to greet me.

"Hi, how are you doing tonight?"

I looked up and met those blue eyes surrounded by a mountain of silky black hair pulled back into a French braid. Our eyes locked, and there was just a nanosecond of silence, a silence that seemed like the world had ceased spinning. It was that moment when you feel you'd known this person your whole life, but you never laid eyes on them before, when your heart is shouting in your ear, *This is the one. This is the piece you've been looking for. It fits, you'll see.*

"I'm fine," I said hesitantly.

"That don't sound too convincin'. Maybe a glass of wine will help ya feel better," she declared.

"Sure, that will be fine," I stuttered.

"You like that word *fine*, dontcha," she remarked. She left me, and just like that, my whole world was changed in that moment. No warning was given, no signpost along the way, just Wham! Tag! You're it! Now run and get her.

My newfound goddess returned with the wine. I needed to know more. Who was she? Where did she come from? Was she available tomorrow night?

"This is really a nice restaurant the owners opened up," I said.

"Yeah, the workers did a pretty good job with the place. I like it," she said with a chuckle.

"I'm Emma," I said, extending my hand politely.

"I'm Toni, nice to meet you." And she took my hand with a firm handshake from which I was not willing to let go.

"You're Toni," I exclaimed. "I'm sorry, I didn't know."

"How could you. First time here, right? Don't worry about it." We had a second moment smiling smiles of embarrassment and understanding and holding on to each other with a simple clasp of ten fingers. She didn't let go but gently squeezed my hand and grazed her thumb against my wrist, sending a tingle through my arm.

"You know, you're the first person to introduce herself to me. That was pretty nice of you People aren't too cool around here with a woman of my background openin' up a place of her own. If you know what I mean."

"What do you mean, 'a woman of your background'?" I inquired.

"You know . . ." and she pointed to the little rainbow flag hanging in the corner by the kitchen door. "But I ain't takin' it down. It took me too long to get to where I am with myself, you know what I mean?"

"I know exactly what you mean." And I squeezed her hand in acknowledgment of our sisterhood, and she felt the connection.

"Yeah, all right! Pleased to meet you, Emma," she exclaimed with a grin from ear to ear. "How 'bout I make you a Toni personal pan pizza, special just for you."

"That would be great," I answered with a wink and a grin of my own.

"OK, I'll be right back with it." And she slowly released her hand, letting her middle finger press slightly against my palm as she and her fingers slipped from me.

I pulled out some papers to grade, trying to look busy, keeping myself distracted, forcing my eyes to focus on the papers and not on Toni behind the counter flipping and spinning the dough into the air. She was marvelous to watch in her tight white undershirt and her white chef's apron hiding a pair of extraordinary breasts underneath. My eyes moved from paper to person like a muscle reflex—spontaneous, impulsive. She caught my eye at one point and smiled.

A few minutes later she arrived with a steamy pizza in hand.

"Now, I think you'll like this," she declared.

I picked up my fork and knife and was ready to dig in.

"No, you mustn't use them. You gotta eat it with your fingers! You gotta feel it with your hands and bring it to your mouth. You gotta experience it," she instructed adamantly.

Ooh baby, did I want that experience with her.

I gingerly pulled a slice from the pie and cradled it in my hands. I felt the warmth of the crust like the warmth of a lover's breast cupped in a familiar hand. I took a bite, igniting an explosion of taste sensations in my mouth. The sweetness of the red peppers infused with the spiciness of oregano and basil, the soft melted cheese dripping over my lips. They were all lapping over my tongue, wreaking havoc on my taste buds.

"Mmmm . . ." I moaned, experiencing culinary ecstasy.

"Now that's a moan worth workin' for," she announced.

I met her eyes again as I swallowed my mouthful. "Yes, it is," I responded, feeling my own heat rise from under the table.

"You let me know if there is anything else I can do for you, OK . . . Miss Emma?" she added with a small smile that had "interested" written all over it.

She left me to enjoy my orgasmic pizza after educating me that food is her turn-on, her foreplay, not the intellectual banter I had experienced with others. I ate slowly, deliberately, savoring every last bite, letting it play in my mouth, tantalizing my tongue with its oral stimulation until I was full. I gathered my possessions and headed toward the counter.

"That was wonderful, Toni, what do I owe you?" I inquired, pulling out my wallet.

"This one is on me," she stated. "I'm sure you'll be back for more." And she winked discreetly.

"Thank you. It was an experience," I said with emphasis.

I headed to my car with my head still reeling. I drove along the coast, past the shops, and parked near the harbor. I sat staring out at the calm sea with its twinkling lights in the distance. I needed to think this out. Or did I? *Babe, you think too much. Just let it be—go for it, girlfriend! Remember the lap dances? Remember the book stacks? It's been a while, hasn't it?*

I started my engine, threw into drive and started back toward town. I sat idling for a while, staring at the stars and listening to the sounds of the night. Finally I saw the last light go off and heard the turn of the lock. I stood leaning against my car as Toni approached.

"How's about a second helping," I seductively suggested.

Toni stood in front of me; her fingers gently touched my cheek. The fingers that kneaded my dinner I wanted now to knead me. I closed my eyes, feeling a sweet sensation rise by her simple touch.

"Babe," she said, "I definitely want a pizza this."

Chapter Forty-one
Crack of Dawn

She got up early every morning. She made one sarcastic joke after another at my expense. Her ass was just incredible. That's why I guffawed with secret laughter every time someone used the term "the crack of dawn." I was Dawn's girlfriend.

When you date someone you pick up on their name every time it's used in a sentence. Some trucker might say, "It never dawned on me," and I'd think, that's right, big boy, and she never will. Or radio songs. There seemed to be dozens with her name in the title or the first lyric: *Dawn, go away, I'm no good for you . . . Delta Dawn, what's that flower you got on?*

And worst, best, or funniest of all was my course in Greek mythology at the community college. We were reading *The Odyssey*. I don't know if you've ever gotten into it but practically every chapter begins with "When Dawn stretched out her finger-

170

tips of rose," or my personal favorite, "Rosy-fingered Dawn." Sometimes, bored in class and thinking about my girl, I'd get the highbrow culture and pop culture confused and start singing to myself. "Rosy-fingered Dawn, what's that perfume you got on?" At basketball games—I was a big WNBA fan—I'd hear hundreds of dykes all around me joining in the National Anthem: " . . . can you see by Dawn's early light . . ." No, I sure couldn't. Like I said, I was always asleep when she got up. At the crack of dawn.

All she wanted was a lover, and she got a comedian as well. But let me tell you about the time we went to a sex toy party together. I don't know what I was expecting but it wasn't Tupperware, no ma'am. Dawn and I sat as comfortably as we could pretend to be in vintage beanbag chairs, sipping cabernet and munching puff pastry while our hostess modeled fur cuffs, dramatic vibrators and edible body powder in twenty fruit flavors. Suddenly Dawn was selected to try out a hot product and report on its effects—some sort of sensational stimulant our hostess handed to her on a clean Q-tip with the instruction, "Go into the bathroom and apply it to your little man in the boat." Nothing about Dawn was a *little man*, but with women buzzing each other teasingly all over the room and a general atmosphere of drunken seduction, it wasn't the time to get politically correct.

Dawn disappeared into the penthouse bathroom and I got busy reading the order sheet, wondering if I really needed spray-on vag tightener. After a few minutes Dawn emerged with a wild expression on her face, as though she'd sat on an anthill at a Hebrew School picnic and was trying not to scream "*Jesus!*"

"Good stuff?" I remarked casually. And she moved her neck in my direction, opened her mouth, and said so low only I could hear, "I'm having a crack attack."

That got my attention. I was a slave to the crack of Dawn. Where could we go? There weren't enough women present that our discreet exit into a bedroom wouldn't be noticed. We'd have to answer to delighted gossip later. But had that ever stopped Dawn? No. It never dawned on Dawn to care what people thought. So I

171

allowed myself to be pulled up from the beanbag and into our hostess's bedroom.

Lee Biden was a woman of taste and her elegant bedroom showed it. Lace curtains rippled in the spring breeze and rare artwork graced the seafoam pastel walls. Above the large bed was an original Maxfield Parrish of two women in languid flirtation, and a Daphne Scholinski sketch gazed at us from a redwood dresser top. All of the party guests' coats were stacked neatly on the bed, mostly leather jackets, since it was warmer than winter now and the occasion demanded sex-fashion. Dawn vaulted backward like an Olympic gymnast and spread out on top of our two leathers. "God, I'm heating up!" she gasped. "It's like a mentholated tongue, it's like a Peppermint Patty lube, it's like the hot sauce of the Goddess!" She laughed maniacally. "I actually feel almost stoned— it's that strong. Come on, baby. *Do me now!*"

"In Lee's bed?" But she who hesitates is lost. I knew better than to resist the crack of Dawn. In seconds I was on my knees, tasting her. The hot/cool stimulant Dawn had applied met my tongue and shot its pheromones into my palate. Now I was drooling, Dawn was moaning, and out of nowhere Lee's pesky little lap dog shot from under the bed and began licking our legs.

"What in hell? How many tongues do you *have*," shrieked Dawn, hips pumping.

"Ignore it or enjoy it," I advised. Now I was panting, Dawn was panting, and the little black dog was panting, too. Knuckles rapped on the bedroom door.

"Oh, shit," sobbed Dawn.

"Uh . . . I'm really sorry, but my purse is in there," a meek voice called in to us. "I have to go pick up my daughter in twenty minutes."

"*One second!*" I bawled, sounding like Elmer Fudd with my tongue wet and curling from the fiesta combo of party product and Dawn effluvia. "Dawn," I whispered. "Get going."

"I've got somebody's handbag strap up my crack!" Dawn wailed.

"It's, um, a red alligator purse with a long strap?" called the anxious voice from the other side of the door. I looked down and saw the red strap emerging out of the Dawn I loved.

"*We're coming!*" I yelled, and no lie, then I took one swift yank and pulled the handbag strap out of Dawn, tumbled on my knees toward Lee's private bath and scoured the strap quickly in soap and hot water. Dawn rose to a sitting position and pulled up her jeans, wadded our leather jackets together so that the wet places weren't visible, and tidied up the other coats, sweaters, and backpacks on Lee's bed. Then we each took a deep breath and opened the bedroom door.

"Is this one yours?" Dawn asked sweetly, handing the red purse to Jackie, a friend from our poetry group. "We were just looking for our checkbooks. I think I might buy me some sex toys."

Jackie gestured carefully to my face, trying—and failing—to quench a smile. "You have a pubic hair dangling from the tip of your nose."

"She's always nosy," cracked Dawn, patting down my face with a Kleenex and not seeming the least embarrassed. I, of course, wanted to die. But that was life with Dawn. I wouldn't change a thing about her—about us. So we took out our checkbooks, and we took some of that special lotion home.

Chapter Forty-two
To Eire Is Human

It was early morn when I rose from my slumber. The dew lay sweetly below the mist of the new day. I took a last look at the soft green hills that stood outside my bedroom window. A tear trickled down my cheek as I bade my world good-bye. I had to leave my small village of Traymore, a place that has been home to me and my kin for generations. I had to bid farewell to my friends and folk and begin my new life, a life without secrets or lies or the "talk" behind my back, a life where I could be me without the shame and the heavy silence that surrounded me and the judging eyes that followed me when I entered a room. I had experienced such things each day since winter's end when my mom came to the barn one late evening after hearing voices and saw a single light burning. She thought it was my father, lost after a night in the pub. But instead she found me and Molly Magee rolling in the hay in the loft with our hands enjoying each other's bare breasts as our lips fed on each other's wanting bodies. We had secret rendezvous for over six months, making love in the green fields, lying in the purple heather of the mountains, or when we were adventurous, we would sneak off to each other's bed when our parents were away on holiday. I loved Molly. I loved her vivacious spirit, her boisterous laughter, and her flaming red hair that fell softly to her breasts when she unfastened her hair clip while straddling my hips. She would smile with excitement of what pleasure was to follow. Her love for me made me come alive, wanting our kisses to go on endlessly and longing for her lips and her touch when we were apart.

Molly and I were childhood friends, but our innocent girl play had now become the play of two grown women who discovered the pleasure and ecstasy of making love together. Our discovery occurred after completing our university exams. We celebrated with our classmates at the town pub. After a few pints and the hour growing late, we walked along the road to home under the light of the stars. Molly held my hand more to steady her, so I believed, until she pulled me toward her at the cemetery gate and kissed me with a sweetness that I had never felt when kissing the likes of Seamus or Ian or Sean. I felt a fire in my belly that ignited an explosion of desire. I wanted to feel more of it. I wanted that feeling in my heart forever.

Molly smiled and giggled. "Did you like that?"

I was speechless, trying to understand what had just happened and how my whole world had changed with that one kiss. I leaned into her and kissed her mouth, gently pressing my tongue against her lips, hoping she would take my invitation. She filled my request with her tongue's greeting. I moaned softly as her hands held my waist and our breasts met in the darkness, sending shivers down my spine. Molly's mouth found my neck and began kissing it rapidly. I felt her breath as she whispered, "I have wanted to do this with you for some time now, Fiona. You are so beautiful, and I have desired you from afar not knowing if you felt the same way, yet hoping I could have you someday."

"Yes, Molly, yes, I understand," I whispered back. I did understand. For the first time I felt that which was missing within me. The void I experienced within my heart was no more. I had tried filling it with those boys, but they could not touch me, kiss me, or excite me as Molly was doing at this moment. Yes, this is it. This love that I now discovered within me and found with Molly was the missing piece of me.

Molly took my hand and led me across the road into the fields. I was ignorant as to how to make love to a woman, how to touch her, how to move the earth beneath her as Molly was doing to me. The moon cast its light upon us as Molly pulled my shirt out of my skirt and began to unbutton my blouse. I mirrored her actions, following her lead. She reached inside and held my breasts in her hands, lifting them as an offering to her mouth. My head fell back with the rush of sweet sensation pulsating through me. She moaned in delight as her tongue moved masterfully over my nipples. My knees began to weaken and I instinctively lowered myself to the grass below. Molly followed me down, instantly kissing my mouth as I felt her hand under my skirt dragging her fingers along my thigh. No words were necessary. All was spoken in our touch. It was natural and familiar as if we had made love a hundred times over. No one ever touched me in the places Molly found within me. I was thrilled by her exploration, wanting her to stay for a lifetime.

"Fiona, my fair lady," she whispered into my mouth, "join me in this pleasure." And she knelt beside me, inviting me to enter her secret place. Our fingers joined our two worlds and with all of the heavenly beings above as witnesses to our love we became one with each other.

I could smile now in front of the window knowing that my love for Molly was real. I began my descent to the kitchen where my mother stood fussing in front of the stove. My brothers and sisters gathered around the table in silence, knowing I was leaving but confused as to why. Perhaps one day they will learn the truth and welcome me back into their lives. I smiled at their lonely faces and softly blew a kiss their way.

"Good-bye, Mum," I said with a bit of a cheer in my voice.

"Be on your way." She spoke into the pot of porridge she stirred incessantly. "And mind you not to set foot on this land again." I smiled at her hurtful words, feeling only pity for her. Pity in knowing the deprivation she experienced in her own life in never having a love as beautiful as Molly and I.

My walk to the train station took me through town where I found a gauntlet of faces standing in front of the different establishments. Women huddled in cliques in front of Miller's dress shop while the men stood strong in numbers in the town square. They all turned to see me pass and then whispered their gossip to one another. I bade them all a "good morning" and smiled, quite pleased with myself. I knew at the end of this tunnel of judgment stood my emancipation and a new life founded on self-knowledge and love.

I climbed the stairs to the train's platform and walked through the pillows of steam escaping from the train. The smile on my face widened as I spotted my Molly halfway down the platform. I made my way to her side and, with our bags in hand, we ascended the steps to the train that would keep us on our journey that began that night under the stars, and now will continue in a new place where our love will prevail.

Chapter Forty-three
Box of Crayons

The pen hung limply from my calloused fingers, like a stalk of wilted celery. Never had I had so much trouble describing a woman I loved. I scowled, jiggled my feet, kicked off one shoe, cued up the Ferron CD in my boom box, ate a spoonful of peanut butter from the jar beside my desk. What had happened to me? I was never at a loss for words.

Once upon a time, I didn't just write. *I fucked writing.* When I didn't have a lover I'd write a book. I'd write all afternoon at work, come home and reread what I'd written and *get off*. And I'd write the real thing, about love and desire and ex-lovers, and wanting and having, and wanting and not having. I told the writing what to dress like, and had it on its back. I had ink spurt and drip and dry on my fingers, and I could smell that ink settling into my pores and leave it on all day. I had my journal in my lap rubbing my hand up and down. I jacked my DNA off that hand and into a couple of

ISBN numbers at the Library of Congress. Lean years, famous years, book years, girlfriend years, and suddenly I was forty and, like most gals, had to *shave*.

Every lover I ever had became a chapter or a verse, a thesis or an anti-thesis, and knit together it was the never-ending story; oh, man, it was the "Song of Songs." But then the ratio changed. I was in more books than I'd ever been in girls. The writing outpaced the partners in duration. The writing became sex, took up the slack. So I fucked writing. I had a date with queer theory. I went out to dinner with postmodernism. I had an affair with slam. Poetry and I made love for thirteen years.

It was fun. If you wrote about sex, you were cool. You *owned* the experience, on paper, which is timeless, far better than any instant replay, than any reality TV, than any fear factor; all scrawled out without makeup, just verbs and images. I had her. I took her. I bit her. I ate her. I lived on the page as comfortably as on the bed. Interchangeably, sometimes, sheets of paper, sheets of girl. It was all so easy, then.

But this one. This relationship. The big one. I could barely find a word. I was just as undecided as I used to be, at seven, opening a box of crayons to draw. Should I use magenta, that pretty color most second-grade girls chose? Even then I was different, drawn away from what would later be called "Barbie colors," magenta, turquoise, teal. I liked the earth tones for their earth words: sepia, burnt sienna. Crayola boxes offered not just colors but new words.

And that was what I needed, all new words, words that burned with feelings, color, mood. The woman I loved was pale, after all my years of olive-skinned partners, how to write of pale? What was a color for tall, or long, or safe, or strong, or tender? Things I felt, locked in her arms. Geez, I was corny. Pen still limp. Was I impotent? Not hardly.

Her eyes, though. Here the Crayola box could help me. Cornflower, midnight blue, aquamarine. Oh, yeah. Every stroke of blue scribbled together into a solid.

Funny the Crayola box didn't have *baby blue*, because that

described my girlfriend's eyes, and I had become a big baby, reduced to absolute babble in her presence. No wonder I couldn't write.

I slipped off my leather desk chair and knelt on the floor with a fresh piece of paper and my box of crayons. How familiar it felt—body contact with the floor, back to childhood when I'd lie on my belly and draw. I could remember the smell of the wooden table legs in my parents' first house and the knots in the shag rug under my skinned knees. The smell of crayons and pens, the thick pad of Academie writing paper, the Crosby, Stills and Nash album endlessly playing on my father's hand-built hi-fi, my mother practicing modern dance exercises in her black leotard as I scrawled. How far we've come, up at our desks with computer screens even in elementary schools, now. Do kids still lie on their bellies and draw? Now, a big long adult, I had to shift around a good deal to fit on the floor of my city apartment, and the hand holding the crayon had a grown-up's watch and ring. But something told me I would have to draw my lover's eyes if I ever wanted to move on to writing about her, about us, about this *thing* between us.

I opened the box of crayons. Here was the row of blue. This blue for her eyes when she looked at me and loved me. This blue for the sadness when we'd had a fight. This blue for the wet, slack drama in our heat of lovemaking. This blue for the day we swam in the ocean, and I had blue water, blue sky, blue eyes, and a blue hooded sweatshirt I wrapped her in afterward. This was what I wanted to remember, the light in her eyes, the space and color around her, the way I moved against her body, the way she looked at me.

I drew her with every blue crayon in the box. I drew her eyes from memory and her love for me was brick red, was magenta, and the coming days were gold, silver, and bronze. Finally I was done. The crayons rolled on the carpet, and I fell asleep with the drawing under my heart.

Her phone call came at seven: "Did you write today," she asked.

Chapter Forty-four
Lion in Wait

You call me at my office to tell me we are giving a dinner party for ten of our closest friends. I am seething with anger inside from this short notice. "Fine," I respond through my clenched teeth.

"So get home about six," you order in your nonchalant tone that compounds my frustrations because you can't hear my ire.

I hang up and try to resume reading my patients' files, but my mind is swirling with all sorts of homicidal thoughts. I decide to leave my office to clear my head so I don't put the lives of my patients in jeopardy. I take a seat on a bench in the park across the street. I close my eyes and take a few deep breaths, letting the cool, soft breeze roll over me. My thoughts, entwined in this anger and frustration, surge through my mind as they say to you things I could not say face to face.

You always pull stunts like this on me. For the past five years I had to be on call for one of your parties or dinners or cocktails with some group of your artsy friends who seem to just entertain their life day in and day out. But not me, I am precise, direct, a planner. I keep my work organized and my appointments exact. I have all my ducks in a row while yours just waddle randomly around in our life. Maybe it was the way you danced through life that made me attracted to you from the beginning. I spotted you in the shoe store, which wasn't difficult to do. You had three salesgirls doing your bidding while boxes upon boxes of shoes lay at your feet. You were flamboyant and alive and I craved that for myself. If I couldn't be that way then I wanted to be with someone who was. I wanted to be close enough so your energy would pass though me. I prayed for such moments when we made love. I prayed that our kisses would send me your spontaneity. I prayed your laughter and excitement would be branded into my heart when I touched your skin, kissed your sweet breast or moved my fingers in you. I cried for our physical connection to ignite a spiritual fusion. I resolved to accept only being close to you and letting myself experience your élan from the external. I would shake with desire during my doldrums days at work wanting you, fantasizing taking you right there on my office desk or in my examination room, but I would compose myself, regain my control, and continue my work. I would glance over at you while we took one of our long drives into the countryside and I would surge with impulses to pull to the roadside and go down on you like a voracious lover. Instead I would clench the steering wheel and stare at the road ahead. So many times, so many opportunities when I could have unlocked the passion lying within me like a caged animal. But I resisted its roar. Your understanding is admirable as well as your efforts to seduce me, to coax me into letting go and to step out from the sexual perimeters I created inside.

"Sometimes, Alex, you can paint outside the lines," you would say.

Why do I torture myself with such discipline while the roars grow louder in my head begging for emancipation? The continuous surge of heat rising in my chest, the moisture seeping between my legs beckons for satisfaction, yet I go through the procedure—sterile, precise, organized. How it must drive you crazy! Yet you never complain. You smile and giggle and tell me how good it was. But I can see it in your eyes. Your spirit is crying for more. It hungers for the same excitement you experience with your friends during your little soirees. I am envious.

I return to my office and clear off my desk. I leave at four and begin my commute home. I purposely left my briefcase at the office. There will be no work done tonight. I serpentine through the traffic on the expressway. The roars inside of me are louder than ever as I tighten my grip on the steering wheel.

Focus, concentrate, get yourself under control. No, not tonight. Unlock the cage and let no holds be barred . . .

I can feel the mighty waves of desire fill my chest. My heartbeat accelerates with the car, and I brush beads of sweat away from impeding my vision. I can see clearly now. I can unleash the hunger within and let it feed on the flesh of my lover. I can let it please her appetite and delight in its meal.

I pulled the car into the driveway, cut the engine and headed for the door. Judy must have heard the door close.

"Honey, you're home early," I heard my beloved say from the kitchen.

I walked with a mission to accomplish, dropping my bag and jacket on the hallway floor, indifferent to my negligence, fixated on my true goal.

"Hey, baby, how was your day?" She turned to greet me.

I met her with my own new salutation. I kissed her lips with a force that freed my lust for this woman, enslaved for years. I pressed my tongue deeper into her mouth, taking her breath away, hoping the breath of her passion would possess me. I felt my own spirit rising within me and I urged it on. I released her mouth as I kissed her neck in rapid fire.

"Oh, baby, don't stop," she gasped.

I pressed her against the counter with my body, feeling her breast against my own. I ripped through her blouse, sending buttons through the air. I devoured her breasts, pushing them together and slipping my tongue into her beautiful cleavage. My hands clung to her magnificent orbs, squeezing her nipples between my fingers.

"Yes, keep going . . . don't stop." She cheered me on.

She began to join in, pulling my blouse out of my pants, and I quickly grabbed her hands and held them against the counter top as my tongue had its way with her chest, sucking her nipples, letting my enslaved covetousness spring free and take possession of me. She acquiesced to my newfound power that howled with joy in its first victory. It wanted more, and it urged me on as I pushed her skirt up and placed my hands fully on her buttocks, pressing my thigh between her legs. I felt the juices of her passion seep through her panties, wanting it to seep into my pores and merge with the spirit now soaring through my body.

"Take me now," she gasped into the back of my neck.

How could I refuse her? In the past I would have pulled back. I would have stood at the edge of the cliff and at the last moment I would move back to my place of refuge, locking the cage and resuming my routine. There was no going back now. I could not deny my lover as I had done too many times before, nor could I ignore the fire burning through my whole being. I knelt in front of my queen and began to feast on her bounty, wanting to drink the juices of her life force. This time my fingers clenched her thighs instead of the steering wheel and I devoured my diva. Every past fantasy, my office, the examination room, the car on the roadside emerged in my mind, exploding in one sexual blast as my goddess encountered her own implosion, releasing a resounding "*Yes!*" I ascended to her embrace, letting my body fall limp in her arms while catching my breath as my beast within gave a champion roar.

"Alex," Judy whispered into my neck.

"Yes," I murmured.

"I'm canceling dinner."

Chapter Forty-five

If You Can't Swap Spit, Swap Chocolate

We wanted to be near each other that summer we fell in love. Being apart was agony. But with the salary cutbacks we'd both endured as teachers that year, we needed summer jobs to tide us over, and that meant trying to find nonhumiliating work where we'd be together every day. Maybe we wouldn't share an office or a work table, but at least we'd take our breaks and lunches together and steal a few kisses in the ladies' room, we hoped. The solution seemed to be taking jobs as temporary coders at the Science Foundation.

Ever done grunt work for a think tank? It's an amusing scene. The foundation had issued five-page survey forms to professors and scientists all over the nation. These mad scientists were supposed to describe the research they were doing, in short sentences.

Our job, as coders, was to "score" these survey forms onto answer sheets that were fed into a computer. We boiled down the respondents' scrawled remarks into A, B, and C categories on corresponding answer sheets. If you did well on the SATs, if you had a sick love for filling in little circles with a Number 2 pencil, this was the job for you—thousands of surveys had to be scored in a three-week period so the foundation could issue its annual report.

Jenny and I were just two of three hundred temps hired to do the grid sheets. All of us had to pass a practice test, an IQ test, and an eye-hand coordination test intended to weed out lesser mortals. On our first day all of us were separated into groups of ten and assigned to thirty long tables in an enormous, over-air-conditioned conference room. The goal was for each coder to score at least one hundred surveys a day, and the regimen was strict: at your table by eight in the morning, first break at ten, two half-hour lunch shifts between noon and one, second break at three, turn in final folders by five p.m. To keep us working rapidly with no cause to get up for coffee or a snack, the foundation did an interesting thing. They encouraged each "table leader" to bring in bags of candy and pour little mounds of chocolate where we could reach out and grab whatever kind we liked during the day.

"There goes my diet," Jenny complained, but I was more dismayed that we were assigned to different tables light-years away from one another in that room. Damn. Worst of all, her group took their lunch in the first shift and mine in the second. The only time we could see one another, except to wave across the room, was at our morning and afternoon break times. The challenge was whether we could manage to have sex on a ten-minute break, with every bathroom filled with other workers racing to pee and every lounge jammed with smokers.

During the first week, it just didn't happen. We wanted to make a good impression, to be good workers. And Jenny wasn't really out as a lesbian yet. Morning break sex seemed too risky. Instead Jenny would scoop up Hershey chocolates from her table—she knew I loved the Special Dark kind, and my own table leader only

186

provided Mr. Goodbars—and pass them from her hand to mine when I brushed against her in the hallway at break. The warmth from her palm melted the chocolate just slightly, and the scent of her perfume melted the rest of me.

"If you can't swap spit, swap chocolate," she'd murmur.

By the second week, though, we had cased the joint. I knew who took which lunches, and Jenny was sure a certain bathroom on the third floor was always empty at the afternoon break. We compared notes until we had a floor plan—how quickly could we get up to the third floor, do it, and get back to our tables on a ten-minute break? Especially if we took different stairwells to avoid rousing suspicion? We had the shortest possible routes planned. But we still would need more time.

Our prayers were answered when, midweek, the foundation announced it would extend our afternoon break to fifteen minutes. *Fifteen! Whee!* A gravel-voiced science babe informed us that we were being rewarded for good behavior—the coding was going very well, our efficiency pleasing the survey directors, plus several women had complained that after lunch everyone felt more tired and droopy and needed coffee by three p.m.

We made a date for three p.m. on Thursday of Week Two.

My heart was pounding when I got off the subway that day. Could we really pull this off? I was a nervous wreck—horny, anxious, amused, paranoid, a whole color wheel of drama. I caught up with Jenny at the water fountain and saw that she, too, was sweating. The perspiration of romantic scheming froze on our brows as we entered the air-cooled cavern of our workroom.

At the ten a.m. break, I attempted to pass a handful of butterscotch drops—Jenny's favorite—into her hand as I passed her table. I missed and they clattered all over the floor. We froze.

"That's all right," smiled Jenny's table leader, a wizened gay man in bow tie, suspenders, and hairy gold blazer. "I swapped candy myself, yesterday!" We searched his face for any indication of a deeper meaning to his words. If he did guess about us, he seemed a likely ally.

I could barely touch my lunch. My teeth were tender from days of munching chocolate, and my whole being was focused on the clock. As I exited the cafeteria with my group, I saw Jenny come in. She gave me a thumbs-up signal and a wink, then held up three fingers. We were still on for afternoon break.

How I coded surveys in those next two hours, I'll never know. The lines of information blurred before my eyes. My underwear was soaked. My thighs were trembling. Then the voice of our "room leader" cut through my haze: "It's time for afternoon break."

"*Yaaaaaayyyy!*" screamed everybody. This was our first fifteen-minute treat.

Feeling like one of the spies from "Mission Impossible," I rose from my seat, knocking over my chair. I quickly righted it, apologizing to everyone. Then for the first time I took the back exit and turned left into the rear stairwell that nobody used. I whisked up two flights as silently as possible—I'd worn old sneakers that day—and then poked my head around the corner. The third floor was a research think tank with silent glass cubicles behind which visiting scholars sat at computer terminals, their backs to me like so many white-coated human lab rats.

I tiptoed down the hall to a door marked "Station." It was the oldest bathroom in the building, Jenny had told me, and the original door sign once read "Comfort Station." All the temporary employees had assumed it was a lab. No one but Jenny ever went in to use the still-functional ladies' bathroom.

I pushed gently against the door. "Hello," I breathed. Jenny was sitting on the first sink—naked, her work clothes in a neat pile on the floor. I gaped, and she mouthed at me, "*Lock the door.*"

Three minutes down. We'd need at least two or three to return down the stairwell at the end of break. We had, at most, nine minutes. I locked the door.

And I loved that girl one minute at a time. I surveyed her body and coded her. I searched, with my tongue and hardy hands, for the right answers buried in her questionnaire. I noted her responses—with every fiber of my physical being. And Jenny. Jenny read me like a form. She left her marks all over me, filling in my circles. We made a proper scientific study of it, no aspect unexamined. I'd remember, later, the tiny dripping sound of the sink and the click of my summer sandals against that old tile floor and Jenny fogging up an unused mirror, finally giving the janitorial staff something to clean up in that space.

Racing with two minutes left, we fumbled our clothes back on, fit belts into loops and pulled slacks up over trembling thighs. A button flew off my shirt and went down the drain. Jenny's hair was in her eyes, a kiss mark on her jaw. Laughing hysterically, I dabbed makeup on her hickey and straightened my own collar. Then we poked our heads out the door, shook hands firmly and took separate paths back to work, arriving just as the table leaders bawled out, "Let's get started."

On the table in front of me, a little mound of chocolate. My favorite kind, today. But no thanks. I didn't need it. My mouth was full of sweetness from my midafternoon break.

Chapter Forty-six
Floor Model Only

Completing my course work at the School of Arts and Design was a piece of cake. People said I had a gift for this kind of thing. From the age of twelve I was helping my mother pick out wallpaper designs and drapes for the living room. I was told over and over again by my female relatives how I was the next Laura Ashley. Little did they know how I wanted to do her more than be her. My roommate and recent lover, Adrienne, celebrated our graduation with a bottle of champagne and a night of hot sex, releasing four years of pent-up sexual tension. But this was a temporary engagement. Adrienne was heading for Los Angeles to work in the film industry as a set designer, while I remained in New York pounding the pavement for employment.

"You were the best graduation present a woman could ask for," Adrienne said as she moved out of my bed to get dressed for graduation.

After the graduation ceremony, Adrienne packed her bags and headed for the airport. We promised to stay in touch, but we both knew that was just a formality. I bid her good luck and wished her well while contemplating my own fate.

The next day I decided to hit some of the big interior designers and see if I could get more than just my foot in the door. I even visited Laura Ashley's showroom, thinking kismet was present. No luck. So I lowered my expectations a bit and headed for some of the major department stores in the metropolis. I got lucky on my first attempt. Martindale's was looking for a window dresser and I qualified. I lugged my portfolio through the store to meet with the head of the department that same day. I got to her office with my life in my hands and sweat dripping down my backside.

"Come in, Ms. Lane. You look like you just did a twenty-mile hike," my future boss remarked. "I'm Charlotte Withers. It is a pleasure to meet you." I took a seat across from her as she handed me a bottle of spring water.

"Thank you. I could use a drink right about now."

"Well, I can certainly use someone of your talents in my department. Your portfolio is quite impressive, though you lack working experience. I am sure I can teach you some of the tricks of the trade," she said slyly.

"You'll see that I am a very quick learner, and I am willing to work overtime," I interjected.

"I'm sure you are." She maintained her familiar tone, one that I found myself being drawn to. "Can you start tomorrow?"

"Yes, of course. I would love to jump right in and get started," I said enthusiastically.

"That is exactly what I am looking for, a willing employee. I will fill out all of the necessary papers to get you in the system and I will see you back here tomorrow at nine a.m. ready to work."

I said my good-bye while shaking her hand, which lingered in mine, then slowly pulled away.

"You have beautiful fingers, Ms. Lane," my new employer remarked.

"Thank you, Ms. Withers, and please call me Penny," I said politely.

"Please, call me Charlotte. I like to be very informal with my workers."

"OK, Charlotte," I said with a big grin on my face.

I left the store skipping down Madison Avenue. I was bursting with joy from my accomplishment and was ready for a night of celebration.

That night I headed to my former college bar, Mermaids, for a celebratory drink and hopefully a nice sweet dyke who could share my good fortune. The place was crowded with graduates still in party mode. I made my way to the bar and got the bartender, Dolores's attention. Dolores was a tough middle-aged dyke who didn't take any nonsense from anybody.

"Whadda ya have, Penny?" she said while holding a cigarette between her lips.

"Tequila, Dolores, with a beer chaser," I ordered.

"Comin' right up," Dolores declared.

I threw back the tequila, sucked on the lemon and grabbed the bottle of beer. I scoped out the crowd, looking for any familiar and cute faces that I might want to get up close and personal with later. I felt a tug on my arm that made me jerk around.

"Well, Ms. Lane, funny finding you here." The voice was very familiar. I found my boss as of today standing in front of me with a gin and tonic in her hand and a smile on her face like she just caught me red-handed.

"I'm glad I ran into you here. It makes our working relationship so much more comfortable when we can be, shall we say, candid with each other. Don't you think?"

I still didn't have my breath back in my body, and my eyes were still looking like a deer's in headlights.

"I . . . I guess so," I stammered, chugging my beer.

I couldn't stop looking into her eyes. They were mesmerizing, like Dracula's in those old movies. They would pull in their victims not with fear or intimidation but with a sensuous power that clasped on to the person's heart and reeled them in. Charlotte's eyes were pulling at my heart and other parts further south. Her smile and her dark eyes were turning my fears into desires. I was drawn to her power not as my boss, but the sexual power, the mystery that she exuded through her eyes. She could sense my curiosity and sense the effect she was having on me. Charlotte leaned her body closer to me, bringing her mouth into my ear.

"You do have such long beautiful fingers," she whispered in my ear as her hand slid up the back of my thigh. "I believe they can work magic on a woman. Perhaps I can experience some of their magic." She took my earlobe between her teeth as her hand gently squeezed my ass. I felt a heat wave rise inside as I tried to fend off the magic of her spell. She released my earlobe.

"Let me show you where you will work tomorrow," she whispered again in my ear.

She took my hand and led me to the exit. I felt no resistance to her ways. I was powerless over her doings, wanting her to do with me as she would, knowing the immense pleasure I was bound to experience.

Charlotte hailed a cab, and she pulled me into the backseat. She gave the driver the address and draped her jacket over both our laps with her hand underneath. She began to massage my thigh, watching for my reaction, seeing if I would resist her seduction. My heart was pounding from the motion of her hand on my thigh, grazing between my legs and onto the other thigh. There was no need for conversation or small talk. She understood my desires and tempted me with her fingers. I wanted her over me, below me, in me. The driver pulled up to the store. Charlotte led me to a side employees' entrance. She used her key, and we quickly made our way through the aisle on the first floor. Charlotte stopped abruptly and pulled me toward her. She moved behind me and began to gently squeeze my breasts as her lips sucked on my neck. Was she a vampire, some immortal being that possessed such powers to render their sex prey helpless as she was doing to me?

"Look in the mirror, my sweet," she murmured to me. "You are so beautiful to touch, to look at." I looked in the mirror and watched as her hands moved along my torso, caressing my breasts, gliding along my stomach and my hips, her fingers pressing between my legs. My head fell back against her shoulder as I released a moan of pleasure from her touch. She stopped instantly and turned me to face her.

"No, not yet my dear, we haven't reached our work area," she said as she kissed my lips for the first time, sending quakes of pleasure through my body. She took my hand and led me through the aisles of merchandise until finally arriving at our destination. Charlotte opened a small door against the front wall of the store. We climbed up into the store's magnificent front window.

The window was dressed in an Asian motif. Large decorative pillows with pictures of tigers and dragons, a fake golden Buddha, and red Chinese silk fabric were spread in a harem-like way. Charlotte began to undress me like one of the mannequins in the window. I stood willing, watching her remove my shirt and jeans and yet not wanting to disturb her as she worked by joining in. She lowered me to the floor covered with pillows and silk. I felt her power as she knelt beside me, lightly brushing her fingers across my body. They moved with the delicacy of a geisha; no words were spoken, only through our eyes did we convey our desires. She smiled, watching my hips rise from her touch, and beads of sweat appeared on my breast. I felt wave after wave of pleasure move within me. I fended off the tsunami that was building inside of me. I wanted her to go on forever riding the waves of pleasure she created in me. She moved her body beside mine as her fingers dipped into my wetness.

"Now it is time, my love," Charlotte murmured into my cheek, penetrating my body with her fingers, sending my hips into the air, releasing the tsunami.

"Oh yes . . . oh Charlotte . . ." expelled from my mouth into the air as my arm clasped onto hers, my body shaking in ecstasy.

I collapsed back onto the silk sheets. Charlotte caressed my face and wiped away the perspiration from my brow.

"You are so beautiful, we will work well together, and you have so many fans," Charlotte remarked with a slight chuckle in her voice.

"What? What do you mean," I asked, somewhat confused by her words.

"Look." And she nodded at the window where a small crowd had gathered.

"I don't think they are window shopping, baby." Charlotte laughed.

Chapter Forty-seven
After-School Snack

Libby and I agreed that the fantasy of time travel was our personal fave. Wouldn't it be cool, we told each other over endless cups of tea, to go back in time with what we know now? Or, best of all, to re-experience certain treasured moments of the sixties and seventies with our present-day dyke savvy?

Our motives were purely selfish.

"I don't mean, like, going back and preventing the assassination of Kennedy," Libby clarified, aiming right at the pivotal moment from our baby boom girlhoods. "Or getting gay marriage onto Jimmy Carter's platform or something. I just look around at what queer teens are doing and demanding these days and think, gee, I wish I'd been capable of making out with *my* best friend at age fifteen. It never occurred to me, you know, that we could try, or that we were allowed. And yet the music we listened to was so *hot*, with all its bad-boy, sexist limitations. Man, I'd just love to go back to the mid-seventies for three hours of tenth grade. Come home from school and, instead of my typical after-school snack, eat Trina Glenn. Play air guitar for her in my Levi's boot-cut jeans and my gauze shirt unbuttoned to the waist and my roach-clip necklace and *get down* on the girl with the wing-feathered hair. That's my time-travel pick. Dumb, huh?"

Not dumb. I was aroused. I put down my women's music festival tea mug and thought about this. "I'll be Trina," I offered. "What am I wearing? Come on. Be detailed."

Libby's a commercial artist now, and she had her sketchpad out in two seconds. "Like this," she illustrated. "Painter's pants from Count's Western Store. A French-cut T-shirt and a little brown vest over that. Leather clogs. Love's Baby Soft perfume. Kissing Potion roll-on lip gloss. Your hair is long, straight, parted in the middle and then rolled at the ends to make Farrah Fawcett feathers. But not too much, though—you're on the field hockey team, real active. Kind of a good girl/athlete femme. You keep your hair sweet-smelling with that Earth Born natural shampoo, apricot scent, and Rose Milk face cream. You wear a ring on every finger—mood ring, zodiac ring, Turkish puzzle ring. And a woven string bracelet from Martha's Vineyard. You're not wearing a bra, but you have long knee socks on under your pants, and a denim purse sewn and cut to look like a pair of Levi's, with an outside red-tag pocket."

I moved closer and examined the drawing. "What do I carry in that handbag?"

"Oh, you know, a hash pipe. A copy of *Jonathan Livingston Seagull* or some other trendy, mega-meaningful book of poetry—maybe *Reflections on a Gift of Watermelon Pickle*. Zit makeup. Clearasil and Erace. Bonne Bell Lip Smackers—root beer flavor. Your math and English homework with little circles for dots over the I's. A permission slip for a youth group sleepover. A half-eaten Marathon bar."

"And in your handbag?"

"Well, I don't have a purse. I have a backpack with cigarettes, *National Lampoon, Flowers for Algernon, Rubyfruit Jungle*. An enamel pendant I made in art class that I'm going to give you for Valentine's Day. An eight-track of The Who's *Tommy* album. My unwashed gym suit. A bag of Funyuns. A baggie of Colombian."

I was clearing off the sofa and getting out the Who albums. Now they were on CD, of course, and we had a DVD player, too. Now we were nonsmokers, nontokers, our tastes running all the way to Donna Karan and Ann Taylor and CK1 and Nautica cologne. But I could see it: that past we had both known, decades before we met each other at a library book sale. I could taste it— that longing, that field-party recklessness twisted up into desire for the special girl, the self-doubt and sublimation. I could see Libby, at fifteen, in Dallas, coming home to crumbly Toll House cookies on her mother's dining room table and wondering, *What is wrong with me?* Her desperate talks with the P.E. teacher who yielded no further information, her forays into the 301 section of the local library for anything about women. Anything. These were the memories we peeled back like shucked oysters when we heard certain songs on the radio, our hearts in love with each other here and now but our minds secretly tinkering with those first crushes, those other girls, her Trina Glenn, my Kimmie Kominsky with the self-pierced ears and the floppy suede hat. And if I could go back? To Kimmie, for three hours?

Libby, meanwhile, had taken off her sweater and disappeared into our bedroom, emerging in her ancient varsity club jacket and an Acupulco Gold T-shirt I thought we had agreed to throw out. She began to play air guitar, singing along with The Who, "It's only teenage wasteland."

I was wet in seconds. I looked at the little clock on our end table and moved its hands around to read 3:35 p.m., the magic hour my old high school let out back in 1976. "It's the Bicentennial," I reminded Libby, and went to the kitchen drawer for leftover Fourth of July picnic napkins to add historically correct décor. Then I got even with Libby's varsity jacket by popping my old algebra book off the shelf where we stored all our schoolbooks from high school and college—in case, for some reason, we needed to resolve New Math word problems in our adult lives as caterers.

Prim, legs drawn up beneath my ass, I studied page 137, shocked to realize I had once penciled *I love Kimmie* on the right-hand margin. "Hi, Kimmie," I breathed at Libby, remembering to sound faintly nasal since in 1976 I'd be wearing my required after-school dental retainer. "I liked what you said in student council today. You totally told Miss Ebersole to shove it!"

"Yeah, and I got detention tomorrow," drawled Libby/Kimmie, who had magically regained the Texas accent of her adolescence. She stood with her thumbs hooked in her pockets. "I'll miss practice. I'm already in trouble with my coach, my math teacher and now the vice-principal. Shit."

"I can help you with your math."

"I guess that's why I came over."

"Mmm. Sit down. You want anything to drink? A & W root beer?"

"Naw. Say . . . you smell nice."

"Oh. It's just Love's Baby Soft." I felt myself blushing just as if I was fifteen again, the way Libby/Kimmie was looking at me. The Who album changed tracks to "Love, Rain on Me."

Her fingers drummed on her knee, then on my knee. Then her fingers touched my hair. "Looks pretty that way. Not too Farrah."

"You're making me feel funny inside," I managed, and that was no lie. We were in the time tunnel and she was my dream girl, my Kimmie, and there weren't any parents around. No one was going to burst into the room this time. I risked some tougher talk. "You know, around school they say you're a queer. Does that bother you? Do you ever feel like fighting back?"

"The truth shall set you free." Libby/Kimmie shrugged off her jacket and squared her shoulders. "I'm me. So what?"

"I don't care, I'm just wondering what it's like."

"Why don't we find out?"

"You mean . . . now?"

"Yeah." Her eyes gazed at me intently. I could smell the old leather patches on her varsity jacket, musty from years in the closet, but authentic. That was my lover—years in the closet. But authentic. I could take her back and make her feel powerful in her memories. Right now. On the armchair.

We moved together very slowly, our lips barely touching at first. I closed my eyes. Would it be like my first kiss? Could I really pretend that Libby was Kimmie? But then a funny thing happened. We couldn't go back. We couldn't *fake* inexperienced first-time kissing. We knew each other too well, had loved each other too long, and automatically we were moving our tongues and lips in the ways our here-and-now grown selves liked and looked forward to. We didn't want to go back to when we were awkward and clueless virgins, as unsure with our kissing as we were with the unfamiliar demands of a gearshift knob and Volkswagen clutch in driver's ed class. We had learned the long, hard way how to kiss and drive, and now no one was going to take away our licenses or doubt our expertise. The hard years were behind us—no more algebra, no disapproving parents, punitive principals. No more SAT tests or meetings with the youth minister about our shameful and dangerous "tendencies." Had our old crushes made it through all that? Were Kimmie and Trina now satisfied adults? I hoped so. I didn't want Kimmie Kominsky anymore. I had the love I wanted, in my lap.

Libby's eyes opened. "That was weird, but fun." She looked like she had just stepped off a time-train subway ride and didn't have any money left on her Metro card to go farther. I felt the same way. We stared at each other, blinking. The Who fell silent.

"Well," Libby began, and stopped. She took off her varsity jacket and carefully hung it in its place. I filed the math book on our shelf. The clock rang eight, the real time, not after-school at all, and I stood up to make dinner, knowing Libby liked her love-making at ten.

Chapter Forty-eight
Call Me Jiffy

A long day's journey into night is nothing compared to a night home alone during a snowstorm. That was my predicament. My baby left me home alone to help out a stranded motorist. She got the call about an hour ago, threw on her boots and parka, grabbed her keys, and headed out to her tow truck.

"I'm sorry, babe, but duty calls," she said as she kissed my forehead. "I'll be back in an hour, I promise."

I walked her to the door with my eyes anxious. "Call if something happens, OK?" I said in my high-pitched femme voice.

"Don't worry, everything will be OK. I'll be back in a jiffy."

So here I sit watching the blanket of snow blowing in front of the window. I move from the living room to the kitchen and back to the living room. *Where could she be? I hope she's all right.*

The wind whistled through the walls, grabbing my attention

and raising my anxiety. I decided to build a fire in the living room's fireplace, poured myself a snifter of amaretto, and tried to relax.

The fire is warm and assuring as I stretch out on the overstuffed sofa in front of it. Letting all of my surroundings comfort me, I stare quietly into the fire. My mind begins to drift while a soothing warmth from the amaretto eases my body.

Oh baby, come home soon. I want you here with me. I want you lying next to me—safe in my arms, kissing my lips, stroking my hair . . .

The lights flickered as the last surge of wattage dissipated. I came out of my mellow state to one of worry. I grabbed the box of matches and lit a few candles. The flames of the fire mixed with the glow of the candles created a trancelike presence, returning me to my comforting sofa and thoughts of Tara.

Hmmm, baby, you are so good to help others. I want to make it so good for you after you return from one of your rescue missions. I want to lay you down in front of this fire and kiss your tired eyes. Removing your shirt, I'd let the fire keep you warm as I move my lips from your eyes to your mouth, letting my kisses be your healing balm . . .

My mental desire sent my hand slowly across my chest, discovering my hard nipple and gently squeezing as Tara's hand would please me.

You are my love, my rock, and my precious jewel. You can be strong when needed, yet fragile like glass when in my arms . . .

My mind continues creating my scenario as I gaze into the fire—now my crystal ball. I hear her moan from my slow caress of her body, moving my hand down to free her from her jeans. She is compliant and wanting of my touch, letting me linger over her tight frame and her soft, snow-white skin. I delicately kiss her stomach, letting my tongue fall into her navel as I feel her muscles tighten beneath me.

Outside the wind howls, beating its force against the window panes as the snow swirls in the darkness. My mind is spinning from my mental play and my urgency to have Tara return. I move my hand along my thigh, letting my fingers brush against me between my legs.

I want you . . . I want you home with me. I need your arms to keep me safe, your beautiful body to keep me warm and your lips to comfort me through the storm . . .

I closed my eyes, letting my mind and body converge on the ethereal plane of delight, yet still longing for my lover's company. A short blast of cold air brought me back to my sofa and my solitude. I turned my head and found my beloved standing over me.

"I'm home, sweetie, and just in time, I see," she murmured with a wide grin on her face. She leaned in and kissed my shoulder as I heard the thump from her boots being kicked off below. She removed her sweater, revealing her muscles bound in her tight black T-shirt.

"You're home!" I softly exclaimed, still in my sexual stupor.

"Yes I am, darlin,' and I see you got this party goin' without me. Maybe I need to bring you on home now, too!"

And she climbed on top of me with her tongue plowing its way into my mouth, sending an avalanche of desire to smother all of my anxiety and fears now that she was here with me. Tara's hand found its way along my terrain, blazing its own trail to my soft wet caverns. I entered that place of sexual limbo, wanting to hover in pleasure, but she was my champion, my snow angel for the helpless, and she knew I couldn't resist her ways. I raised my hips like a car lifted effortlessly by her truck. From her fingers furrowing deep within me I called out in a thunderous clamor. The roar of nature encompassed my love and me, finally coming home to Tara.

We lay entangled in each other's embrace, energy spent, limp limbs entwined. My mind was returning to a clearer state, and I played back the scene, quite puzzled.

"How did you know I was in the sofa, and how did you get to me so fast without me hearing you?" I asked.

She chuckled and said, "I saw the light of the fire and peered through the window and saw you doing your thing on the sofa. So I got in here as quick and as quietly as I could." I started to laugh, burying my face in her neck.

"What's so funny?" she remarked.

"I guess I will have to do this more often, to get you home, as you put it, in a jiffy."

Chapter Forty-nine
Better Than a Bike

Possibly it was stupid to do a ten-mile bike ride the morning before my lover arrived for a sex weekend. I'd have a sore crotch and she'd scream, "What the hell were you thinking? Get off the bike! I'm better than a bike!" She was right, of course. I was working out like a maniac these days. But how could I explain I had fallen in love with my bike, with my cycling class at the gym? The sweat! The burn! The thigh control! Couldn't she feel my strong quads and just nod approvingly or marvel at their power? I used to be a runt.

"I don't want to hear one more word about that friggin' cycling class," Whitney announced as she stepped off the train and into my arms, but little did she know what I had in store. I'd signed her up as a guest for the Saturday morning cycling class at my sports club. We'd go together! To sweeten the deal, I presented her with wrapped gift boxes containing top-of-the-line workout shorts and a sleeveless yoga top. Her face softened, then crinkled into a grin. "You had to bribe me, babe?"

I admit it was hard to leave our warm erotic bedsheets the next day and pull on sneakers for the trip across town. At the gym I swiped my membership card and then presented the guest pass I'd set up for my girlfriend. We changed in the locker room downstairs. I could feel Whitney taking in the very pleasant ambiance of muscular buttocks and enormous legs all around us, weekend workout amazons shouting greetings to one another and sucking from water bottles.

Our class was in a long, well-lit side room with state-of-the-art bikes lined up on a slick wooden floor. Jessica, the perky instructor for the hour, showed Whitney how to set up her bike, adjusting the seat and handlebars to the right height levels. "I feel like I'm falling forward," Whitney complained, but Jessica assured her that was normal.

The fifty-minute workout began with stretches, slow pedaling, then "a small hill," with Jessica reminding participants to "increase the tension" on the bike. "I thought you worked out to *reduce* tension," Whitney stage-whispered to me. "To *reduce* stress."

"Heads up, shoulders relaxed, now lift. Feel the point of the seat between your legs. We're going to do a series of lifts. Now lift. And down. Now lift. And down. Remain seated for the rest of the song."

Everyone got busy concentrating, sweat glimmering on the backs of hands. I could smell the faint scent of Whitney's perfume as heat rose from her torso just a few feet away.

"The next song is a long slow hill. Keep pedaling. Adjust the tension one quarter turn."

The pressure of a long, slow, seated burn. I could feel the padded bike seat pressed against my crotch. I was tender from days of cycling and hours of sex, but I was used to the pressure of a bike seat by now. How was Whitney handling the experience?

I looked over and saw a very familiar expression on her face. *Oh, no!*

"*God damn,*" she gasped to me, so low that I hoped none of our classmates could hear. "I'm going to *come any second!*"

Sometimes I, too, would hop off a wet bike at the end of a long ride or a tough class and feel the unexpected reward of a very public orgasm trying to build from my pressed folds down under. What do you do? Well, you laugh it off, hobble toward a bench and stretch it out or discreetly head toward a locker-room shower stall and finish it off with panache. I had forgotten that Whitney grew excited with the merest brush of a skilled finger.

I prayed that the next song from Jessica's cassette player would be a nice, loud, rousing U2 selection or, better yet, Nelly Furtado or one of those maniacal downhill bluegrass mixes, because Whitney was loud. Loud and *wet.* I started to panic, but Jessica commanded "And now an easy downhill! Make this a sprint, everybody! Pedal! Pedal! Pedal!" And we heard the boom box shift over to that great, annoyingly frantic song, the Red Hot Chili Peppers, "Jump."

My eye was on Whitney and her quivering inner thighs. She managed to time her moans—"Oh! Oh! Oh! Oh!" to the Peppers' "Jump! Jump! Jump! Jump!" and I helpfully added a loud cover-up shout of "Wheeehaw!" which I admit I often shout in class, so no one thought anything of it. Then I thrust my bottle of watered-down grapefruit juice at Whitney, offering "Here!" while deliberately spilling half of it into her lap. Now she and her "lap" would be discreetly fruit-scented. "Oh, I'm *so* sorry!" I gleamed, jerking my head in the direction of the ladies' washroom. "Why don't you go get some paper towels and mop up your bike seat? I'm really sorry."

Whitney, panting, came to a stop, shoulders down, legs limp.

"Aaand . . . posture break!" screamed Jessica. "Everyone sit up and stretch. Have a sip of water!" Women let go of the handlebars in grateful gasps, and shifted their seating, reaching for sport bottles and terrycloth towels. As Whitney stalked tremblingly to the bathroom, I eyed my workout buddies. How many of them had also reached orgasm today? Every day, in cycling class? How did we all manage to hide it? Wasn't this God's gift to woman, the ability to get off simply by sitting down? How many out-of-shape women might be lured into workout programs with the promise of in-class orgasms? Did I possibly have a one-track mind?

Later, as I munched an avocado and bean sprout sandwich on wheat toast in the gym snack bar, Whitney chugged a cold soda and laughed at my lunch. "Honey, you won't find me eating a wiggly green sandwich. But now I see why you're so hot for this cycling thing. Secret benefits! Or are you just keeping your equipment in shape for me?"

I knew the right answer. "Babe, you're better than a bike."

"Damn right." She grinned, and slipped her hand into mine under the table. "Maybe you'll let me take you for a ride later. For a spin. Go downhill. Put your leg up on my handlebars and stretch."

I swallowed the last of my bean sprouts. "I think I could *handle* that."

Chapter Fifty
State of the Union

Security was pretty tight for the governor's inauguration day. Ever since the death threats started coming in after the election results, we had to double the man- and woman-power. Winning the election by a slim margin of 10,000 votes particularly due to the gay and women voters, the governor has been a target for all sorts of kooks who just can't accept that the change that was coming is here. I guess it really started the day on the campaign trail when the candidate marched in the Gay Pride Parade. Cheers and jeers resounded down Main Street. I had to keep my senses on high that day, scouting the crowd making sure my charge was safe.

I met the newly elected governor when she was campaigning for the state senate six years ago. She was having a verbal altercation with some bystander over her position on gay marriage, and I stepped in with my blazer pushed back, revealing I was packing.

"We gotta problem here?" I stated in the face of the citizen with my back guarding the future governor. The guy was a bit taken aback by the presence of two women—two women with some clout, and we were taking him on. He stood down real fast. I was hired on the spot. Since that day, Governor Alexander and I have had a truly amazing working relationship built upon trust, respect, and honest communication. But now, I will be happy to get through this day and have her safely in the governor's mansion tonight.

"*Alpha leader, this is detail one,*" my radio blurted in my ear.

"*Go ahead, detail one,*" I responded.

"*We finished security sweep for the main floor and the platform and the surrounding grounds.*"

"*OK, detail one. Begin security check of the reception hall.*"

"*Roger, alpha leader . . . out.*"

My senses were alert and my mind was replaying every detail of today's itinerary. The ceremony, the press reception, and the inauguration ball tonight. I had to make mental checks and then check them again. No mistakes today. She depends on me to keep her secure and worry free. I am her front line, her shield, her body armor, and I would sacrifice myself for her with no hesitation.

I checked my watch. It was time for the swearing-in ceremony so I headed up to her suite. I walked into the room and found her checking herself out in front of the full-length mirror. I stood at a comfortable distance, not to alert her to my presence, as well as to admire her long tight calves in their skin-toned stockings and blue pumps. She looked so dignified and powerful in her navy blue suit. It spoke of her inner strength, conviction, and sensuality. I felt that warm feeling pour over me and a smile crept onto my face.

"Olivia, is it time?" She spoke, jolting me from my reverie.

"Yes, Governor Alexander," I said, emphasizing the *governor* part. She turned with a smile on her face.

"Amazing, isn't it," she said. "If you told me six years ago that we would be standing here together ready to lead the state after spending countless hours on street corners shaking hands and distributing flyers, I would have said you were crazy."

"But it's real, and there is nobody better to lead than you, Governor," I remarked.

We began our walk toward the stateroom where dignitaries, the legislature, the justice of the state supreme court, and an array of press people were waiting for us. I took the point and led my charge to her destiny.

The ceremony went smoothly. The governor was greeted with applause and cheers as she gave her inauguration speech. I stood to the side checking the perimeter, watching the crowd and checking in with my detail. All was fine, so I took a moment and enjoyed her words, her gestures, and her beautiful face.

"We, together as one, can do so much more for this state. We can bring financial security, the opportunities for a better quality of life and most important, the blessings of liberty for all people. I believe we are a can-do people. And together, we can do it all."

The crowd came to their feet in an ovation of cheers and applause affirming their belief and support of my governor. I jumped into security mode and escorted her off the stage as she waved to the crowd. I had one eye on her and one on the masses. I did a double take as we headed down the stairs. A face in the crowd grabbed my attention. We made eye contact, but I couldn't place him. A reporter perhaps? A councilman? Lobbyist? Who was that guy? I radioed my detail.

"Detail one, this is alpha leader."

"Go ahead, alpha leader."

"Detain individual in stateroom for identification purposes. Description: Male, five foot ten, late thirties, dark hair, gray suit, red tie, and red handkerchief in jacket pocket."

"Copy, alpha leader, will proceed."

I felt a bit relieved that I went with my gut and made the call. My instincts were speaking volumes to me about that guy, but I couldn't put my finger on it. I shook my brain and put my focus back on the governor. She saw the concern on my face.

"What's wrong, Olivia?" she asked as we proceeded back to the suite.

210

"It's nothing, Governor, just a routine security check." I wasn't going to worry this woman on the most important day of her life. This was her day, her finest hour, and I wanted her to take it all in and savor the moment.

Back in the suite, the governor threw off her suit jacket and kicked off her shoes. From spending hours with her I have learned that as dignified and austere as she was in her power suit, she was more of her real self when wearing a pair of sweatpants and a T-shirt. That was just her style inside and out—soft and comfy. I checked in with my security team as my Wonder Woman showered.

"Detail one, report . . ."

"Alpha leader, this is detail one. Individual was detained for security check."

"Give specifics," I ordered.

"Individual is Thomas Landry, a reporter for the Herald. *He claims he just began position this past month. Individual had credentials. We released him."*

"Roger, detail one."

I heard the report, but my gut was still sending me signals. I just couldn't place this guy in the right scenario. It's like having one piece of the puzzle still out of place but no open spots.

"Olivia, you have a minute?" she called from the bedroom.

The governor stood in her bathrobe; her hair was wrapped in a white terry cloth towel and the scent of lavender permeated from her skin. She was holding up two gowns in front of her.

"I need another woman's opinion. Which one for the ball? The crimson red or the emerald green?"

This was a tough decision. I had seen her in both and she looked spectacular.

"Well, honestly, either one . . . you look fantastic in both of them," I blurted, a bit surprised by my candid remark. Up to this moment I had not revealed my admiration for her in such familiar terms. I blushed slightly as I became self-conscious of my words.

"Really, Olivia! I didn't know you noticed!" she said playfully.

I stood staring at my feet in embarrassment, feeling like the fourteen-year-old who has a crush on her gym teacher.

"Can I be honest with you," she asked. I shook my head, still staring at my feet, not wanting to meet her eyes.

"When I see you in your business suits, I think you look pretty hot."

I raised my eyes in disbelief of what she had just spoken. I never thought she noticed how I dressed, yet I always wanted her to notice.

"Olivia," she said so sincerely.

We stood encompassed by that thick air of anticipation, ready to cross that line and take our relationship to a much deeper level. She slowly made her way toward me, dropping her gowns on the floor. I stood frozen, never taking my eyes away from her smile.

"There. I said it. We both said it," she murmured. "And it feels so good to finally say it."

She grabbed hold of my jacket's lapels and kissed my lips, sending an earthquake through my whole body. She removed my communication headset and it fell to the floor, along with my jacket.

"I think it's time for me to do my own investigation," she said as she wrapped her arms around my neck, burying her tongue into my welcoming mouth. I felt every muscle in my body melt with her embrace as I untied her robe and began my own security sweep of her voluptuous body. We kissed with a sense of urgency in our limited time before the ball, as well as to make up for six years of desire held in check.

She pulled me toward the bed. I removed my shirt, shoes, pants, as quickly as dismantling and assembling a gun during my training days. She positioned herself in the center of the bed, her robe removed, her long hair falling over her shoulder and onto her magnificent breasts as she lay on her side watching me disrobe.

"I've waited so long for this moment, Olivia. I have dreamt about you coming to me in the middle of the night, making sure I was safe and then lying with me to keep me safe."

"You are safe with me, my Governor. No harm will ever come

to you. I vow my life to you." And I placed myself next to her, moving her back against the bed and kissing her tender lips, touching her perfect frame, watching her hips rise and fall with each stroke of my fingers. She was my Governor, my leader, my goddess and I would always do her bidding.

"I will always be here for you," I declared.

Her eyes were closed from the pleasure she was experiencing.

"I will protect you, watch over you, be here by your side and any where you may go. I am your servant and now your lover." I made my own oath of love to her, sealing my declaration with my fingers within her that sent waves of ecstasy through her body.

"Yes." She gasped. "Yes, Olivia . . . always."

We rested in each other's arms, wanting to remain so for the rest of the night, but we both knew we had to get back to business.

"Will you come to me tonight?" she softly asked.

I held her face in my hands and gazed into those dark eyes. Those eyes could whittle any political figure down to size, but now they were as soft and as gentle as a newborn kitten. "I will be here," I declared.

We both rose from our bed and began to dress, reassuming our professional mode.

The ball was majestic—a reincarnation of the glorious days of kings and queens. I circulated the room with my head clear and my eyes fixed on both the rank and file and, now, my love. She was dazzling in her emerald gown, shimmering from head to toe and so graciously receiving her guests. My earlier gut feeling returned in a split second as I spotted Thomas Landry, now dressed in a tuxedo, standing in the reception line. I felt my instincts pulling me toward the governor with my eyes plastered on this man. Who was he? How did I know him? Where had I seen him before?

I kept searching my memory as my feet carried me across the room. Finally, the sinking feeling in my stomach exploded as I remembered my first chance meeting with the governor on the street. He was the citizen in her face. I picked up speed as he drew closer to her. Three people were ahead of him in the line. I politely excused myself, making my way through the crowd, not wanting to arouse suspicion. Two people before he'd reach her. I quickened my pace as the voice in my head grew louder.

Get to her! She is in danger . . . get to her!

One person to go before he was in front of her.

She is your goddess, your lover . . . you are her protector . . . save her.

The governor is distracted by my approach and I can see the concern in her eyes as he stands in front of her, and she recognizes him. He reaches into his breast pocket and I feel as if I am in a dream, restricted from moving any faster than I am allowed.

I must stop him . . . he can't take her from me . . .

I lunge at Landry, knocking him to the floor, pushing my love out of harm's way. We struggle for control with our hands clasped around his gun.

"She must die! She must die!" he is shouting, as a single shot expels through the confusion surrounding us.

Over the ringing in my ears, I hear my governor's voice. "*Noooooooo!*"

My muscles fall limp as I collapse back onto the floor. From the corner of my eye I can see my security detail rushing my love out of the room. In my mind I know this is procedure, but in my heart I plead for her to come back to me, to kneel by my side, to kiss me again and to let me tell her once more I love her. The rest of my detail apprehends her assailant as I feel my energy begin to slip away.

For six years I vowed to myself my loyalty to my first lady. I vowed that I would protect her with my body if needed. And now my words have come to fruition. I shielded her from harm and made the ultimate sacrifice for my charge, my love. Landry had failed to take her from me and me from her, since I had slipped on my vest before the ball. I suffered a nasty bruise and some sore ribs, but I was standing tall once again.

I softly knocked on the door of the governor's suite. With all of the police action and radio silence, she hadn't been told of my survival. I requested that it not be released until I spoke to her, guarding against any personal reaction she might show, revealing our secret.

The words "Come in" came through the door in a voice that was filled with sadness and remorse. In the darkness I could see her silhouette sitting in the chair, staring out the window, motionless as if in a catatonic state induced by grief.

"What do you want?" she asked, still staring out the window. "I asked to be left alone."

Her voice had hardened from tonight's events and from what she believed was the tragic outcome. I smiled to myself, knowing all of this would be dispelled with the sound of my voice. I had to save her one more time. But this time it was from her false grief.

"Now why would you want to be alone on the night of your inauguration, Governor Alexander?"

"*Olivia! You're alive!*" She jumped from her chair straight into my arms.

"Of course I am. Didn't I promise to be with you tonight? I always keep my promises. Especially to you, Governor."

Chapter Fifty-one
The Captain and Chenille

Gazing at the half-million rainbow-clad bodies stretched as far as she could see on the national Mall, Robyn thought that Gay Pride rallies had to be her favorite holiday. Beauty and pageantry, joy and humor, yet there were no Hallmark cards to send, no wrapping paper for Pride gifts. Not yet. But someday soon. She thanked God she had lived to see so many sweeping changes in gay rights, the end of punitive sodomy laws, the marriages in Massachusetts, the openly gay celebrities and television show hosts like Ellen and Rosie.

She shifted her backpack and unclasped its buckles to take out her wrapped sandwich lunch. The thing about giant gay rights rallies was that you never knew who you might run into from your past—an old crush, a gym teacher, the ex-lover who had vanished off the face of the earth. They all turned up here at the Lincoln

Memorial. And she didn't want romaine lettuce hanging out of her face when those encounters began, so she wolfed down her lunch early in the day and took a long sip from her water bottle. Then she squirted a bit of cologne on her wrists from the tiny Nautica sample vial tucked in the left pocket of her cargo shorts. There. She was ready for love! And it was only ten thirty in the morning in a lovely, long day.

Beautiful humanity, flowing from every corner of the earth. One group carried signs lettered in Urdu-Hindi that read "Khush: South Asian Gays for Justice." There was a large contingent of lesbian Mormons. Gay dads with toddlers in bright wagons. P-FLAG moms, beaming; the warm response they elicited from onlookers always made Robyn cry. She caught a glimpse of a gay rabbi her parents knew, holding hands with his partner, Moishe, and spotted several coworkers from her computer lab, but so many in the crowd were strangers. Robyn marveled at the sheer number of gay and lesbian Americans. Surely their day would come . . . surely, in her lifetime, marriage and adoption would no longer be considered controversial . . . look at the couples, the children. The *families*. She shivered with an unavoidable regret at her own single, childless status. *Temporary*, she told herself, *just temporary*.

A pickup basketball game was underway in a little public park near the Mall and Robyn was amused to see an atypical "shirts against skins" arrangement: men in gay pride tank tops vs. several topless lesbians. Wait a minute. Wasn't that . . . *the Captain*?

Oh, the Captain! The big, buff, redheaded older girl from Robyn's term at Camp Shalom, way back in 1977. The captain of the camp basketball team. Game after game, practice after practice, Robyn had crept into the bleachers to watch the Captain scream out game plans and swish in baskets. She'd never been caught watching, and as far as the Captain knew Robyn was one of the arty/drama kids at camp, not an athlete. They'd barely spoken, the single year of age between them a canyon of difference at fifteen and sixteen—the Captain *drove a car*. Just once, finished with her dishwashing chores and free for an hour at twilight, Robyn had gone into the camp gym and tentatively picked up a basketball, unsuccessfully hurtling it toward the basket, where it bounced off the backboard and slammed her in the face. "Are you OK?" A voice had gasped. A tall figure strode out from the shadows, and it was the Captain moving toward her with concern, the Captain who took her to the infirmary. Robyn would never forget the feel of the older girl's steady hand on her shoulder as the camp nurse applied a cold compress to the rising egg-shaped bruise, the thrilling way that the Captain had asked familiarly, "Feeling better, babe?"

But there she *was*. It was *her*: Dina Edelson. Robyn found her feet moving of their own volition to the blacktop sidelines of the court. The Captain's creamy breasts swung freely as she bashed in free shots. Boy, she hadn't aged a day.

"All right, cool it," screamed an angry voice, and the action ground to a halt as an orange-vested Pride rally "peacekeeper" approached the shirtless women. "I don't know what group you're with, ladies, but we have an agreement in our permit for this Pride march—no nudity. Please get your shirts back on this minute. I'm already worn out trying to keep the Radical Faeries out of the reflecting pool. Help me out here!" She cocked an eye at the Captain's breasts disappearing into a roomy V-neck sweatshirt and added in a low voice, "Honey, you're good," then stalked off to issue her next protocol violation.

Laughing, the players changed roles—the women taking their time putting old polo shirts over damp armpit hair and tattoos, the men pulling off their own tops to wipe sweat from gleaming, shaven chests and pierced nipples. Robyn unconsciously smoothed the folds of her own chenille sweater, then approached the Captain, who was resting on the grass and tousling the hair of a small child.

"Excuse me. Um, aren't you Dina Edelson? I think you were the basketball captain at my summer camp. About a million years ago. Except you sure look the same as I remember."

The Captain looked up in surprise, her red hair backlit by the morning sun and absolutely ablaze. "Holy shit. Aren't you that kid who took a basketball to the head one night? What were you doing, trying to work on a hook shot after hours or something?"

She remembers. "The same. Robyn." They shook hands.

Dina's face creased into a smile. Now a few wrinkles did show, but they were laugh lines, and Robyn wondered what it would feel like to touch that long nose with her own, to taste those dimples with her tongue. She looked at the child by Dina's side—a strawberry blond four-year-old—and asked, "Yours?"

"You bet. This is Hannah. I'm a single mom." Hannah reached out with one tiny, sticky hand and stroked Robyn's chenille sweater in wonder, piping, "Soft. Soft." Robyn squatted down to Hannah's level, and the little girl put her hand on Robyn's shoulder, patting the sun-warmed material. "Soft." Had it been a full generation since Hannah's mom, the Captain, had patted Robyn's shoulder in just that place?

"Hannah," the Captain began remonstrating, just as Robyn said, "I love kids." They laughed awkwardly as their words overlapped. Then Robyn squatted down to Hannah's level, and said, "Go ahead. You can pet my sweater."

"Feels good, huh?" the Captain asked her daughter, and Robyn though, *Oy. Petting, feeling good, what are we saying? Let's leave the kid out of this.* But then Dina said the magic words: "What are you doing with yourself these days, babe?"

Babe! Oh, there it was, the word from camp, the throwaway endearment! The doorway to possibilities of more! So Robyn seized the day and said "I guess I turned out gay—like you."

"Ah." Dina shrugged. "There's that. You know, I knew I was gay at camp. I threw myself into basketball because I thought if I was good at sports I'd still be popular if any, you know, rumors started. I wanted a job as a junior counselor at that camp, and I had to keep it clean." She sighed. "But dig this"—gesturing to the Pride rally surging around them—"I actually ran into one of the old camp *administrators* here!"

"No way!" Robyn squealed, delighted.

"Yeah. That's the fun thing about these million-homo events. You never know who you'll run into."

"That's exactly what I was thinking this morning," Robyn agreed. Dina smiled. Their eyes locked.

Meanwhile, Hannah had not stopped playing with Robyn's sweater, chanting, "Soft, soft."

"Cool it a minute, hon." Dina gently removed the little girl's hand and reached out with her own tough fingers. "Let Mommy see. Hmmm. It *is* soft!" She smiled at Robyn, who knelt paralyzed by the tingling rays emanating from the touch of her ancient crush.

"Gotta go number one, Mommy," Hannah interrupted.

"There's a porta-Jane over there," Robyn suggested.

Dina looked at her. "A porta-*Jane*? Not a Porta-John? You must have spent a couple-three years working at the Michigan Womyn's Music Festival."

"How'd you know?"

"I was there eight years in a row, before I had Hannah."

"But I never saw you! Shit, that's weird!"

"Well, come on, babe. Five thousand women. I hid out with my posse in the RV area. You wouldn't have liked me much, anyway. I partied hard and skipped out on work shifts. I got my act together eventually."

"Bathroom, mommy," Hannah whined. They all rose and without further discussion headed together toward the portable toilets. Hannah trustingly held hands with both Dina and Robyn.

This could be my child, thought Robyn. My little family. As Hannah abruptly let go and banged into the toilet, the grown-ups' hands bumped. They laughed awkwardly again.

"Would you like to spend the rest of the day with us?" the Captain asked, now, without preamble. At the exact same moment, Robyn began blurting out, "I always liked you."

"Huh? Oh. Sure," they then fumbled, as each gradually understood what the other had said.

Then the Captain reached out and touched Robyn's sweater again. "*Soft.*"

"You might be surprised by how tough I have become," Robyn answered.

"Babe, I wouldn't be surprised at all."

"But I never perfected a hook shot."

"That's my department. I bet you're good at other things."

"You might be surprised," Robyn said again, and smiled, and Hannah came out and took each of their hands, and they continued on together. It was just eleven thirty a.m., and they had all of Pride Day and the rest of their lives ahead.

Chapter Fifty-two

52 Pickup

It was game night at the Tri-Lambda sorority house. This was a weekly gathering of some of the most exquisitely delicious dykes on campus. No one ever left from one of our game nights unsatisfied or wanting. We aimed to please and were quite accurate with our aim. The ladies always came back for more, week after week. This was our way of releasing all that pent-up frustration and getting the juices flowing after dealing with classes, papers, or exams. We all felt it, we all wanted it, and we all got it every Saturday night. There was someone in charge of picking the "game of the week" and bringing the necessities—just a few things to whet our appetites. They were both pleasing to the palate and arousing to the senses.

Betsy was the first to arrive. She was our flag-burning radical who was always spewing some new left-wing socialist theory as she stormed through the door. Despite her politics, she had nice tits.

"Hey, Bets, what's shaking?" I asked, as she barreled past me into the living room.

"Shaking? I'll tell you what's shaking. The whole political system is! And the people are shaking with anger, ready to take it back," she declared, standing in the middle of the living room.

"Bad day in class today?" I chuckled

"Naw. It was the same old boring bourgeois rhetoric. I'm just angry because I lost my favorite Lenin-lover pin."

"Yeah, I hate when that happens," I remarked, shaking my head in amazement at her fiery spirit.

A knock at the door saved me from Betsy and her ranting. Tania and Lia were all smiles when they saw me.

"Hey, girlfriend, ready for some action tonight?" Tania asked as she laid a wet one on my cheek. Tania didn't pull any punches when it came to our Saturday nights. She came ready to play and was always the one to initiate the fun. Lia was the yin to Tania's yang. Some might say she was the quiet one of the bunch, but I saw that as a seductive air. She liked to sit back and take in the atmosphere before she engaged in any activities. I liked that about her. It was a quality of self-control, but underneath that quiet demeanor was a firecracker that could explode with the right match.

"Hey, baby," Lia said, brushing her finger across my cheek. "You're lookin' good tonight."

My heart be still. I stood holding the door, watching their backsides move into the living room where Betsy was still pacing. The door pushed back and in walked Mel and Jen. They were the lesbian version of Siamese twins, always together, roommates for all four years but not lovers, and they took ninety-five percent of their classes together. They were our token jocks, borrowed from the soccer team. Both sported blond ponytails and legs that could bend steel.

"Hey, girls, come on in," I said with a swooping arm gesture and a chivalrous bow. "Welcome to Saturday night game night. It's always a pleasure."

"The pleasure is all ours," they chimed.

They skipped into the living room to join the three amigos, who were sharing their week of torture. I stood for a moment, looking at them all, wondering how such a motley group of women got along so well once a week. What was our common bond? What's the tie that binds us to our weekly soiree? I was brought back from my thoughts by the knock on the door.

"Hey, sweet cakes, what's the word?"

It was JoJo—the hottest, coolest, bad-ass number of the bunch. JoJo was short for Josephine Joanna Jackson, and she was a triple threat to any breathing babe with boobs. She was all decked out in her leather jacket and boots, her button-fly blue jeans, and her slicked-back hair. This girl was born ready for anything and anyone that came her way.

"Well, well, if it isn't our fearless leader," I announced. "Whatcha got in the bag?" JoJo was clutching a crumpled brown paper bag very close to her chest.

"What, this? This contains a few of our game pieces."

"Can I see?" I said, reaching for the bag.

"Oh, no, my dear, you must wait your turn like a good girl." JoJo clutched the bag tighter, not letting her precious toys out.

"Well, if they are game pieces, then I want to be either the thimble or the race car," I joked.

"Very funny, my friend. But you will not find such things in my secret compartment," she returned. "These are special props to enhance the excitement. And I, your game master, will reveal them all in good time." JoJo left me standing in the doorway and proceeded to join the crew.

I was ready to participate in the banter going on in the living room when a soft knock landed on the door. I was a bit surprised, since everyone was present and accounted for. I opened the door to a real sight for sore eyes.

"Hi. I'm Cleo. I'm a friend of Betsy's. She invited me tonight. Is she here?"

"I'm a Pisces. Sure, come on in."

"No, my name is Cleo, not Leo," she corrected.

"Yeah, sure." I stood looking into a pair of hazel eyes that seemed to go on forever. I was lost in them, deaf to the chatter in the living room and blind to Betsy standing there beside me.

"Cleo, I'm glad you could make it!" Betsy's words shook me out of the spell Cleo's perfect lips had cast me under. "Cleo, I'd like you to meet the woman of the house, Andrea. You can call her Andy."

"Nice to meet you, Andy. Betsy has told me about your Saturday night game nights so I thought I would join the fun."

I turned to Betsy with a look of surprise. Our game nights were a well-kept secret—members only. Betsy read the expression on my face.

"I thought we could use some new blood in the group. You know, branch out a bit," Betsy explained. "From the reaction you had opening the door, I don't think it was a bad choice on my part, wouldn't you say," she said with a smile and a raised eyebrow.

"No, I guess it will be OK, just this time," I responded without taking my eyes off the brunette.

"I thought you would approve," Betsy remarked, with a satisfied look on her face.

"I love playing games," Cleo declared. "I'm really good at Scrabble and Pictionary, but I also really enjoy a good game of backgammon."

I turned toward Betsy and gave her my evil eye, which screamed "*You didn't tell her?*" Betsy got my message, and it almost knocked her back against the wall.

"Cleo, honey, why don't you go inside and introduce yourself to the rest of the girls; I'll be right with you," Betsy suggested.

"Sure, no problem. Can I use the bathroom first?" she asked.

"It's inside on the right," I stated between clenched teeth, never taking my eyes off Betsy, who was hoping for some ally to come through the door, but I had bolted it shut and was not letting anyone else in tonight.

"How could you not tell her," I said in my loudest whisper.

"I thought I did. I guess she didn't catch on when I said we play female games," Betsy said in her own defense.

"I never knew backgammon had a gender!" I said, as I felt the heat rise up to my neck.

"Andy, calm down. She'll be all right. I'm sure she'll catch on and will go along with the game." Betsy tried with all her debating skills to convince me, but I wasn't buying it. I took some deep breaths and ran my fingers through my hair, trying to get myself back under control.

"Besides," Betsy continued, "she's pretty hot. And I saw the look on your face when you opened that door." Betsy's voice went to the cutesy pitch that made me remember the jolt I got in the pit of my stomach when I first saw Miss Hazel Eyes.

"Yeah . . . OK . . . you're right." My heart was overruling my head and I smiled, thinking of her in my bathroom. We both looked at each other as if we were communicating through telepathy.

"JoJo!" we both resounded. We headed into the living room to find all the girls reclining on the couch or on the rug.

"Hey, who's the brunette in the bathroom?" JoJo inquired for the group.

"She's my new friend that I invited," Betsy stated firmly.

"Not bad, Bets," JoJo declared. " 'Bout time we had some new pickin's around here."

"*Hey!*" the girls retorted.

"I'm only kidding. Can't you take a joke?" JoJo played the antagonist jokingly, but I was ready to protect Cleo. Except it was JoJo's turn as game mistress so I had to be careful not to be too vigilant.

Cleo finally came out of the bathroom, and Betsy did all the formal introductions. JoJo stood in the middle of the room without her secretive bag of tricks.

"Ladies, welcome to game night!" JoJo announced like a ringmaster at a circus. "Tonight we have a special treat for all of you, and especially for those with us for the first time." JoJo reached down toward Cleo and lifted her chin with the tip of her fingers so she could look deep into those hazel eyes and turn her on with her charm. Little did she know how little Cleo knew about tonight's game. Cleo smiled back innocently and JoJo's smile was like a wolf in sheep's clothing. JoJo continued her introduction.

"The name of the game is 52 Pickup," JoJo announced.

"I don't think I know this one," Cleo stated in her innocent voice, while the rest of the women smirked under their breath. It didn't matter what she called it or how she played it, it was still the same game to us. JoJo took out a deck of cards and displayed them for all of us to see.

"It's very simple, my dear," JoJo directed Cleo. "I will drop the cards onto the floor all facedown. Each of us will pick up one card during each round and the person holding the highest value card gets to choose the lady of her liking for two minutes of heaven in the next room, where you will find some items to play with awaiting you and your partner." JoJo then pulled out, from behind the couch, a small gong.

"This will be used as our timer to start and stop each round," she added.

"Not bad, JoJo," Tania acknowledged.

"We can dig this," Mel and Jen said in sync.

My eyes widened and I shot another evil stare toward Betsy, who was watching Cleo's reaction. She shrugged at me in confusion, not seeing much reaction from our novice player. JoJo dropped the cards on the floor, and they fanned out in every direction, all upside down.

"Ladies, let the game begin." JoJo reached down and picked up a card at her feet. We all reached for a card and I began to pray for an ace. I closed my eyes and said a quick prayer before revealing my ten of hearts. JoJo had a jack of diamonds and my stomach sank to the floor. Cleo displayed a three of spades and I cringed, thinking what would happen if JoJo won. Tania let out a short scream, showing her king of clubs. I began to breathe again.

"Come, baby, let's see what mistress JoJo brought for us." And Tania took Lia's hand and led her toward the bedroom. JoJo rang the gong as Lia slammed the door shut. The Siamese twins began to giggle as we heard a thud, which was probably Lia's back hitting the wall.

"What was that?" Cleo asked.

"Oh, nothing. Tania probably just slipped," I interjected before JoJo could make some comment. JoJo ran to the door, banging her gong, letting them know time was up. Tania came out first with a big grin on her face, and Lia was making a futile effort to button her blouse.

"Round two!" JoJo announced.

I took another deep breath and pulled a card from under a small pile. JoJo knelt down behind Cleo and pulled her card from the pile, reaching over Cleo's shoulder.

"I wish you luck, my dear," she whispered in Cleo's ear.

I took a quick glance at mine and found I was holding a seven of clubs. I winced at my poor pick. I waited for JoJo to show hers. She looked disappointed. She dropped a two of hearts back onto the floor. I smiled at her defeat.

"Yeah, baby!" came from Betsy's direction. "I got the queen of spades," she declared cheerfully.

No one claimed a higher card, so I shot her the hardest evil look I could find inside of me, conveying with my telepathic powers, *don't you dare do it*. Betsy caught my look and the smile quickly dropped from her face.

"How's about two minutes with a radical?" she said as she stood up and offered her hand to Jen.

"I would love to talk politics with you," Jen said, this time solo.

The two skipped off to the bedroom with JoJo and gong in tow. I looked over at our little sheep, and she still had that look—like wondering when we were going to break out the Trivial Pursuit.

Moaning started to seep through the bedroom door. My insides were twisting in conflict, wanting to be in that bedroom yet wanting to stay here and guard my precious jewel from the thief. Perhaps, if luck is a lady, I will get the best of both worlds. JoJo ran to the door and tried to bang the gong over Jen's mantra of "yes, yes, yes." Finally the door flew open and Betsy scowled at the smiling JoJo leaning against the doorjamb dangling her gong. Jen staggered through the door on her newly acquired rubber legs. She collapsed on the floor with her head landing in Mel's lap.

"Is she OK?" Cleo asked, concerned, yet still confused.

"Baby girl, don't you worry about her. She's feeling just fine," JoJo commented while dragging her hand across Cleo's shoulders.

"Round Three!" JoJo proclaimed, and everyone reached for another card.

I was feeling desperate, turning to my pathetic knowledge of probability to calculate my chances. *Eight women in the game, two rounds gone, that's sixteen cards out of fifty-two* . . . I reached into the pile and pulled my choice close to my heart, hoping my strong desire would will me a high card. I peeked, and a grin came to my face—the ace of diamonds. I looked over at JoJo and she was practically drooling over her card.

"I guess it's my turn to choose," she declared, revealing her ace of clubs.

"I don't think so," I said sternly, letting her see my ace of diamonds.

"Well, I guess we got ourselves a quandary here, don't we," JoJo intimated. "But being the mistress of the game, I guess I can override your ace."

"Where did that rule come from? That wasn't mentioned at the beginning of this game of yours," I said. I was standing now and shooting darts at her with my eyes. I don't know why I was feeling this way. Why was I protecting Cleo? She was Betsy's friend. Why was I feeling so angry toward JoJo? She was my good friend. Was it anger, or was I jealous? I acknowledged to myself the feelings I had for Cleo. She was beautiful and sweet and I wanted her. Even if it was only for two minutes alone in the bedroom staring at each other, I would be satisfied.

"OK, partner, I got a way to settle fairly. Since both of us want the same thing, why don't we let our fair maiden here choose," and she turned toward the oblivious Cleo. "Baby, you decide your destiny."

Cleo looked at both of us, happy with her newly granted power. "Well, it is your game, JoJo," she stated with this falsely authoritative voice.

I looked into those hazel eyes with all the compassion I could muster and pleaded inside for her to choose me. She held my gaze and I felt a hint of the same coming back at me.

"But . . ." she continued, "it is Andy's room and in cards, the tie always goes to the house," and she smiled and winked at me.

I was thrilled, yet shocked by her card savvy. She stood up and took my hand. "Sorry, JoJo, but that's my decision."

"Ooooh! You were dissed, girlfriend," came from the peanut gallery.

I took Cleo by the hand and started toward the bedroom. She closed the door, and I heard the click of the lock. I turned to see what she was doing and I was flung onto the bed by the force of her body hurling toward me. She pinned me to the bedspread with her mouth clinging to mine, her hands ripping at my shirt. They claimed my breast like a lioness claiming her territory. She straddled my legs as her mouth serpentined along my body, intensifying my arousal that had begun the moment I answered her knock on the door.

"Oh, God, Cleo, slow down," I gasped.

"Two minutes only," she murmured over my hard nipple.

I tried to push her off of me to gain top advantage, but she was exerting a strength I hadn't counted on, considering her petite frame. She shed my jeans from my body like a snake's skin and with the first contact of her tongue I clutched the bedspread to keep from catapulting toward the ceiling. My head was spinning, clouded by the incredible sensations she produced in me. I could hear JoJo frantically banging her gong and then turning the knob on the locked door. I finally gave in to her, my sheep with the deceptive wolf hunger, and exploded with the ferocity of a volcano from her play.

Cleo moved to my side, holding her head up with one hand as

230

the other soothed my drained body with a large feather that JoJo had left as one of her props.

"Surprised?" she asked.

"Very," I stated as I pulled myself up and gently pushed her back onto the bed.

"Andy, our two minutes are up," she asserted.

"That was my two minutes. We still have your two minutes," I claimed.

"Mine?"

"Yes. Those are my house rules."

Round Four.

Publications from
BELLA BOOKS, INC.
The best in contemporary lesbian fiction

P.O. Box 10543, Tallahassee, FL 32302
Phone: 800-729-4992
www.bellabooks.com

THE NEXT WORLD by Ursula Steck. 240 pp. Anna's friend Mido is threatened and eventually disappears . . .   1-59493-024-4 $12.95

CALL SHOTGUN by Jaime Clevenger. 240 pp. Kelly gets pulled back into the world of private investigation . . .   1-59493-016-3 $12.95

52 PICKUP by Bonnie J. Morris and E.B. Casey. 240 pp. 52 hot, romantic tales—one for every Saturday night of the year.   1-59493-026-0 $12.95

GOLD FEVER by Lyn Denison. 240 pp. Kate's first love, Ashley, returns to their home town, where Kate now lives . . .   1-1-59493-039-2 $12.95

RISKY INVESTMENT by Beth Moore. 240 pp. Lynn's best friend and roommate needs her to pretend Chris is his fiancé. But nothing is ever easy.   1-59493-019-8 $12.95

HUNTER'S WAY by Gerri Hill. 240 pp. Homicide detective Tori Hunter is forced to team up with the hot-tempered Samantha Kennedy.   1-59493-018-X $12.95

CAR POOL by Karin Kallmaker. 240 pp. Soft shoulders, merging traffic and slippery when wet . . . Anthea and Shay find love in the car pool.   1-59493-013-9 $12.95

NO SISTER OF MINE by Jeanne G'Fellers. 240 pp. Telepathic women fight to coexist with a patriarchal society that wishes their eradication.   ISBN 1-59493-017-1 $12.95

ON THE WINGS OF LOVE by Megan Carter. 240 pp. Stacie's reporting career is on the rocks. She has to interview bestselling author Cheryl, or else!   ISBN 1-59493-027-9 $12.95

WICKED GOOD TIME by Diana Tremain Braund. 224 pp. Does Christina need Miki as a protector . . . or want her as a lover?   ISBN 1-59493-031-7 $12.95

THOSE WHO WAIT by Peggy J. Herring. 240 pp. Two brilliant sisters—in love with the same woman!   ISBN 1-59493-032-5 $12.95

ABBY'S PASSION by Jackie Calhoun. 240 pp. Abby's bipolar sister helps turn her world upside down, so she must decide what's most important.   ISBN 1-59493-014-7 $12.95

PICTURE PERFECT by Jane Vollbrecht. 240 pp. Kate is reintroduced to Casey, the daughter of an old friend. Can they withstand Kate's career?   ISBN 1-59493-015-5 $12.95

PAPERBACK ROMANCE by Karin Kallmaker. 240 pp. Carolyn falls for tall, dark and . . . female . . . in this classic lesbian romance.   ISBN 1-59493-033-3 $12.95

DAWN OF CHANGE by Gerri Hill. 240 pp. Susan ran away to find peace in remote Kings Canyon—then she met Shawn . . .   ISBN 1-59493-011-2 $12.95

DOWN THE RABBIT HOLE by Lynne Jamneck. 240 pp. Is a killer holding a grudge against FBI Agent Samantha Skellar?   ISBN 1-59493-012-0 $12.95

SEASONS OF THE HEART by Jackie Calhoun. 240 pp. Overwhelmed, Sara saw only one way out—leaving . . .   ISBN 1-59493-030-9 $12.95

TURNING THE TABLES by Jessica Thomas. 240 pp. The 2nd Alex Peres Mystery. *From ghosties and ghoulies and long leggity beasties . . .*   ISBN 1-59493-009-0 $12.95

FOR EVERY SEASON by Frankie Jones. 240 pp. Andi, who is investigating a 65-year-old murder, meets Janice, a charming district attorney . . .   ISBN 1-59493-010-4 $12.95

LOVE ON THE LINE by Laura DeHart Young. 240 pp. Kay leaves a younger woman behind to go on a mission to Alaska . . . will she regret it?   ISBN 1-59493-008-2 $12.95

UNDER THE SOUTHERN CROSS by Claire McNab. 200 pp. Lee, an American travel agent, goes down under and meets Australian Alex, and the sparks fly under the Southern Cross.   ISBN 1-59493-029-5 $12.95

SUGAR by Karin Kallmaker. 240 pp. Three women want sugar from Sugar, who can't make up her mind.   ISBN 1-59493-001-5 $12.95

FALL GUY by Claire McNab. 200 pp. 16th Detective Inspector Carol Ashton Mystery.
                    ISBN 1-59493-000-7 $12.95

ONE SUMMER NIGHT by Gerri Hill. 232 pp. Johanna swore to never fall in love again—but then she met the charming Kelly . . .   ISBN 1-59493-007-4 $12.95

TALK OF THE TOWN TOO by Saxon Bennett. 181 pp. Second in the series about wild and fun loving friends.   ISBN 1-931513-77-5 $12.95

LOVE SPEAKS HER NAME by Laura DeHart Young. 170 pp. Love and friendship, desire and intrigue, spark this exciting sequel to *Forever and the Night.*
                    ISBN 1-59493-002-3 $12.95

TO HAVE AND TO HOLD by Peggy J. Herring. 184 pp. By finally letting down her defenses, will Dorian be opening herself to a devastating betrayal?
                    ISBN 1-59493-005-8 $12.95

WILD THINGS by Karin Kallmaker. 228 pp. Dutiful daughter Faith has met the perfect man. There's just one problem: she's in love with his sister.   ISBN 1-931513-64-3 $12.95

SHARED WINDS by Kenna White. 216 pp. Can Emma rebuild more than just Lanny's marina?   ISBN 1-59493-006-6 $12.95

THE UNKNOWN MILE by Jaime Clevenger. 253 pp. Kelly's world is getting more and more complicated every moment.   ISBN 1-931513-57-0 $12.95

TREASURED PAST by Linda Hill. 189 pp. A shared passion for antiques leads to love.
                    ISBN 1-59493-003-1 $12.95

SIERRA CITY by Gerri Hill. 284 pp. Chris and Jesse cannot deny their growing attraction . . .   ISBN 1-931513-98-8 $12.95

ALL THE WRONG PLACES by Karin Kallmaker. 174 pp. Sex and the single girl—Brandy is looking for love and usually she finds it. Karin Kallmaker's first *After Dark* erotic novel.
                    ISBN 1-931513-76-7 $12.95

WHEN THE CORPSE LIES A Motor City Thriller by Therese Szymanski. 328 pp. Butch bad-girl Brett Higgins is used to waking up next to beautiful women she hardly knows. Problem is, this one's dead.   ISBN 1-931513-74-0 $12.95

GUARDED HEARTS by Hannah Rickard. 240 pp. Someone's reminding Alyssa about her secret past, and then she becomes the suspect in a series of burglaries.
                                                          ISBN 1-931513-99-6 $12.95

ONCE MORE WITH FEELING by Peggy J. Herring. 184 pp. Lighthearted, loving, romantic adventure.   ISBN 1-931513-60-0 $12.95

TANGLED AND DARK A Brenda Strange Mystery by Patty G. Henderson. 240 pp. When investigating a local death, Brenda finds two possible killers—one diagnosed with Multiple Personality Disorder.   ISBN 1-931513-75-9 $12.95

WHITE LACE AND PROMISES by Peggy J. Herring. 240 pp. Maxine and Betina realize sex may not be the most important thing in their lives.   ISBN 1-931513-73-2 $12.95

UNFORGETTABLE by Karin Kallmaker. 288 pp. Can Rett find love with the cheerleader who broke her heart so many years ago?   ISBN 1-931513-63-5 $12.95

HIGHER GROUND by Saxon Bennett. 280 pp. A delightfully complex reflection of the successful, high society lives of a small group of women.   ISBN 1-931513-69-4 $12.95

LAST CALL A Detective Franco Mystery by Baxter Clare. 240 pp. Frank overlooks all else to try to solve a cold case of two murdered children . . .   ISBN 1-931513-70-8 $12.95

ONCE UPON A DYKE: NEW EXPLOITS OF FAIRY-TALE LESBIANS by Karin Kallmaker, Julia Watts, Barbara Johnson & Therese Szymanski. 320 pp. You've never read fairy tales like these before! From Bella After Dark.   ISBN 1-931513-71-6 $14.95

FINEST KIND OF LOVE by Diana Tremain Braund. 224 pp. Can Molly and Carolyn stop clashing long enough to see beyond their differences?   ISBN 1-931513-68-6 $12.95

DREAM LOVER by Lyn Denison. 188 pp. A soft, sensuous, romantic fantasy.
                                                          ISBN 1-931513-96-1 $12.95

NEVER SAY NEVER by Linda Hill. 224 pp. A classic love story . . . where rules aren't the only things broken.   ISBN 1-931513-67-8 $12.95

PAINTED MOON by Karin Kallmaker. 214 pp. Stranded together in a snowbound cabin, Jackie and Leah's lives will never be the same.   ISBN 1-931513-53-8 $12.95

WIZARD OF ISIS by Jean Stewart. 240 pp. Fifth in the exciting Isis series.
                                                          ISBN 1-931513-71-4 $12.95

WOMAN IN THE MIRROR by Jackie Calhoun. 216 pp. Josey learns to love again, while her niece is learning to love women for the first time.   ISBN 1-931513-78-3 $12.95

SUBSTITUTE FOR LOVE by Karin Kallmaker. 200 pp. When Holly and Reyna meet the combination adds up to pure passion. But what about tomorrow?   ISBN 1-931513-62-7 $12.95

GULF BREEZE by Gerri Hill. 288 pp. Could Carly really be the woman Pat has always been searching for?   ISBN 1-931513-97-X $12.95

THE TOMSTOWN INCIDENT by Penny Hayes. 184 pp. Caught between two worlds, Eloise must make a decision that will change her life forever.   ISBN 1-931513-56-2 $12.95

MAKING UP FOR LOST TIME by Karin Kallmaker. 240 pp. Discover delicious recipes for romance by the undisputed mistress.   ISBN 1-931513-61-9 $12.95

THE WAY LIFE SHOULD BE by Diana Tremain Braund. 173 pp. With which woman will Jennifer find the true meaning of love? ISBN 1-931513-66-X $12.95

BACK TO BASICS: A BUTCH/FEMME ANTHOLOGY edited by Therese Szymanski— from Bella After Dark. 324 pp. ISBN 1-931513-35-X $14.95

SURVIVAL OF LOVE by Frankie J. Jones. 236 pp. What will Jody do when she falls in love with her best friend's daughter? ISBN 1-931513-55-4 $12.95

LESSONS IN MURDER by Claire McNab. 184 pp. 1st Detective Inspector Carol Ashton Mystery. ISBN 1-931513-65-1 $12.95

DEATH BY DEATH by Claire McNab. 167 pp. 5th Denise Cleever Thriller.
ISBN 1-931513-34-1 $12.95

CAUGHT IN THE NET by Jessica Thomas. 188 pp. A wickedly observant story of mystery, danger, and love in Provincetown. ISBN 1-931513-54-6 $12.95

DREAMS FOUND by Lyn Denison. Australian Riley embarks on a journey to meet her birth mother . . . and gains not just a family, but the love of her life. ISBN 1-931513-58-9 $12.95

A MOMENT'S INDISCRETION by Peggy J. Herring. 154 pp. Jackie is torn between her better judgment and the overwhelming attraction she feels for Valerie.
ISBN 1-931513-59-7 $12.95

IN EVERY PORT by Karin Kallmaker. 224 pp. Jessica has a woman in every port. Will meeting Cat change all that? ISBN 1-931513-36-8 $12.95

TOUCHWOOD by Karin Kallmaker. 240 pp. Rayann loves Louisa. Louisa loves Rayann. Can the decades between their ages keep them apart? ISBN 1-931513-37-6 $12.95

WATERMARK by Karin Kallmaker. 248 pp. Teresa wants a future with a woman whose heart has been frozen by loss. Sequel to *Touchwood*. ISBN 1-931513-38-4 $12.95

EMBRACE IN MOTION by Karin Kallmaker. 240 pp. Has Sarah found lust or love?
ISBN 1-931513-39-2 $12.95

ONE DEGREE OF SEPARATION by Karin Kallmaker. 232 pp. Sizzling small town romance between Marian, the town librarian, and the new girl from the big city.
ISBN 1-931513-30-9 $12.95

CRY HAVOC A Detective Franco Mystery by Baxter Clare. 240 pp. A dead hustler with a headless rooster in his lap sends Lt. L.A. Franco headfirst against Mother Love.
ISBN 1-931513931-7 $12.95

DISTANT THUNDER by Peggy J. Herring. 294 pp. Bankrobbing drifter Cordy awakens strange new feelings in Leo in this romantic tale set in the Old West.
ISBN 1-931513-28-7 $12.95

COP OUT by Claire McNab. 216 pp. 4th Detective Inspector Carol Ashton Mystery.
ISBN 1-931513-29-5 $12.95

BLOOD LINK by Claire McNab. 159 pp. 15th Detective Inspector Carol Ashton Mystery. Is Carol unwittingly playing into a deadly plan? ISBN 1-931513-27-9 $12.95

TALK OF THE TOWN by Saxon Bennett. 239 pp. With enough beer, barbecue and B.S., anything is possible! ISBN 1-931513-18-X $12.95

MAYBE NEXT TIME by Karin Kallmaker. 256 pp. Sabrina has everything she ever wanted—except Jorie. ISBN 1-931513-26-0 $12.95

WHEN GOOD GIRLS GO BAD: A Motor City Thriller by Therese Szymanski. 230 pp. Brett, Randi, and Allie join forces to stop a serial killer. ISBN 1-931513-11-2 $12.95

A DAY TOO LONG: A Helen Black Mystery by Pat Welch. 328 pp. This time Helen's fate is in her own hands. ISBN 1-931513-22-8 $12.95

THE RED LINE OF YARMALD by Diana Rivers. 256 pp. The Hadra's only hope lies in a magical red line . . . climactic sequel to *Clouds of War*. ISBN 1-931513-23-6 $12.95

OUTSIDE THE FLOCK by Jackie Calhoun. 224 pp. Jo embraces her new love and life. ISBN 1-931513-13-9 $12.95

LEGACY OF LOVE by Marianne K. Martin. 224 pp. Read the whole Sage Bristo story. ISBN 1-931513-15-5 $12.95

STREET RULES: A Detective Franco Mystery by Baxter Clare. 304 pp. Gritty, fast-paced mystery with compelling Detective L.A. Franco. ISBN 1-931513-14-7 $12.95

RECOGNITION FACTOR: 4th Denise Cleever Thriller by Claire McNab. 176 pp. Denise Cleever tracks a notorious terrorist to America. ISBN 1-931513-24-4 $12.95

NORA AND LIZ by Nancy Garden. 296 pp. Lesbian romance by the author of *Annie on My Mind*. ISBN 1931513-20-1 $12.95

MIDAS TOUCH by Frankie J. Jones. 208 pp. Sandra had everything but love. ISBN 1-931513-21-X $12.95

BEYOND ALL REASON by Peggy J. Herring. 240 pp. A romance hotter than Texas. ISBN 1-9513-25-2 $12.95

ACCIDENTAL MURDER: 14th Detective Inspector Carol Ashton Mystery by Claire McNab. 208 pp. Carol Ashton tracks an elusive killer. ISBN 1-931513-16-3 $12.95

SEEDS OF FIRE: Tunnel of Light Trilogy, Book 2 by Karin Kallmaker writing as Laura Adams. 274 pp. In Autumn's dreams no one is who they seem. ISBN 1-931513-19-8 $12.95

DRIFTING AT THE BOTTOM OF THE WORLD by Auden Bailey. 288 pp. Beautifully written first novel set in Antarctica. ISBN 1-931513-17-1 $12.95

CLOUDS OF WAR by Diana Rivers. 288 pp. Women unite to defend Zelindar! ISBN 1-931513-12-0 $12.95

DEATHS OF JOCASTA: 2nd Micky Knight Mystery by J.M. Redmann. 408 pp. Sexy and intriguing Lambda Literary Award–nominated mystery. ISBN 1-931513-10-4 $12.95

LOVE IN THE BALANCE by Marianne K. Martin. 256 pp. The classic lesbian love story, back in print! ISBN 1-931513-08-2 $12.95

THE COMFORT OF STRANGERS by Peggy J. Herring. 272 pp. Lela's work was her passion . . . until now. ISBN 1-931513-09-0 $12.95

WHEN EVIL CHANGES FACE: A Motor City Thriller by Therese Szymanski. 240 pp. Brett Higgins is back in another heart-pounding thriller. ISBN 0-9677753-3-7 $11.95

CHICKEN by Paula Martinac. 208 pp. Lynn finds that the only thing harder than being in a lesbian relationship is ending one. ISBN 1-931513-07-4 $11.95

TAMARACK CREEK by Jackie Calhoun. 208 pp. An intriguing story of love and danger. ISBN 1-931513-06-6 $11.95

DEATH BY THE RIVERSIDE: 1st Micky Knight Mystery by J.M. Redmann. 320 pp. Finally back in print, the book that launched the Lambda Literary Award–winning Micky Knight mystery series. ISBN 1-931513-05-8 $11.95

EIGHTH DAY: A Cassidy James Mystery by Kate Calloway. 272 pp. In the eighth installment of the Cassidy James mystery series, Cassidy goes undercover at a camp for troubled teens. ISBN 1-931513-04-X $11.95

MIRRORS by Marianne K. Martin. 208 pp. Jean Carson and Shayna Bradley fight for a future together. ISBN 1-931513-02-3 $11.95

THE ULTIMATE EXIT STRATEGY: A Virginia Kelly Mystery by Nikki Baker. 240 pp. The long-awaited return of the wickedly observant Virginia Kelly.
ISBN 1-931513-03-1 $11.95

FOREVER AND THE NIGHT by Laura DeHart Young. 224 pp. Desire and passion ignite the frozen Arctic in this exciting sequel to the classic romantic adventure *Love on the Line*. ISBN 0-931513-00-7 $11.95

WINGED ISIS by Jean Stewart. 240 pp. The long-awaited sequel to *Warriors of Isis* and the fourth in the exciting Isis series. ISBN 1-931513-01-5 $11.95

ROOM FOR LOVE by Frankie J. Jones. 192 pp. Jo and Beth must overcome the past in order to have a future together. ISBN 0-9677753-9-6 $11.95

THE QUESTION OF SABOTAGE by Bonnie J. Morris. 144 pp. A charming, sexy tale of romance, intrigue, and coming of age. ISBN 0-9677753-8-8 $11.95

SLEIGHT OF HAND by Karin Kallmaker writing as Laura Adams. 256 pp. A journey of passion, heartbreak, and triumph that reunites two women for a final chance at their destiny. ISBN 0-9677753-7-X $11.95

MOVING TARGETS: A Helen Black Mystery by Pat Welch. 240 pp. Helen must decide if getting to the bottom of a mystery is worth hitting bottom. ISBN 0-9677753-6-1 $11.95

CALM BEFORE THE STORM by Peggy J. Herring. 208 pp. Colonel Robicheaux retires from the military and comes out of the closet. ISBN 0-9677753-1-0 $11.95

OFF SEASON by Jackie Calhoun. 208 pp. Pam threatens Jenny and Rita's fledgling relationship. ISBN 0-9677753-0-2 $11.95

BOLD COAST LOVE by Diana Tremain Braund. 208 pp. Jackie Claymont fights for her reputation and the right to love the woman she chooses. ISBN 0-9677753-2-9 $11.95

THE WILD ONE by Lyn Denison. 176 pp. Rachel never expected that Quinn's wild yearnings would change her life forever. ISBN 0-9677753-4-5 $11.95

SWEET FIRE by Saxon Bennett. 224 pp. Welcome to Heroy—the town with more lesbians per capita than any other place on the planet! ISBN 0-9677753-5-3 $11.95

Visit

Bella Books

at

BellaBooks.com

or call our toll-free number

1-800-729-4992